D0922171

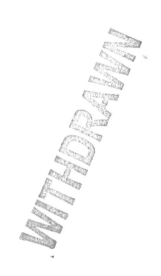

The Perfectly Proper
PARANORMAL
MUSEUM

The Perfectly Proper
PARANORMAL
MUSEUM

by

KIRSTEN WEISS

MIDNIGHT INK
WOODBURY, MINNESOTA

FIRST EDITION
First Printing, 2016

Book format by Teresa Pojar
Cover design by Kevin R. Brown
Cover Illustration by Mary Ann Lasher Dodge

Midnight Ink, an imprint of Llewellyn Worldwide Ltd.

This is a work of fiction. Names, characters, places, and incidents are either the product of the author's imagination or are used fictitiously, and any resemblance to actual persons living or dead, business establishments, events, or locales is entirely coincidental.

Library of Congress Cataloging-in-Publication Data

Names: Weiss, Kirsten, 1968- author.
Title: The perfectly proper paranormal museum / Kirsten Weiss.
Description: First edition. | Woodbury, Minnesota : Midnight Ink, 2016. |
    Series: A perfectly proper paranormal museum mystery ; #1
Identifiers: LCCN 2015039301 (print) | LCCN 2015047756 (ebook) | ISBN
    9780738747514 | ISBN 9780738748269 ()
Subjects: LCSH: Mystery fiction. | Paranormal fiction.
Classification: LCC PS3623.E4555 P47 2016 (print) | LCC PS3623.E4555 (ebook)
    | DDC 813/.6--dc23
LC record available at http://lccn.loc.gov/2015039301

Midnight Ink
Llewellyn Worldwide Ltd.
2143 Wooddale Drive
Woodbury, MN 55125-2989
www.midnightinkbooks.com

Printed in the United States of America

To my father

ONE

Friendship can be a minefield.

Okay, terrible analogy. In a real minefield, it doesn't matter how gingerly you tiptoe. If you step on a mine—boom.

But I was stepping carefully as I squinted at the watercolor my friend Adele Nakamoto had handed me. In the dim golden light from the microbrewery's stained-glass lamps, I had a hard time making it out. The drawing was supposed to be a design plan for her new tea room, but the blocks of pastel looked like something a talented kindergartner might have drawn. Shifting in the booth, I glanced at our friend Harper Caldarelli for support. The red Naugahyde squeaked beneath my jeans.

Adele brushed a cascade of fine black hair behind her ear and leaned across the table. Her open, Jackie Kennedy–esque blazer drifted close to a blot of barbecue sauce on our table. "Well?"

A roar of sound from the jukebox scorched my eardrums. "The colors are soothing," I shouted. That, at least, was true. They reminded me of Neapolitan ice cream.

Harper snatched the drawing from my hands. Brows furrowing, she stretched back in her seat. Her leather jacket parted, revealing sleek curves beneath her tight designer T-shirt. With her cascading, nearly-black hair, sculpted cheekbones, and olive skin, she looked a little like Penelope Cruz. But Harper's eyes were a startling green.

A man at the bar gaped at her, beer dribbling down his chin.

I didn't bother being jealous. Blue eyes and fair, freckled, central European skin was my heritage. I'd carried an extra ten pounds since my abrupt departure from my job. And the three of us had polished off a wedge of pumpkin bread pudding. I was basking in the warm, contented glow of a full stomach.

Harper snorted. "This is an architectural drawing? It looks like paint samples."

"Don't be boring." Adele made a face and crossed her slim legs, twisting her pink pencil skirt. "My designer is an artist. This is a representation of the *essence* of the tea house. You can't expect one of those dull architectural drawings."

"Actually," Harper said, "you can."

Happy to be home, I let their bickering fade into the background din. I turned the beer mat in my hand and stared at the microbrewery's giant copper vat. Patches of it were tarnished, and it looked like under the right conditions it might explode, pelting us with bolts and metal shards. Leather-clad bikers and rough-and-tumble cowboys rubbed shoulders along the polished wooden bar.

I was home.

Adele snapped her fingers in front of my nose. "Earth to Maddie. Seriously, what do you think?"

Having no idea what they'd been talking about, I played it safe. "You've got great taste, and I'm sure it will be a success." But a part of me wasn't sure. The tea room meant a lot to Adele, but she'd never run a business before. I hoped she wasn't in for more heartbreak.

"Exactly!" Adele sat back in the booth.

The kid in the booth behind me kicked his heels, a rhythmic thump that rattled my teeth.

"My tea house will be an elegant and restful oasis from the hustle of everyday life," Adele added.

Harper laughed into her beer, choking. "Hustle in San Benedetto?"

"You are both philistines." Adele sniffed.

I couldn't argue. I liked burritos and country bars and my '58 Ford pickup. Harper owned a successful financial planning business and had developed more refined tastes. But at root she, too, was a small-town girl.

My phone vibrated, and I checked the number. My mother. Turning the phone off, I jammed it into one of the slots in my canvas messenger bag.

Harper tapped the drawing. "So this is going into that building your father gave you as a wedding gift?"

Adele made a wry face, rubbing her bare ring finger. "My dowry. It's a good thing Daddy doesn't believe in take-backs after you-know-who did you-know-what."

You-know-who was her now ex-fiancé, Michael. Adele had caught him doing you-know-what with Christy Huntington in the back of an old sedan. I'd never trusted Michael, but how do you tell that to a friend who's in love? So I'd kept my mouth shut, and Adele had been hurt. How badly, she never quite let on.

She examined her French manicure. "I still can't believe I misjudged him." Her voice dropped, and I leaned closer to hear. "An affair is one thing, but doing the deed in an '87 Buick was just tacky."

Harper turned the drawing upside down. "Sorry, I'm still not seeing it. And these plans look too small for the space that held Chuck's Chicken Shack and Paranormal Museum."

Adele shuddered. "Please don't mention the Chicken Shack. I'm exorcising it from the town's memory." She reached below the table, her black hair swinging forward in a silky curtain. Straightening, she pulled out two ebony wine bags from her pink Chanel purse. "Daddy wanted me to give you each a sample of his latest vintage with his new Haunted Vine label. Harper, return my drawing before you get ketchup on it."

Harper swapped the drawing for the wine, and I drew my bottle from its sleeve. The bottle was almost black, with a ghostly image of a twisted vine. It was a zinfandel—no surprise, since our tiny Central California town specialized in that grape. We were farmers who made wine, not like those snooty vintners in Napa. San Benedetto was off the beaten wine trail, but our wines could hold their own against our better-known competitors. Adele's family owned a vineyard and tasting room, thanks to which the three of us had developed an illicit taste for vino well before the legal drinking age.

"Why 'Haunted Vine'?" I asked.

A furrow appeared between Adele's brows. "It's a play on San Benedetto's second-biggest tourist attraction, the Paranormal Museum."

"I thought the giant flaming Christmas Cow was our second-biggest attraction," I said.

Every year, the local dairy farmers' association created a thirty-foot straw cow for Christmas. And nearly every year, someone—I suspected high school kids—burned it down. I'd bring marshmallows if I knew the timing of the next cow flambé, but it was always a mystery. Last month, just when we thought the cow might survive the season, it went up two days before New Year's.

"Back to your drawing," Harper said. "It looks like your tea room takes up the Chicken Shack space. So what's up with the Paranormal Museum?"

"It's …" Adele stiffened. "Oh, no."

We tracked her gaze toward the entryway. Michael St. James had walked through the door. His business jacket was slung over one arm, his blue striped shirt open at the collar. Tall and broad shouldered, he looked like he'd stepped out of a Ralph Lauren ad. He looked around the microbrewery and caught Adele's eye.

Adele's expression turned stony. She sank back in her seat and gazed straight ahead. Hurt flickered in her dark eyes.

"We can go somewhere else if you want," I said. Michael St. James wasn't my ex-fiancé, but I could feel my blood pressure rising.

Adele's jaw set. "We were here first."

A shadow fell across our table. Harper and I looked up. Adele sipped from her empty beer glass.

"Adele, Maddie, Harper … hi," Michael said. "Adele, can I speak with you alone?"

"No," she said.

"It's important."

Harper's eyes narrowed. She made a strange, rocker sign of the horns and stabbed it at the floor.

"Don't be such a stalker," Adele said, her attention riveted on a brass light fixture high on the wall. "We have nothing to talk about. And if we did, the answer would be no. Now please depart, go away, vamoose."

"Adele …" Grimacing, Michael shook his head, his shoulders crumpling inward. For a moment I almost felt sorry for him. And then I remembered that terrible day, Harper calling me with the news of his defection. My pity evaporated.

He opened his mouth as if to speak, caught Harper's gaze, and seemed to think better of it. He walked away.

"Unbelievable," Harper muttered, watching Michael's exit. "It's been less than a month, and he wants to be friends."

"Well, that's not happening." Adele pressed her hands flat on the table and cleared her throat. "Anyway. My tea room. It's going to be elegant, sophisticated, modern. With teas I'll blend myself."

"What do you know about blending teas?" I followed Adele's lead, moving the conversation to safer territory.

"Oh, please." Adele tossed her head. "It's simple. It's not as if I'm cooking. I've already found a supplier for my scones and tea cakes, so I won't have to wake up at an ungodly hour to supervise any food preparation."

I smothered a laugh. The idea that Adele might do any baking herself hadn't entered my mind.

Adele held out her hand to me. "By the way, Mad. May I have a dollar?"

"Sure." I should have been suspicious. Adele was never short of cash. But like a dork, I dug my wallet out of my purse and handed her a dollar.

She took the money and handed me an envelope.

"What's this?" I asked.

"It's the Paranormal Museum. You were looking for something to do, and now it's yours. Isn't it marvelous? Now we can work right next to each other!"

"What?" I tore open the envelope and pulled out the legal document inside. "This isn't … What is this?"

"You're our witness, Harper. She just bought the museum."

Harper snorted beer, coughing. "I don't think it works that way."

"Oh pleeease, Maddie. I've wanted to get rid of the thing but Daddy forbade it. The mayor doesn't want to lose the museum. They've had the Wine and Visitors Bureau running it for the last few months to keep it going. Besides, it's not as if you have anything better to do."

My chest hitched. I'd left my overseas job nine months ago, due to a difference of opinions with the CEO and a longing for home. I was still unemployed. "This is really generous, Adele," I said. "But I can't accept it."

"Well, that's gratitude," Adele huffed. "I'll have you know, Chuck made more money on that museum than he did selling chicken."

"It was terrible chicken," Harper muttered.

"Besides," Adele added, "I can't own a paranormal museum."

"Why not?" I crossed my arms, knowing the answer. A paranormal museum was too gauche for Adele. She flitted through the higher echelons of San Benedetto society, doing good works and running the occasional wine tasting at her family's vineyard.

Her dark eyes widened. "I'll be too busy with the start up of the tea room. Do you have any idea how much work goes into a new business?"

I resisted smiling. It was a smooth deflection, and it was all true. Adele would be busy. But there was no way she'd touch anything as lowbrow as a paranormal museum.

"The remodeling alone is nearly killing me," Adele continued. "I had to fire my first contractor."

"I told you not to hire Benny," Harper said.

"But he was so cute. You can't really say no to someone who looks like a young George Clooney."

"But you fired him," I pointed out.

"Charm has its limits. Benny never started the project. We were a month behind schedule, and good looks will only go so far. Though my new contractor doesn't exactly fall short in the looks department. So what do you think? Will you take the place off my hands?"

"No." I knew exactly what would happen. I'd get sucked into the museum and my job hunting would get derailed. "I can't buy your museum for a dollar. It isn't fair to you—it's got to be worth more than that."

"Yeah," Harper said. "It's worth at least twenty."

We glared at her.

"Besides," I said, "I can't make that kind of decision over drinks. I'm job hunting, you know."

Adele pouted. "But you'd be perfect for it. You always put on the best haunted houses and Halloween parties. And your tarot readings are amazing. You could go pro."

"You know I read the cards once, for fun, and made things up as I went along. And there's a big difference between a haunted house and a museum."

"Not if the rumors are true," Harper said. "They say the Paranormal Museum is haunted."

"That's not an argument for working there," I said.

"I know." Harper stood and stretched. At the bar, her admirer's lips parted with longing. "It's late. I'm headed out." She dropped some bills on the table and left, wine bottle in hand.

Adele stared at me with feverish, over-bright eyes. Her hands fluttered. "The Wine and Visitors Bureau has told me they can't manage the museum anymore. I'm desperate. If I don't figure out a way to keep it open, Daddy says he'll take my dowry back. The mayor is really leaning on him. Please? Please?"

My stomach tightened with guilt. "It's thoughtful of you, Adele, but I don't know if I want to be a paranormal museum owner. Plus, I've got applications out all over the Bay Area. What if I have to go in for an interview?"

This was looking less and less likely, but it could happen. I'd spent my first seven months in the States living and job hunting in spendy San Francisco; my bank account had dropped faster than a pair of shoes on prom night. Two months ago, I'd returned inland to low-cost San Benedetto, where my aunt had offered me her garage apartment at bargain basement prices. But I'd recently applied for a job with a financial services company in the Bay Area that I was perfect for. I had a real shot. If they didn't ask me for an interview, no one would.

"Okay, fine," Adele said. "Don't buy it now. But will you at least manage it temporarily and think about it? Just for a few weeks until I can get things organized? You can keep job hunting from the museum and see if you like it. The work's not hard. You can submit resumes between ticket sales. And the museum is closed Mondays and Tuesdays—you can interview then!"

My resistance crumbled. What was a few weeks? "Fine."

"Thank you! You're a lifesaver."

"Mmm."

"Have you seen the museum lately? It's super spooky at night." Adele rose from her seat. "Come on. Let's go take a look, and I can show you my progress on the tea room."

She hustled me out of the bar. San Benedetto's wide streets were dark and empty, the glow from the iron streetlamps blunted by low fog. Bare cherry trees lined the brick sidewalks, casting weak, skeletal shadows. We walked past the stone library, past the hardware store, past the little park with its WWII-era cannon. I heard, but couldn't see, the creek that cut along the other side of the park, rattling over stones, rushing against its high banks.

In front of the tea room—once Chuck's Chicken Shack—Adele fumbled with her keys. At the top of the building was the number 1910: not the address, but the year it was built. The light from the motorcycle shop next door spilled onto the sidewalk. I stopped in front of the shop's window, blowing into my clenched hands for warmth and admiring a baby-blue Harley. I'd never ride one—they were way too dangerous. But they sure were pretty.

"Got it," Adele trilled. The paneled wood door snicked open. "Isn't the door marvelous? I considered updating it, but I love its shabby-chic feel."

I followed her inside, and she flipped a switch. Above, a fluorescent lamp flickered to life. The Chicken Shack had been stripped to its concrete floor. Translucent sheets of plastic covered part of one wall, and they rustled in the draft. Shivering, I jammed my hands into the pockets of my frayed gray pea coat. I should have brought a hat. It was colder inside than outside.

Adele tugged me to the front corner of the room. "I'm going to build bay windows over here. And the counter will go there." She pulled out her drawing and frowned at it. "There'll be white-painted shelves behind the counter with teas and tea accessories for sale. Probably some houseplants as well, because plants warm a room. I'm going to close up the wall next to the Paranormal Museum, build more shelves over there..." She pointed to the plastic sheeting and faltered.

Dutifully, I turned in that direction.

One corner of the plastic fluttered back, like a tent opening. Beneath it a woman lay sprawled, her face angled away, her blond hair a golden tangle. A dark pool of blood stained the concrete floor.

TWO

ADELE SQUEAKED AND GRABBED me around the waist.

My reaction wasn't any better. I stared, disbelieving. Prying Adele loose, I hurried to the fallen woman on the cold cement. Her eyes stared, sightless. Shocked, I took an involuntary step back.

It was Christy Huntington.

That was bad.

I glanced at Adele, wide-eyed, frozen.

My hands went clammy, my muscles growing rigid. I didn't need to take Christy's pulse to know she was dead. But I did it anyway, squatting beside the fallen woman, pressing my fingers to her still-warm neck. "Call 911."

"Is she …?"

"Dead. Call 911."

Adele gulped and dug in her Chanel bag.

The plastic shifted again, covering Christy's shoulders. With the back of my hand, I lifted the makeshift curtain and peered into the darkened museum next door. The light filtering into it from the tea room made weird silhouettes of the objects in the museum. Christy's torso lay on the bare concrete of the tea room, but her legs sprawled on the Paranormal Museum's checkerboard linoleum. It looked like she'd been leaving the museum when she'd fallen.

A charcoal-colored Egyptian obelisk, about eighteen inches long, lay beside Christy's red stiletto heels. Bits of blood and hair stuck to its base.

"Yes … yes …" Adele was saying into the phone. "The Paranormal Museum. Hurry!" She hung up. "Are you sure she's dead? I know CPR."

"She's gone."

Something small and black shot toward me. I shrieked, wobbled, and fell on my butt.

A black cat arched its back, hissing at me, one of its paws raised as if to strike.

I clutched my chest to keep my heart from slamming free. "A cat! What's that doing here?"

"Poor GD Cat. Did the big lady scare you?" Adele pressed her face to the cat's side and turned from Christy's body.

"What's a cat doing in a museum?" Rattled, my mind clung to trivia. Christy. I'd seen her parents in the grocery store last week. This was horrible.

"It's GD Cat." Adele's voice wobbled.

"GD for … gosh darned?"

"Ghost Detecting. Chuck claimed the cat sees ghosts." Taking a deep breath, Adele put the animal on the floor and brushed black cat hairs from her jacket. "Okay. I'm calm. It's an empty building. These things happen. This poor woman, a vagrant no doubt, broke in through the museum—"

"Adele—"

"This sort of thing happens all the time. Not here of course, in San Benedetto, but it happens."

Christy was no vagrant. Adele couldn't see her face, angled as it was. But I wondered how much of this was denial. I cleared my throat. "What did the police say?"

"The dispatcher said they'll be here in ten minutes. That's enough time to move the body. Grab her feet."

My head jerked back. "What? I'm not going to move the body!"

"Of course not. Not by yourself. We'll do it together." She pushed back the plastic. Heels click-clacking, she walked inside the museum, stopping by Christy's feet.

"You're contaminating a crime scene! We can't move her. It's illegal."

"Madelyn." Adele straightened and put her hands on her hips. Her dark eyes glittered. "A corpse cannot be found in my tea room. We have to move her into the Paranormal Museum."

"Adele, I think you're in shock," I said gently. "This isn't you. You cannot be seriously suggesting we move the body."

"Why not? It's perfectly reasonable."

"It's a felony. Besides, the police will know in a minute what happened. There's blood on the concrete in your tea room."

"We have to," Adele wailed. "Don't you see—a corpse is perfectly proper in a paranormal museum, but not in my tea room!"

"Adele … it's Christy Huntington."

Adele's face sagged. "Oh." Emotions shifted across her face. Sadness. Horror. And … relief?

"What was she doing in here?" I asked.

"How should I know?" Adele's voice was threaded with hysteria. "She probably came to torment me, or steal my ideas, or sabotage the tea room. I was telling Harper about a new menu item—a coconut cinnamon scone—while we were shopping yesterday. I caught Christy eavesdropping. She's out to ruin me."

I rocked back on my heels. None of that seemed likely. I didn't know Christy well, though I knew firsthand she had a temper. But she was also a lawyer, and I didn't think she was stupid enough to cross the line into criminal trespassing.

Adele looked down. "What's this?" She reached for the obelisk. "Don't—"

She picked it up and stared at it, a crease forming between her brows. "Do you think it fell from one of the shelves and hit her?"

"Adele! That might be a murder weapon."

"I certainly hope not. If it fell and hit her, you know someone will sue me for negligence. The museum is still mine—unless you took ownership before she died."

I gaped at her from my crouch on the floor. "Adele!"

Distant sirens wailed.

Shuddering, Adele dropped the obelisk. It clattered on the linoleum. She covered her mouth with her hands and moaned. "I can't believe I said that. I'm so sorry. What's wrong with me?"

I clamped my jaw shut, wondering the same thing. "Wait outside. I'll check the doors."

"Alone? You can't stay here alone." Clinging to my side, Adele watched me examine the museum's front door. It looked okay.

"There's a door to the alley too, through the tea room," Adele said. We checked it out, and it didn't look broken into either.

Wordlessly, we went out front and stood on the brick sidewalk.

A black-and-white police car screeched to a halt at the museum. A uniformed cop jumped out of the car and jogged over to us. "What happened?"

"We found a body." I pointed to the open tea room door.

An ambulance, lights staining the street red, pulled up, followed by a fire truck.

"Stay here." The cop hustled into the tea room, one hand on the butt of his gun.

A black SUV rolled to a halt in front of us, and a long-legged blonde stepped from the passenger side. Her hair was in a bun, and she wore a black windbreaker with a gold badge embroidered on its chest. A gun belt was slung low about her hips.

From the driver's side, an African-American man exited. High cheekbones, chiseled face, and dark-chocolate complexion. Our gazes locked. His eyes were flecked with gold, and the connection jolted me. The moment froze, a hitch in time, and it seemed as if he looked all the way inside me. And then the seconds resumed, ticked forward. He walked past, into the building.

His companion strode to us and flashed a detective's badge, a spark of recognition lighting her eyes. Scrunching my brows, I tried to remember how I knew her. She looked about my age—early thirties—and there was something familiar in her rolling strut. A sense of defeat, humiliation, and claustrophobia wormed in my stomach.

Her lips thinned. She dug a notepad from her inside pocket and flipped it open. "What happened here?"

Adele gaped at the fire truck, her almond-shaped eyes dull.

I nudged her to answer.

When she didn't respond, I picked up the slack. "We came to see Adele's renovations," I said, "and found a body in the building."

"Kind of late for a tour, isn't it?"

I glanced at Adele, who was still in the Land of This-Is-Not-Happening. "It was a spur of the moment thing," I said.

"You two been drinking?"

I blew out a breath. "Just a beer. We came from the Bell and Brew. You can ask them if you want."

"Thanks for giving me your permission." Her upper lip curled.

Great. A cop with attitude. I could see where this was going, and attempted to make nice. "I'm Madelyn Kosloski, by the way. This is Adele Nakamoto. It's her building."

"I know who you are. Did either of you know the victim?"

"Slightly," I said. "It's Christine Huntington. And, er, you are?"

Her pen paused over the notepad. "The same Christine Huntington who got caught schtupping your friend's fiancé?"

Adele roused herself. "In a Buick."

I didn't know where Adele's Buick obsession came from, but I didn't think the detail helped.

"What was she doing in your building, Nakamoto?"

Color rose in Adele's cheeks. "How should I know? She didn't tell me she was coming."

"How did she get inside?" the detective asked.

"She must have broken in somehow," Adele muttered.

"How?" I asked. "The doors and windows look okay."

"Who has a key?" the detective continued.

Adele looked at the fire truck. "Only myself, my contractor, and the Wine and Visitors Bureau. They've been running the Paranormal Museum during the transition."

The detective sighed. "Does your contractor have a name?"

"Dieter Finkielkraut."

"Finkielkraut?" She spat the word, her lips twisting.

"What's wrong with her contractor?" I asked.

Ignoring me, the detective turned to go. "I'll be in touch."

"Uh, it looked like Christy got hit in the head with a miniature stone obelisk," I said.

"I'll decide what she got hit with," the detective snapped.

"I brought it up because Adele might have accidentally picked up the obelisk," I said.

Mouth slackening, the detective rubbed her brow. Adele looked at me like I'd returned her favorite Manolo Blahniks covered in mud.

"She was sort of in shock," I added.

"You two stay here." The detective slapped her notebook shut and strode inside.

"Thanks a lot," Adele hissed.

"They're going to find your fingerprints on it anyway. Better you tell them now."

"But I didn't tell them. You did."

I hunched my shoulders. "Sorry."

Adele stared at her designer shoes. "No, you're right. I shouldn't have touched it. It was like the thing hypnotized me." She crossed her arms. "Laurel must be loving this."

"Laurel?" A coldness knifed my core.

"The detective."

I stepped backward, shaking my head. It couldn't be.

"Laurel Hammer?" Adele said. "From high school? She was a year ahead of us. Ran with the smoker crowd? Had three tattoos by the time she graduated? Shoved you into your gym locker? How could you forget? The fire department had to pry you free."

I swallowed. "I must have blotted it from my mind." But I hadn't. You didn't forget being stuck inside your ninth grade gym locker for over an hour, wearing only your ninth grade cotton underwear.

Laurel Hammer. She'd been shorter and bulkier in high school. But she still had the same hard edges.

My high school bully emerged from the tea shop with two uniformed officers. "We've got more questions." She motioned toward the squad car. "Get in. We'll give you a ride to the station."

"No need," Adele said. "My Mercedes is a few blocks from here."

Laurel's expression was granite. "Leave it. Gonzalez?"

One of the uniforms nodded and came to stand beside us. The other opened the back door of the squad car. Feeling criminal, I slunk inside. Adele, muttering, slid in beside me.

"Cheer up," I said. "We're not cuffed. They only want to talk to us." But even I knew this wasn't a good sign.

At the police station, they put us in separate cinderblock rooms, and I waited. And waited. The floor was green, and somewhere I'd stepped in something sticky. I lifted my boot experimentally, listening to it peel off the floor. Ewww.

The good citizen in me was programmed to help the police. And I wanted to help. A murder in San Benedetto was shocking. Of course the police had questions. What was Christy doing in Adele's locked building? Why had we been there so late at night? The sooner I cleared things up, told them what happened, the sooner they could solve the crime.

I tried to think zenlike thoughts and look innocent for the video camera high up in one corner of the wall. But the longer I sat, the more I thought about Christy and Michael and Adele. Picking up the obelisk had been stupid, and I half-wondered if Adele had done it intentionally.

Berating myself for my disloyalty, I propped my head in my hands, elbows on the table. It wobbled beneath me. Adele might be pampered, privileged, and pushy, but she was a good person at heart. She didn't spend time at the head of all those charitable committees because she wanted to network. She cared about her projects. And she'd been a good friend, there for me for everything from my senior prom disaster to my latest career hiccup. Adele wasn't a killer.

I'd know if she was a killer.

Wouldn't I?

Laurel Hammer banged open the door to the interview room. "So which one of you two idiots killed her?"

I sat up. "Um, neither?"

She sat across from me and braced her elbows on the table. I removed mine, and her end thumped to the ground.

She scowled. "If you cover for her, that makes you an accessory. It's not looking good, Kosloski."

My gaze darted around the room, landing on the metal door in front of me. I willed someone—anyone—to walk through it. If Laurel was playing bad cop, where was the good cop? Unless Laurel was the good cop, in which case Adele was in real trouble.

"I'm not covering for anyone," I said. "We met for drinks with Harper Caldarelli at seven o'clock. We were at the Bell and Brew until nine. Then Harper went home, and Adele and I walked to the Chicken Shack. I mean the tea room."

"Why?"

"Adele wants me to run the Paranormal Museum. Taking me there was her way of talking me into it."

"Must be nice to have a friend give you a business." Laurel's eyes narrowed with dislike. "Most people have to work for it."

My voice hardened. "She isn't giving it to me."

"Right. Nakomoto said you bought it for a dollar."

"I'm not buying it. I don't want it. I'm doing a favor for a friend."

"Like covering for a murder?"

"Of course not." I ground my teeth into a smile. High school was more than a decade ago. I'd changed. Laurel had changed too, at least on the outside. She was doing her job.

"Let's go over this again."

"I've already told you—"

"And I'm asking nicely. Let's go over this again."

And we did. And again.

I rubbed my eyes. "Detective Hammer, I can't tell you anything more."

"Don't tell me what you can't do."

The door clanked open, and her partner with the remarkable golden eyes entered the room.

"She's free to go," he said.

Laurel jerked to her feet. "What? Slate, I'm in the middle—"

He silenced her with a look.

Her hands balled into fists.

"Thanks," I muttered. Heart thumping, I scuttled past him.

He touched my arm, his expression impassive. "By the way, the mayor wanted me to tell you that you can reopen on Saturday."

I stared, taken aback. The mayor? Was the Paranormal Museum that important? And how had the mayor found out about the murder so quickly? But the answer was obvious: Adele and her connections.

My stomach bottomed out. It was the worst sort of favoritism. If I were Laurel or her partner, I'd despise us.

I fled the station before they could change their minds.

THREE

Slumped on Adele's snow-white couch, Harper stretched out her legs, bumping the briefcase near her feet. It wobbled but didn't fall. She wore gray wool slacks and a starched white blouse, and I assumed she had an appointment later with a client. As a financial adviser, she set her own hours. I knew they were long.

"I can't believe someone killed Christy," Harper said. "San Benedetto hasn't had a murder in at least a decade. What happened?"

"It looked like someone bludgeoned her to death." I rubbed my eyes, gritty from lack of sleep. I gazed past her, through bay windows overlooking rows of grapevines, shrouded by morning mist. The living room of Adele's Victorian was a study in white—white chairs, white shag rug, white-brick fireplace—as if the fog had made its way inside.

Adele was a contrast in black: black turtleneck, black pencil skirt, and black tights in black Jimmy Choos. I think she was going for a mourning look, but she looked chic. "They're going to arrest me," she said. Her voice was flat, defeated.

Adele's pug, Pug, snuffled my ankles, and I bent to scratch behind his ears. "No, they won't," I said.

Harper ran a hand through her loose mahogany hair. "What was Christy Huntington doing in your tea room?"

"In the Paranormal Museum," Adele corrected. "She was clearly attacked in the Paranormal Museum. It's not my fault her body fell into my tea room."

"That's sort of a moot point, isn't it?" Harper asked. "You own the whole building. What was Christy doing inside?"

"I don't know." Adele gnawed her lower lip. "I don't know how she got inside, or why she was there. The police said she had a key on her. They asked me if I'd given it to her and lured her there. If I wanted to lure her there, I wouldn't have had to give her a key! But they think I have a motive. Let's face it. They're right."

"But you were with us from seven o'clock on," I said. "Christy was still warm to the touch when I tried to take her pulse. She couldn't have been dead long." My gorge rose at the memory. I crossed my arms over my chest. "When was the last time you were in the tea room?"

"I met with Dieter around three o'clock, and then I left. He usually works until five. Christy must have let herself in after that."

Unless the contractor was the killer. Last night's shock had been replaced by a sick, creeping feeling. I told myself that Christy's murder had nothing to do with us. Adele and I were incidental to the crime. But my gut didn't believe it.

I cleared my throat. "All right. You were with Dieter at three. Where were you between three and seven, when you met us?"

"I had a manicure at four. And then I went home and took a nap and had a light dinner before we went out."

"Why do you always eat before we go out?" Harper asked.

"You know I dislike eating in public. What if someone sees me with half-chewed spinach between my teeth?"

"Forget the food," I said. "Was anyone with you at home?"

"I was alone with Pug." Adele picked him up and rubbed her face against his fur. He panted, tongue lolling, depositing fawn-colored hairs across her black sweater.

"So we need to hope she was killed when you were with us at the microbrewery," Harper said. "Then you'll be off the hook. I wonder how long it takes a body to cool?"

We scrambled for our phones and began tapping for answers.

"Okay." I felt I'd won a prize for finding the information first. "A body normally loses 1.5 degrees of heat every hour, until it reaches the room's temperature. But that varies by how the corpse is dressed, what it was lying on, etc. Half of Christy was on bare concrete, the rest on linoleum, and it was pretty cold inside."

"She was dressed lightly," Adele said, "in a blazer and slacks, like she'd come from work."

"So we have no idea when she was killed—it could have been right before we arrived, or earlier." I dropped my phone on the couch cushion.

"This is not making me feel better," Adele said.

My phone buzzed. The number was my mother's, and I rubbed my lower lip. I come from a family of overachievers, and my mother was losing patience with my extended unemployment. I was losing patience with my extended unemployment too. I sent the call to voicemail.

Harper checked her watch. "Client appointment. Gotta go." She picked up her briefcase and rose. "Adele, if there's anything you need…"

Adele waved her hand. "I know. Thanks, Harper."

I stood as well.

"Mad," Adele said, "I hear they're going to let the Paranormal Museum open tomorrow. Seriously, can you manage it?"

"I've never run a museum before."

"It's easy. It's not as if the exhibits do anything. All you have to do is take money and hand out tickets. You can keep the profits. It'd be like you owned the place." She clawed a hand through her silky black hair. "I know you're not totally sold on the museum, but I don't have anyone else." She lowered her voice. "And I've got a bad feeling I'm not going to be around to help."

I waffled. "Adele, you've talked to a lawyer, haven't you?"

"Of course. Only an idiot would be interviewed by the police without one."

I gave her a fixed smile, lips clamped together. I'd had no lawyer for last night's interrogation.

"So you'll do it?" she asked.

"Until you can find someone to buy the museum." Helping out at the museum might not be such a bad idea. I needed to do something.

She exhaled. "Good. Thanks." She handed me a key from her purse. "On Saturdays, it opens at ten." Her phone rang, and she grabbed it off the polished coffee table and checked the number. "Would you mind seeing yourself out? I have to take this."

I felt strangely eager to see myself out.

Harper's departing BMW had left dust trails settling along the dirt and gravel driveway. The air smelled faintly of cow manure, and I wrinkled my nose. A blur of movement caught my eye—two crows harrying a red-tailed hawk. The hawk soared, plummeted, veered.

The crows stayed on him. They were smaller, but it was two against one, and I hated unfair fights. The birds vanished behind a row of trees. I waited, watching, hoping to see the hawk escape, but the birds didn't reappear.

It was kind of disturbing.

But the past twenty-four hours had brought all new dimensions to disturbing. I leaned against the hood of my beat-up red truck and listened to the message my mother had left.

"Madelyn, this is your mother. Big news about Melanie. She's going to be singing at the Bolshoi in Moscow this summer! It's too bad you quit that job—it would have been so nice for her to have her sister around. How's your job hunt going? And I've got news about your brother as well. Call me."

My sister Melanie was an opera singer. The Bolshoi. Good for her. I wondered about Shane's big news. A promotion to ambassador? I smiled. The family gossip grounded me back in the normal world, where murder was just a news item, something that happened to people you didn't know.

But I didn't want to call my mother back. I knew that threaded between all the stories about my siblings would be questions about my own job situation. Questions I didn't want to answer. With my mother living in San Benedetto, it was getting harder to avoid them.

I drove toward my studio apartment, past rows of grapevines and through downtown San Benedetto. The shops weren't open yet, but a few people wandered the sidewalks in search of coffee or breakfast, bundled up against the cold. A familiar-looking face stalked past, moving in the opposite direction. Adele's ex.

I wrenched the wheel sideways, pulling into an empty spot on the street, and leapt out of my faded pickup.

"Mike!" I knew it drove him crazy when people called him Mike. He preferred Michael, no doubt thinking it sounded more dignified.

He turned, seeking the source of the shout.

I waved. I'd swear he spotted me. But he turned on his heel and strode in the opposite direction, hands jammed in the pockets of his elegant black wool coat.

"Mike!" I hurried after him but was no match for his long strides. I broke into a jog.

Shoulders hunched, he ducked his dark head. His hair was slicked back, each strand in its place. I reached out and touched his elbow. "Mike."

He whirled. The fabric of his coat sleeve grazed my chin. "What? And don't call me Mike."

I stepped back. "It's …" Now that I had his attention, my certainty drained away. I felt awkward, intrusive. "I'm sorry about Christy."

He looked at me blankly, his expression slack.

"She told me you were engaged. You have my deepest sympathies."

He didn't move, didn't speak.

"Um, have you heard about Christy?" I asked.

His lips whitened. "I heard. And you shouldn't be talking to me about it. You'll make things worse for yourself."

"For myself?" Mentally, I scratched my head. A mother pulling two toddlers in her wake brushed past us, and I lowered my voice. "What are you talking about?"

"Christy told me what you did last week. I had to tell the police."

"Last week? What?"

"Yeah," he said bitterly. "She told me you'd deny it." He left me standing on the sidewalk, gaping.

I hadn't known Christy well. With all the travel I'd been doing at my old job, I'd lost touch with most of my friends. And frenemies. My mind went to my encounter with Christy last week—the first and last time I'd spoken with her since I'd returned nine months ago. And I hadn't done anything. I'd run into her outside a bridal shop. She'd boasted that she and Michael had gotten engaged— shocked, I'd burst out, "He was engaged to Adele a month ago!" It had been maladroit, and she wasn't happy. But it had also been true. Yet nothing had happened. No histrionics. No fisticuffs. No pistols at nine paces.

I hadn't told Adele about the engagement.

I couldn't.

But what had Michael told the cops? Stomach churning, I walked back to my battered pickup. I hadn't even thought of getting a lawyer last night. I was innocent. A woman had been killed. I wanted to help. But maybe Adele had been right. Maybe I should have had a lawyer during the police questioning.

As I approached my apartment, I saw an unfamiliar blue Mercedes in the gravel drive. Since I was living, for now, over my aunt Sadie's garage, I didn't give much thought to any visitors she might have. I trudged up the wooden stairs to my studio; the steps creaked beneath my feet. At the top, I unlocked the door and walked inside.

My brother rose from the couch and spread his arms wide. "Hey, sis."

"Shane?" My messenger bag thunked to the floor.

He walked to me and gave me a hug.

I reciprocated, thumping him on the back. Shane was a cultural attaché for the U.S. Embassy in Moscow. He was blond and chiseled, and his smile was as blindingly white as his shirt. Did I mention I came from a family of overachievers? It held true in the genetics department as well, at least when it came to my brother and two sisters.

He took a step back, his hands bracing my shoulders. Shane was my brother, so I pretty much had to love him, but he made life seem effortless. When you've been dealing with nine months of rejections, that's irritating.

"So you got Sadie's garage," he said. "Nice."

He was right. I was lucky. The studio had distressed wood floors and was done up in a nautical theme of soft blues, whites, and grays. We were over a hundred miles from the ocean, but my grandfather had been a sea captain. Shadow boxes with starfish and coral hung from the white-washed walls. Old mariners' equipment worked as bookends. There was a telescope in a battered leather case. A sextant. A captain's hat.

And then there were the stacks of boxes I hadn't gotten around to unpacking. In my defense, with all Sadie's stuff there wasn't much space for my things.

"What are you doing back in California?" I managed to ask.

"Vacation. Moscow is miserable this time of year, and I wanted to see Mom. How've you been?" He jammed his hands in the back pockets of his expensive jeans and rocked on his loafered heels.

"Great," I said brightly. "Just great. Great." My gaze slid to the empty pizza carton on the coffee table, the bunched-up socks in front of the TV, the half-empty bottle of wine. "Well, not really. Adele and I discovered a dead body in her building."

"A dead body?"

"Yeah. Christy Huntington."

He shook his head. "Should I know her?"

"Probably not. She was in my class at school."

"So you knew her? I'm sorry, Mad. That's terrible."

"What's terrible is that I'm more sorry for Adele and the people Christy left behind than for Christy herself. I didn't really know her well, and I didn't really like her much. But I can't imagine losing a child. What must her parents be going through?"

We paused, thinking of our own loss—our father's death—last year.

I pushed that thought away, grabbed the bottle off the TV, and clutched it to my chest. "Drink?"

"Too early."

Sweat trickled down my back. I put the wine on the coffee table and tugged my earlobe. "So how's Moscow?"

He frowned. "I told you. Cold. Mom told me you were career transitioning. What's next for my little sis?"

Of course she'd told him. When she hadn't gotten any good answers from me, she'd sicced my long-lost brother on the case. "I'm, er, talking to a museum."

"About being a collector? That would be right up your alley—traveling the world, finding objects, swinging deals. I could put you in touch with some amazing folks in Eastern Europe."

"More like a … curator."

"Curator? Whoa, that's high-powered stuff. Way to go, Mad. About time we got a curator in the family." He grinned. "Mom will be over the moon."

Yeah, when she heard about the Paranormal Museum she'd be over the moon all right. "Let's not talk about it. It might not happen. I'm not even certain I want the job," I fudged.

He winked. "Got it. I see why you haven't told Mom. She'd brag to all her friends."

I laughed feebly. "So how's Moscow?"

"That's the second time you've asked me."

"Are you going to make me go for thirds?"

"Nothing's changed. The city reeks of money, power, and organized crime. It was exciting at first, but now … Let's say it's good to be home. You know how it is."

"Yeah." God, what had I done? Why had I come home? I should have done what they'd asked and kept my job. But no, I had to get indignant. I had to have principles. I had to be an idiot.

I had to pull myself together. "Speaking of home, how long are you here for?"

"Three weeks. I might make a run down to San Diego to visit friends, but I've got to get back in time for a joint U.S.-Russian exhibit the embassy is sponsoring. Moscow has a lively surreal art scene."

"I'll bet."

"So how about I take you out to lunch? Hey, remember that wacky paranormal museum? If it's still open, want to go take a look at it for old time's sake?"

"It's closed today," I said repressively.

His brows drew together. "On a Friday? That's weird. Oh well, we can do it some other time." Draping one arm around my shoulders, he grabbed his leather bomber jacket off the back of the chair. "Lunch it is."

FOUR

At nine thirty Saturday morning, I slunk into the Paranormal Museum. It had been hard keeping the museum from my brother. He's one of those men who's good at getting other people talking. And he really listens. The big jerk. But I'd managed to route him away from any discussion of my new "work."

And now it was time for me to get to work. I felt a little nervous.

This was my first real chance to examine the museum. The walls were white-paneled, their ornate moldings painted shiny black. Two doors in the right wall led to other rooms. Opposite them hung that plastic barrier, and the gap in the wall that led to the tea room. The floor was a white-and-black checkerboard of linoleum tiles. A rocking chair stood in one corner. Glass-enclosed shelves filled with haunted objects lined the rear wall. It looked like an undertaker's ice cream parlor.

The only thing that could have completed the grim effect would have been Christy's chalk (or taped) outline on the floor. But chalk

outlines were for the movies. Today's police had cameras to record the scene.

GD Cat made a Slinky of himself, dropping from a high shelf lined with old-timey photos onto the floor. He approached me, his strut confident, his meow imperial. Interpreting this as a demand for food, I searched the cupboard beneath the cash register. Next to a dusty and unopened bottle of Kahlua was a bag of kibble and a metal bowl. I filled it and placed it near a bowl of water by the rocking chair.

He turned his back on me and ate, teeth crunching.

I picked up the water bowl to freshen it. And then I realized what was missing: a bathroom. If Adele sealed the whole wall between the tea room and the museum, I'd be on daily liquid restrictions.

I rummaged through the drawers and found a bundle of tickets. Beside them was a small key that fit the old-fashioned register. It was ten o'clock, and I was ready to go.

Walking to the plastic drapes that separated the museum from the soon-to-be tea room, I peered through. A dark stain spread across the bare concrete. So the police hadn't eradicated the signs of the murder. The clean-up was left to us. Shivering, I retreated into the museum.

No customers beat down the door, so I wandered into the two other rooms that constituted my temporary empire. One had shelves filled with antique dolls, their eyes staring sightlessly, their gowns faded. A sign above the door declared this the Creepy Doll Room. It certainly creeped me out.

The Fortune Telling Room fascinated me. Cases filled with Ouija boards, tarot cards, divining rods, and other tools of the trade ringed the room. I ran one finger over an odd wheel-and-pulley device and wiped the dust off on my jeans. In the center of the room stood a lightweight Victorian séance table: *circa 1889, France*, said the card. Against one wall was a spirit cabinet from the 1870s. The placard beside it didn't explain much. Were spirits supposed to live in the cabinet? I opened its doors. A bench had been built inside, against the cabinet's right-hand wall. It didn't look comfortable, even for a ghost. On the wall beside the cabinet hung a framed Houdini poster: *Do Spirits Return?*

Was the poster real or a replica? I'd need to do a thorough inventory of the museum to understand exactly what Adele had and its true value. She'd need that information if she ever found a buyer.

I returned to the main room and the cash register. The plastic sheeting rustled. GD Cat sat in front of the plastic where Christy's body had lain, licking his paws, unconcerned.

"I guess that means we're ghost free," I said.

He paused, fixing his green-eyed gaze on me, and then returned to his ablutions.

I unpeeled the information card taped to the seat of the paint-flecked rocking chair. It read: *A presence has been felt in this chair donated by Gerald Winters. Visitors have reported seeing the chair rock by itself.*

I raised my brows. It seemed silly, but I plowed on, getting acquainted with the objects d'spook under my purview: A colorfully painted magic scroll from Ethiopia believed to entrap evil spirits—*How many are trapped inside? And what will happen if they're released?* A tattered copy of an occult journal from the nineteenth century. A Victorian mourning ring said to attract the ghost of the woman whose hair was woven into the band.

The museum was an Aladdin's cave of the paranormal. I had to admit, it was an impressive collection.

The bell above the door jingled, and I scooted behind the cash register. Two Goth teenagers sauntered in, their faces unnaturally pale, their hair unnaturally black. The boy made a V-sign with his fingers, and I handed him two tickets.

"That will be …" I scanned down the list of instructions and choked. "Twenty dollars for the two of you."

His girlfriend drifted into the Fortune Telling Room. He dug a handful of crumpled bills from the front pocket of his black jeans and handed me the money. I untangled the damp mass, and he followed Girl Goth.

"You gave me too much." I held out a fiver.

He didn't look back, waving a hand negligently over his shoulder. "Keep it."

Shrugging, I dropped the cash in the tip jar. I turned the jar and read the label: *Lunch Money for GD Cat. Our ghost detecting cat has been known to spot ghosts! Watch where he gazes!*

Looking at the cat, I raised a brow. "Really?"

GD sneezed and followed the Goths into the Fortune Telling Room.

The plastic sheeting rattled, and a man in loose denims and a torn, paint-stained tee bounded into the room. From the tool belt slung low about his hips, I deduced he was Adele's contractor, Dieter Finkielkraut. His brown hair was spiked as if he'd plugged his finger into an electrical socket, and his brown eyes gleamed. Tanned and muscled, it wasn't hard to see how brokenhearted Adele had found him appealing.

"Hi! Are you Mad Dog Kosloski?"

I ground my teeth. Adele and her big mouth. Would high school never die?

He loped across the checkerboard floor, his hand extended. "I'm Dieter Finkielkraut, Adele's contractor. She said you'd be opening the museum today. How's it going?" He pumped my hand. His palm was rough from manual labor, but his grip was gentle.

"Two customers so far," I said.

"I'd planned to start up the circular saw. Want me to hold off until they go?"

"Theoretically, customers will be coming and going all day, so there's no point in delaying the noise. If anyone complains, I'll tell them it's the ghost of a lumberjack."

"Hey, do you know if Adele's coming in today? I wanted to ask her about some molding."

The Goths wandered into the Creepy Doll Room.

"I'm not sure. The murder might have changed her schedule."

"Murder?" His eyes twinkled. "Is she planning a murder mystery party for charity?"

I blinked. This was a small town, and murder was big news. I'd have thought word of Thursday night's death would be all over. "You haven't heard? Christy Huntington was found dead inside the Paranormal Museum."

His eyes dulled. "Christy Huntington? Here? When?"

"Thursday night. Were you here on Thursday?"

"I'm here nearly every weekday."

"What time did you leave on Thursday?" I'd no intention of playing detective, but finding Christy's body had left me with an ugly, vulnerable hollow in my gut. I wanted things to be okay, for

Adele to be in the clear. And I wanted to know why, if Dieter was here every weekday, he'd missed the cops in the tea room on Friday.

"I packed up Thursday around four thirty and headed up to Tahoe to get some snowboarding in on Friday. Just got back."

"Did you see Christy when you left on Thursday?"

He shook his head. "The only person I saw was your grumpy neighbor, the biker."

"If you just got back, I guess that explains why the police haven't talked to you," I said, uneasy. But why hadn't the police at least called Dieter to set an appointment for an interview? He was a potential witness.

"Why would the cops want to talk to me?"

"The body was found here Thursday night. I'd imagine they'd want to know when you left, to help figure out when she died, or if you'd seen her around the museum. We had to tell them you had a key. One of the cops seemed to recognize your name."

He hitched his jeans. "Oh? Who was it?"

"A detective named Laurel Hammer."

He grinned. "Oh yeah. Me and Laurel go way back to her pre–Johnny Law days."

"Were you staying at a hotel?"

"Why?"

"It's been ages since I've been to Tahoe," I said, deliberately vague. Oh yeah, I definitely had a flair for detection.

"Well, I was at a friend's cabin," Dieter said. "He gave me the key."

"You went alone?"

"Yeah, there's no special lady in my life."

Drat. So it would be tough to verify his story. Dieter had a key to the tea room—he could have killed Christy and then left for Tahoe, but what was his motive? "Did you know Christy well?"

"No. She's outta my league. I mean, *was* outta my league."

We stared at each other.

"How was the snow?" I asked.

"Icy."

My conversational gambit exhausted, Dieter departed. The whine of a circular saw pierced the air, and the Goths fled the museum.

A jowly businessman in a threadbare suit sidled through the front door. A customer!

I smiled, reaching for the tickets. "Welcome to the Paranormal Museum."

"Uh, yeah. Is Dieter here?"

Sourly, I pointed toward the plastic curtains with my pencil.

"Thanks." He hurried through them.

Between researching the museum's assorted oddities online, I relieved visitors of their ticket money. Saturday should have been a big day for sales. Although there was a steady trickle of guests, I couldn't see earning a living off the place if I bought it. Maybe if it had a gift shop, or a way to bring in repeat visitors. I could put a round table in the center of the room with things for sale. Or Dieter could build some shelves near the cash register to sell tarot cards and stuff. What that other stuff might be, I had no idea. Paranormal Museum postcards? Did people even send postcards anymore? And why was I thinking about this when the odds that I'd buy the place were practically nil?

A weedy-looking man in wrinkled khakis and a gray button-up shirt slouched in. His youthful face was carved in a hangdog expression, his single mark of distinction. Otherwise, he was Mr. Average—average height, average weight, sandy hair, brown eyes. He'd be an ideal bank robber, his identity fading into a million other averages.

I smiled. "Welcome to the Paranormal Museum. Tickets are—"

"I'm not here for a ticket." His voice dropped to a whisper. "I'm here to see where Christy died."

"Then you'll have to leave." An ache throbbed behind my left eyeball. I'd already driven off two reporters. The P.T. Barnum in me told me that no publicity was bad publicity, but it seemed icky, and Adele had enough problems.

The circular saw screamed. I winced, regretting that I'd told Dieter to go ahead with the work.

"You don't understand. Christy was my …" He gulped, his Adam's apple bobbing.

"Your …?"

"We were friends," he said. "I can't believe she's gone. It's denial, I guess, the first stage of grief. Do you know what happened?"

"The last reporter told me he was her brother. Unfortunately, he'd forgotten to remove his press pass from the Stockton Crab Feed."

The man pulled a wallet from his back pocket and dug out a business card: *Sam Leavitt, Esquire.*

So Sam was a lawyer. If the business card was legit. He looked like a harmless young professional, clean cut in business casual.

"Wow. I've never met a squire before," I said. "Is your horse parked outside?"

"It means—"

"I know what 'esquire' means."

He swallowed again. "Christy was my girlfriend," he said in a low voice.

My breath hitched. His girlfriend? Could I be any more insensitive? But what about Christy's engagement to Michael? "Christy told me she was seeing someone else."

"My girlfriend once," he clarified. "Then she dumped me for Michael St. James."

I leaned closer, feeling an unwilling twinge of sympathy.

"I couldn't blame her," he said. "He's rich. Successful. I'm a struggling lawyer, just starting out. At first, Christy and I had so much in common. And then her law career took off and mine flatlined. We were doomed."

He leaned closer. His breath smelled of onions and Tabasco. "What happened?" he asked, his fists clenched. "Were you the one who found her? If I find the person who did this…"

The museum had gone quiet, and I realized we were alone. I looked for something to put between me and Sam besides the counter, not liking the glitter in his eyes. If Christy had jilted him, had Sam killed her for revenge? I shifted the cat's tip jar in front of me as a barrier.

"I don't know what happened." I stared at the door, willing a customer to walk in, anyone. But the museum remained depressingly empty. Even the cat had abandoned me. "What do you think happened?"

He sagged. "I don't know. Christy was so sensitive and smart."

I bit the inside of my cheek. Smart and sensitive were not two adjectives I'd have applied to Christy, but I hadn't known her well. "If you have information, you should talk to the police."

He laughed. "Are you kidding? What do you think they'll do?"

The answer to that seemed obvious. Was there something I was missing? "They're investigating the case."

Brow wrinkling, he looked around the museum. "I can't believe she got killed in a place like this. Christy was very conscious of appearances. She would have hated being found in a paranormal museum."

"If she felt that strongly about it, she shouldn't have broken in."

"Broken in? She would never have broken in! She was committed to law and order."

I doubted that, but it was true that a key to the tea room had been found on her. How had she gotten her hands on it? And were there more keys floating around?

"Haunted chairs, creepy dolls," Sam said. "Christy would have found them tacky."

"I'll have you know that we have a genuine spirit cabinet used by mediums in the nineteenth century to defraud customers." My research that morning hadn't been a total waste. "We also have a Victorian-era spiritoscope designed to catch frauds. The spiritualist movement was an important and much over-looked period in American history." Okay, I made that part up. But it could have been true.

Sam looked unconvinced. "She loved art galleries, but this isn't art."

Now he was just being rude. This was a paranormal museum, not the Met. What did he expect? "A rotating macabre art exhibit is planned," I said stiffly. "The Creepy Doll Room would be a perfect space. Four windowless walls ideal for displaying exhibits, and a skylight above for natural lighting."

His eyes widened. He blinked rapidly, backing away. "Macabre?"

"Or arcane. It's not just a paranormal museum," I said, pointing to the row of old photos, "it's a capsule of our community."

"That's ... that's ..."

The bell tinkled over the door and I turned to it, relieved. "Welcome ..."

My brother walked inside, chic in jeans and a cream-colored fisherman's sweater.

The welcome died in my throat.

I was busted.

FIVE

My brother did a double take, his cornflower-blue eyes bulging. "Mad? What are you doing here?"

For a wild moment I thought of racing around the counter and pretending to be another visitor. But I'd been caught fair and square. "Nothing."

"Wait, you're not working here?"

My heartbeat grew loud in my ears. "I said I hadn't made a decision yet!"

"You mean this is the museum you were telling me about?"

"It's a perfectly proper museum." My voice was shrill. I winced, hearing myself parrot Adele's words.

Shane doubled over, howling with laughter.

Sam's gaze ping-ponged between the two of us. He raised a finger in the air. "I'll just …" He hurried from the museum, banging the door behind him.

My brother wiped his eyes. "The Paranormal Museum? Wait until Mom hears."

"You can't tell her," I hissed. "I'm doing a favor for Adele."

"What does Adele have to do with this? I wouldn't have thought it would be her thing."

"She owns the building now, and the mayor wants the museum kept open." I straightened. "It's the second biggest tourist attraction in San Benedetto."

"What's the first?"

"Duh. The wineries."

"But the wineries aren't *a* tourist attraction. They're multiple attractions, which puts your museum pretty far down the list. Are you more popular than the flaming Christmas Cow, or is that number one?"

"Since the Christmas Cow flames but once a year, the museum beats it. And I told you, it's not my museum."

"Whatever. This place is awesome. Where's the cat that sees ghosts?"

"He comes and goes, and right now he's gone. You're out of luck."

The cat strolled in from the tea room and twined himself around Shane's legs. Traitor. If GD Cat expected a penny of that tip money, he'd better develop opposable thumbs.

Shane bent and ruffled his fur. The cat arched his back in ecstasy.

An old man ambled in, his cabby hat pulled low over bushy eyebrows. "Is Dieter here?"

"Through there." I jerked my head toward the plastic-wrapped opening to the tea shop.

"Thanks." He hurried through.

"Busy place," Michael said. "Hey, you hear about Mel's gig at the Bolshoi?"

I nodded.

"It's not La Scalla," he said, "but she's moving up. She'll be disappointed you won't be in Moscow to hear her sing."

"It's not my fault I …"

"Quit?"

I couldn't tell him I'd been fired. "You wouldn't understand."

"Try me."

When I said nothing, he said, "I won't be there either, if it makes you feel better."

"Where will you be?"

He shrugged. "The State Department's talking about a new posting. But I'm not sure where yet. I'm glad at least one of us is here for Mom."

I looked down at the cash register. None of us had been in the States when our father had died, and it felt like a failure.

Adele bustled through the plastic sheeting, a cardboard carrier with four cups of coffee in one hand. Over her other arm swung a kelly-green purse. Its color exactly matched her '60s-style miniskirt. She plunked the coffee on the counter. Straightening her brown turtleneck sweater, she turned to my brother, arms wide. "Shane!"

He hugged her. "Good to see you, Adele."

She stepped back. "Mad didn't tell me you were in town. What do you think of the museum?"

He laughed. "Weird as ever."

She handed me a paper cup and some sugar packets. "Mochaccino for you, Mad. I know it's your favorite."

"Thanks," I said, surprised by the gesture. I peeled off the plastic lid and inhaled the aroma of coffee and chocolate. Heaven.

"Shane, how do you feel about Ethiopian?"

"Love it."

She handed him a cup.

Dieter bounded into the room. "Do I smell coffee?"

"Not that you need any caffeine," Adele said, "but here's your double espresso."

"If you didn't know Shane was here, why did you bring an extra coffee?" I tore open the sugar packets, dumped them in, and stirred.

"I always get one extra, just in case. It's only polite should you have an unexpected guest." She threaded her arms through Dieter's and Shane's. "Let me show you our plans for the tea room."

I watched her lead the men out of the museum area. When the plastic sheeting closed behind them, a muscle between my shoulder blades released. Was I jealous of Shane's success? I hadn't been when I'd had an international job of my own. I blew out my breath. I was a small, small person.

As penance, I called my mother. She picked up on the second ring. "Madelyn, is it true?"

"Hi, Mom. Is what true?" I found a pencil that had rolled beneath the cash register and tested it on a blank ticket. It was nice and sharp.

"That you've bought the Paranormal Museum."

I stared at the haunted rocking chair. How had my mother found out so fast? "No, I didn't buy it." That one-dollar sale couldn't have been valid.

She sighed. "Oh, thank goodness. Adele's father told me you were taking it over. I knew you wouldn't do something so stupid."

"But Adele and I are talking about it." There was a snap, and I looked down. I'd gouged a hole in the ticket and broken the pencil's tip. Carefully, I laid the pencil down. "I'm helping her run the place until I make a decision."

"Run the place? You mean you're serious?"

"Someone needs to manage it. The Wine and Visitors Bureau can't do it indefinitely."

"Madelyn, not everyone likes that museum."

A middle-aged couple strolled through the door.

"Just a sec." Laying the phone on the counter, I sold them two tickets. I picked up the phone. "What were you saying?"

"The museum is a mistake. You can't ..." My mother breathed heavily. "After everything you've done with your life, you can't run that ridiculous little tourist trap."

"Why not?"

"How will you earn a living?"

"Revenues are a bit low," I said, enjoying the thought that I was about to make her crazy. "But if I added a gift shop for added revenue and maybe some rotating art exhibits to get repeat customers ... it could work. Especially if I put the gift shop online. You have no idea how interested people are in the paranormal." I knew she didn't because neither did I.

"Oh. My. God. You are serious."

"Just thinking aloud." Then I relented. "I haven't made any decisions. Seriously, right now I'm just helping out Adele."

"How is Adele?" My mother's voice softened. "I read about what happened in the paper. Poor Mrs. Huntington. Christy was her only child."

"Do you know them well?"

"Her mother? No. I feel terrible. She's a member of my church, but you know how big that church is. How's Adele doing? Finding the body must have been a terrible shock."

"She's soldiering on." I didn't want to tell her I'd found the body too. It would sound like I was looking for sympathy.

"Please let her know that if there's anything I can do, I'm here for her. The police must consider her a suspect since Christy … well, you know. But anyone who knows Adele knows she couldn't do it."

"I'll pass on the message," I said, oddly touched. Feeling guilty for teasing, I listened to my mother gush about Melanie and the Bolshoi while I hunted for a pencil sharpener. I promised to stop by for dinner and rang off.

A few more people trickled in. I glanced at the computer screen, its window open to a page on Ouija boards. I might as well get started on a more organized inventory of the museum. I needed to get better acquainted with the collection. Someone might ask me a question I couldn't invent a plausible answer for.

My brother stuck his head through the plastic sheeting. "I'm headed out. Call me."

GD Cat slunk into the museum and studied a photo on the wall.

A bespectacled tourist walked in from the Creepy Doll Room. He stared at GD. "Is that the ghost cat?"

I nodded.

Squinting at the spot the cat had fixated on, he snapped a picture and checked the viewer on his camera. "I've got orbs! Your cat really does detect ghosts." He hurried to the cashier's desk and handed me the camera. "See?"

I looked at the screen. In front of a grainy portrait on the wall floated two translucent circles. They were likely dust or reflected sunlight, but who was I to discourage him? "You should post that online," I said.

"I will!" He took a few more shots, but none turned up more orbs. Beaming, he jammed some dollar bills in the tip jar before leaving.

Expression smug, GD Cat looked over his shoulder at me.

"All right," I said. "You earned your keep on that one."

Rooting through the drawers beneath the counter, I found a battered three-ring binder. Each page had a receipt taped to it, a photo of the "haunted" object, and a far-too-brief description. Grabbing a pad of yellow sticky notes, I started matching the objects in the main room to their pages in the binder. The rocking chair was on page one. I stuck a yellow note on the chair and penciled a check mark on its page.

I scratched my head with the eraser end of the pencil, studying the sepia-tinted photo that had fascinated the cat. It hung in a row with other old-timey portraits. The photo was from the 1890s, a husband and wife. The woman's face was expressionless, but there was something in her eyes—a solemn awareness. Her nose was longish, her eyes deep-set. She posed beside a seated man for a formal portrait, one hand braced on his shoulder. The notation read: *Cora M. McBride and husband. Convicted of husband's murder and sentenced to life. Haunted photo.*

Haunted? How? I checked its corresponding page in the binder. The caption there was identical, with one addition: *b.f.h.l.* I flipped the pages. Someone had added those four letters to most of the page corners. This binder was more cryptic than the Egyptian Book of the Dead.

"What the heck does 'b-f-h-l' mean?" I asked no one.

No one answered. Which was a good thing, because I could hear Adele and Dieter in the room next door discussing ceiling treatments.

Dog-earing the page with Cora's photograph, I made a note to do more research on the murderess. Who was Cora? Why had she killed her husband? And what made this photo haunted?

I moved on to the next photo in the row. The information on it was scanty, as it was on the next photo in line. I dog-eared more pages, affixed more sticky notes. Improving the museum wasn't my problem. But better stories about the objects would generate more interest. It was a missed opportunity. Missed opportunities irritated me.

Someone knocked on the door, and Harper stuck her head inside. "Can I come in?"

"It's a public place. You don't have to knock."

She leaned against the counter, her blue pantsuit hugging her curves. "Is Adele here? We're supposed to—"

Adele blew into the room and ran her fingers through her ebony hair. "You have no idea how many decisions have to be made during a remodel. Did you know grout comes in different colors? Hi, Harper."

"I'd have thought you'd be in your element." I closed the binder and returned it to its drawer.

"Normally, yes." Adele's gaze slid to the spot on the floor where Christy's body had lain, and she shuddered. "But now the only color I can think about is prison-jumpsuit orange. What's worse is that there actually was a moment when I wanted to kill her. It's almost like my wish came true, and I'd give anything if it hadn't."

"You might not want to go around telling people that," I said. "I know what you mean, but other people could take it the wrong way."

"Done," Adele said. "I'd rather not talk about it at all."

Harper checked her wide, leather-banded watch. "Hey, Adele, are you ready to go? Your lawyer is waiting for us."

"In a minute. What do you think about seasonal tea services? Like pumpkin scones for Halloween with ginger tea, and a Christmas service, that sort of thing?"

My mouth watered. "I stand ready to assist with the market research."

Adele laughed. "Oh, and Harper, I'd love to sell your special tea."

Harper seemed to contract, pulling her arms closer, looking away. "Uh, I don't make that anymore."

A line appeared between Adele's brows. "But that tea was wonderful! Oh well, the recipe will do as well."

"I lost it. Sorry." A beat passed. Harper frowned.

Adele stared at her. I knew what she was thinking. I was thinking it too. Harper was lying, and it seemed like a stupid thing to lie about. I shifted, awkward. I wasn't going to stick my head in this bear trap, but I couldn't figure out how to change the subject. The silence thickened.

"Adele," I blurted, "I noticed there's no bathroom in the museum."

"So?"

"So if you close up the pass-through between the museum and the tea room, what will the museum customers do?"

She opened her mouth, then closed it.

The door to the museum opened, bamming against the wall. Michael strode inside. His gaze landed on Adele. "We need to talk. Now."

Harper straightened up from the counter.

Eyes narrowing, Adele crossed her arms over her chest. "I don't think that's such a good idea. Christy's death hasn't changed anything between you and I."

"Adele, I'm not kidding around." He stepped between the two of us, turning his back on me.

I leaned across the counter, nudging the tip jar aside. "I'd be happy to talk to you. You never did tell me what you said to the police about me and Christy."

Michael didn't bother looking at me. "Why should I? You know what you did. Christy told me about your fight."

Adele stepped to the side and caught my eye. "You argued with Christy?" A line appeared between her finely plucked brows.

"No." But my cheeks warmed.

"That wasn't Christy's story," Michael said.

It hadn't been a fight, but I'd been shocked and angry when Christy had informed me of her engagement to Michael. I still didn't want to give Adele the details of that encounter—Michael should be the one to tell her about his engagement to Christy, not me. News of that final betrayal would hurt more from an outsider to their relationship.

"I don't care what Christy told you," I said. "It's not true."

Michael's face darkened.

Adele adjusted the purse on her arm. "What do you want, Michael?"

He stepped closer to her, and she arched away. "There's only so much I can do to protect you," he said quietly. "I need to know what happened."

She touched her hand to the hollow at the base of her throat. "Protect me? What are you talking about?"

Dieter brushed through the plastic hangings, hitching up his tool belt. "While you're here, can you come take ..." He trailed off, catching sight of Michael. "Everything okay in here?"

"Everything's fine," Adele said. "Michael was just leaving."

"No, I'm not," Michael said. "Not until we discuss this."

"I think you are." Dieter's voice hardened. His limbs remained relaxed, hands at his sides, but his chin lowered, jaw set.

Michael cleared his throat and backed away. "That's Adele's decision."

"And I think you should go." She looked away.

"Fine." Michael raised his hands in a gesture of surrender. "We can talk later. If you're still free," he said under his breath. He turned and stormed out the door.

"Are you all right?" Dieter asked.

Adele smiled. "I'm fine. Michael's harmless."

"Tell that to Christy," Dieter said.

She yanked the cuff of her brown sleeve. "Michael did not kill Christy."

"How do you know?" I asked. He seemed like a pretty good candidate to me.

"Because," she said, "someone else killed her."

SIX

"MICHAEL COULDN'T HAVE KILLED Christy," Adele repeated. She twisted the gold watch circling her wrist. "He can't even kill spiders."

"The killer was most likely someone she knew," I said, gesturing at the museum. "No one broke in. Nothing was taken. Christy didn't get caught up in a robbery." Not that there was anything to steal—unless you were a fan of paranormal knickknacks.

"It wasn't Michael." Adele checked her watch. "Oh, darn. I nearly forgot, I've got an appointment with my father and our lawyer. Let's not continue this conversation later." Slipping her green purse over her shoulder, she minced out the door.

Harper and I looked at each other.

"Any minute, she'll remember that we're going there together," Harper said. "I'd better go find her." She hurried out the door.

Dieter's shoulders slumped, his hands falling to his sides. "I think I made her mad."

"Christy—the *other woman*—was killed in Adele's tea shop, and she and Michael are the most likely suspects," I told him. "There's nothing you can say to make that better or worse."

He leaned against the counter. "Michael's a jackass. The whole town knows he cheated on Adele, and now he's begging to get her back. At least she's smart enough not to fall for his garbage twice." Dieter raised his eyebrows, questioning.

I chewed my lower lip. I'd witnessed some of Michael's attempts to crawl back into Adele's good graces. But Christy had told me she and Michael were engaged. Had it been a lie? Had Christy been trying to ruin Michael's attempts at reconciliation with Adele? And was that a reason for him to kill her?

When I didn't respond, Dieter returned to his work. The whine of the circular saw punctured the air.

The front door banged open. I looked up, glad for the distraction, and reached for a ticket.

A man walked inside, a five o'clock shadow darkening his chiseled features. His hair was tied back in a short blond ponytail. A motorcycle helmet dangled from his fingers. His gaze lingered on me, and he shrugged his muscular shoulders. They strained against the contours of his black-leather motorcycle jacket. This was a guy who put in some serious gym time. It was embarrassingly easy for me to imagine him bare-chested on the cover of a romance novel.

He plunked the helmet on the counter, rattling the tip jar. "You in charge?"

I smoothed the leer from my features. "I'm running the Paranormal Museum. Would you like to buy a ticket?"

He glowered. "No, I would not like to buy a ticket. I would like you to shut off that damn circular saw and move your dumpster out of my rear parking space."

"Your rear parking space?" I sucked in my cheeks.

"I own the motorcycle shop next door. And I can barely hear myself think over that saw."

A flush of warmth flooded my body. And annoyance. "I'm not in charge of the renovations, but I'll let the owner know, and I'll talk to the contractor about a better time to run the saw. Er, when would be a better time to run that saw?"

"Since I live over my shop, never." The man turned on his booted heal and stormed out, brushing past a tall, older man in a gray suit.

The older man scratched his neatly trimmed beard. His blond hair was streaked with silver, and he was well built. He approached the counter, jerking a thumb over his shoulder. "What's his problem?"

"No refunds. Can I help you?" I took in the briefcase in his broad hand, the silver hair, the expensive suit. He didn't fit my customer profile, but that was a work in progress, so I decided to stay open-minded.

He glanced around. "I was looking for Adele. I'm her lawyer. Is she here?"

I grabbed for my cell phone. "Her lawyer? She left not long ago to meet her lawyer for lunch."

He laughed. "That's okay. She must be meeting with Fred, her criminal attorney. I do estate and business law. We're old friends. I was just dropping by to see how she was doing."

"I'll let her know you stopped by, Mr. . . . ?"

"Just Roger. She'll know who I am." He leaned an elbow against the counter. "So who are you? You don't look like you're with the Wine and Visitors Bureau. I know everyone there."

"I'm Maddie, a friend of Adele's. She asked me to manage the museum until she could find a buyer."

"Rats. I was hoping you'd be the buyer. She needs to unload this albatross."

"It's not so bad. It could make money."

"Not enough. Whoever buys it should give it more flash."

"I do think the museum could do a better job telling the stories of the artifacts," I admitted.

"Artifacts? This junk?" He laughed. "This stuff is boring. An old spirit cabinet? Who cares? The museum needs something sexier."

"Sex sells?" I asked coldly. He was a friend of Adele's so I had to play nice, but I wished he'd shut up about the museum. "I suppose it depends on the sort of client the new owner wants. Personally, I think putting a rotating macabre art exhibit in the Creepy Doll Room could bring in repeat customers. Add a gift shop, put it online, and the owner could really bump up revenues."

"You want to get rid of the creepy dolls? People love the creepy dolls."

"There's empty wall space in this room," I pointed out. "I could shift things around and mount new shelves for the dolls here."

"Those aren't bad ideas. I know a guy who's an art agent. He could probably set you up with the types of artists you're looking for."

"Thanks." Wait. Did I just take over the project? I backtracked. "But I'm not—"

Dieter walked through the plastic curtains. He raked a hand through his hair, spiking it higher. "Hey, I'm going to need to turn off the water for an hour. Oh, hi Roger."

"Dieter!" The lawyer clapped him on the back. "So Adele took my advice and hired you for the job. Dieter has done the remodels on several of my rental properties," he said to me. To Dieter: "How's that caveman diet going for you?" He winked at me. "Well-cooked meat and raw vegetables. That's the ticket to health."

Dieter winced. "Haven't had a chance to try it yet."

"Don't delay. You're only young once. How's the remodel going?"

"The police had the museum shut down Friday, but I was in Tahoe anyway, so I'm still on schedule. But there's something I'd like to talk to you about, Roger."

"Sure. We can talk." The lawyer shook his head. "I still can't believe she's dead. What was Christy doing here?"

"Christy? You knew her?" I asked.

"She's a junior partner at my firm. Was a junior partner, I mean."

"Did Christy do estate and business law too?" I asked.

"Yep," Roger said. "I wonder if she had her own estate in order? So many of us don't."

Dieter changed the subject. "Maddie, I also wanted to let you know I'm done with the saw for the day."

"Oh, good. One of the neighbors was complaining."

Dieter's dark brows drew together. "Let me guess. The motorhead next door?"

Roger clapped him on the shoulder. "As long as you're running the saw during working hours, you've got nothing to worry about."

"I'm not worried," he said. "The guy's pissing me off. Wanna come out back and we can talk?"

"What's the rush?" The lawyer reached for me and drew me into an awkward group huddle, his arms around both Dieter and my shoulders. I tried to edge away.

"Do you two want to know the secret to life?" he asked. "Don't take yourself so seriously. If you can do that, everything else falls into place."

"I'm not sure that applies to our situation," I said. "The police are taking Christy's death very seriously, and they seem to consider Adele a prime suspect."

"Adele?" Dieter asked. "She's half Christy's size. How's she going to take her down? Even if this goes to court, Adele's got nothing to worry about."

The lawyer shook his head. "If this goes to court, she has everything to worry about. Some of my oldest friends are criminal attorneys. I've heard all the stories, and let me tell you something. Defendants, lawyers, cops—everybody lies. Don't count on the truth setting Adele free."

SEVEN

I NEEDED A DIVERSION from inventory-taking. Removing Cora Mc-
Bride's picture from the wall, I brought it to the counter and pried off
the back. On one corner of the photo in ornate Victorian handwriting was a date: 1891. Or was it 1897? The ink was faded, but I was
fairly certain it was '91.

I surfed the Internet, searching for something about Cora. The
old murder either wasn't that notorious or I was spelling something
wrong. I didn't find a thing.

A narrow, mousy-looking man wearing fish-bowl glasses and a
bow tie stuck his head through the open front door.

"Dieter's in the back," I snapped. Nearly a quarter of the men
who'd been in today had been looking for Dieter.

He sidled inside, catching the sleeve of his tattered tweed jacket
on the door handle. Lurching backward, he disentangled himself.
"I'm looking for the proprietor of the Paranormal Museum."

"Oh." I lowered my head, deflated. "That's me."

He smoothed his comb-over. "Excellent. It's about time this fine establishment got adequate replacement management. You can call me Herb."

The cat trotted to him, and he patted its head.

"Er, yes," I said. "What can I do for you?"

The cat sat on his haunches, watching us intently.

Herb wagged a finger at me. "The question is, what can I do for you?"

"All right. What can you do for me?"

"I'm a collector. I've been providing paranormal exhibits to this museum for years." He tapped the photo of Cora still lying on the counter. "That was one of mine."

I perked up. "Oh? Maybe you can tell me something about it. The notes are fairly thin."

"The prior owner of this museum, Chuck, was a paranormal enthusiast, but his record keeping was abysmal. It's nice to see someone taking more of an interest."

"Cora?" I prompted.

"Of course. An interesting tale because it happened right here in San Benedetto."

"Really," I said, skeptical. When a town doesn't have much history, it tends to embroider on what it's got. Before I'd found the photo, I'd never heard of Cora.

"Cora O'Malley married Martin McBride in 1890. It was a tumultuous marriage. The town didn't expect Cora to survive it, but much to everyone's surprise, it was Martin who died prematurely. Cora tried to make it look like a suicide, but it quickly became obvious that it was murder."

"Why was it obvious?" I scratched frantic notes on the pad beside the cash register.

"I have no idea, but they had sufficient evidence to sentence her to life in prison in 1899. She died two years later. At any rate, a donor who shall remain nameless picked up this photo at an estate sale. Having no such photos of relatives of her own from that era, she hung it in her parlor."

"She had a parlor?" People still had parlors?

"But soon thereafter, she began hearing the sound of a woman's sobs coming from the room at night when no one was there. Unnerved, she came to me looking for a recommendation for a ghost buster. I convinced her it would be simpler to sell me the photo instead."

"I thought you said she was a donor."

"Perhaps you would find this tale more enlightening if you listened without interruption."

"Sorry." I coughed. "But how did Cora's husband die?"

"Hanged, I believe. You can probably get more details from the Historical Association. I don't suppose you've heard Cora's sobs yet?" He tilted his head to the side.

"No, but I don't stick around the museum at night."

He smiled, revealing sharp incisors. "You should. Ghosts are with us constantly. But with the hustle and bustle of daily life"—he nodded as two tourists emerged from the Creepy Doll Room—"it is difficult to detect them. One needs silence, stillness, and most importantly a controlled environment to perceive ghosts."

"That's useful information," I said. "Thanks."

"For you, that information is free." He glanced at the visitors. "I heard an object here was used to murder the young woman. Which was it? I don't suppose you still have it?"

"The police have it." I tapped my fingers on the counter, my gaze flicking upward. Herb was just another murder site lookee-loo, and I'd been suckered into a conversation.

"What a shame. I would have liked to have taken EMF readings."

"EMF?"

"Electromagnetic field. We believe that spirit activity can change EMFs." He pulled a small plastic box from his pocket and turned it on. A rainbow of lights lit up the top, then blanked out. He waved it across Cora's photo, and the lights went to orange. "Interesting. It also would have been interesting to see if the EMF on the murder weapon had changed, if it was an object I procured."

"Why did it light up over the photo?"

"There appears to be some energy there, but that's no surprise since it's haunted. I provide a valuable service removing haunted objects from people's homes and businesses."

"And you dump them here?" My voice jumped, hair standing at attention on the back of my neck. Not that I believed in any of that haunted stuff.

"I bind the objects first, of course, though Chuck suggested it would be best if I left some of the less harmful objects be. What's the good of a paranormal object that's no longer paranormal? Now, I can see that you're a woman of discernment. I have come across an amazing object of historical significance, and I wanted to give the Paranormal Museum the right of first refusal."

"I'm breathless with anticipation."

"As you should be." Lifting his heels, he thrust his chest out. "Dion Fortune's scrying mirror."

"Oh?" I understood "mirror," but as to the rest, he might as well have been describing the Federal Reserve system.

"I picked it up in New York." Herb dug into his pocket and unfolded a piece of paper. "You'll want to see the provenance, of course." He handed me the paper. At the top: a photo of a mirror. At the bottom: a notary's stamp. In between was a list of owners by date, and the location where the mirror had been stored.

"I'll need to do some research of my own first," I hedged.

"Of course. I'm asking ten thousand."

I coughed. "Dollars?"

"But for you, five."

"Thousand?" I wouldn't pay five thousand for Ali Baba's mirror. There was no way anything in the museum cost that much.

"And now onto our next piece of business." Herb's eyes narrowed. "My first bit of information was free, as a token of my esteem. But this will cost you."

"Information about what?" I asked, bewildered.

He leaned across the desk, his voice dropping to a hiss. "Murder."

"You know something about the murder here last Thursday?"

He pressed a finger to the side of his nose and nodded. "How much is it worth to you?"

"Since I don't know what you've got, nothing. Besides, if you have information, you need to tell the police."

"The police?" His head reared back, spectacles glinting in the sun from the window. "I don't talk to cops. In my experience, they are completely untrustworthy."

"Fine. Ten bucks."

"Twenty."

I dug into the tip jar and pulled out a wad of cash.

GD Cat meowed, his tail lashing.

"It's for a good cause," I told GD.

"Indeed it is," Herb replied.

Flattening out the cash, I counted out twenty dollars.

The cat stalked into the Fortune Telling Room, his tail a bottle-brush of indignation.

"So what have you got?" I asked.

"I stopped by here Thursday evening, just before six o'clock, looking for the proprietor." He bowed to me. "The light inside the museum was on, but the door was closed and the shades drawn. However, the door to the establishment next door stood ajar—"

"To the tea room?"

"Precisely. I went inside. I heard two people arguing in the museum—the murdered girl and a man."

"What exactly did you hear?" My blood hummed. A clue! Herb would clear Adele, and we could all relax.

"The woman was shouting about trust. I dislike conflicts, so I left."

"What did the man say?"

"I didn't actually hear the person she was shouting at."

"So it might have been a woman. Or she could have been talking on a cell phone."

"Hardly. I saw their shapes through the plastic sheeting. One was definitely a man. Quite large."

"How do you know Christy was the woman?"

"I could see her through the gap in the plastic." He gestured toward the makeshift barrier to the tea room. The two sheets formed a seamless wall, but I'd seen the plastic billow and fold back like a tent. He could have seen Christy.

"Herb, you need to tell the police."

His mouth slackened. "Absolutely not."

"This is a murder investigation. If the police don't have all the facts, someone may be wrongfully charged."

"Then you tell the police." He glanced past my shoulder out the window, and his eyes widened. Turning, he sprinted through the plastic drapes. They whipped around him.

"Hey! You can't go back there!" I hurried after him, but the tea room was empty. Something clunked to the floor on my right. Dodging power tools and stacks of slate-gray tile, I headed for the hallway that led to the bathroom and the alley. Herb's slight form vanished out the back door.

There was a shout and Dieter poked his head around the corner of the alleyway door, his hair thick with sawdust. "Who was that?"

"You mean you don't know him?" I asked, chagrined. All I'd gotten was Herb's first name.

"Your customers have to stay out of the tea room until construction is done. They might hurt themselves tripping over a cable or something and sue."

"What about all those guys who've been coming to see you?"

"Good point. I'll ask them to come through the alley from now on."

I stomped back the way I'd come, brushing through the plastic tarps into the museum.

Detective Laurel Hammer stood in the center of the room, turning slowly and tugging at the wisps of blond hair at the base of her neck. The sleeves of her white blouse were rolled to her elbows, and I detected a flash of blue skin at the edge of one rolled-up sleeve.

Her partner stood beside the counter, engaged in a staring contest with the cat. Without breaking eye contact, the cat reached out a stealthy paw and batted the cuff of his white shirt.

I cleared my throat. "Hello."

The detective turned from the cat, his look speculative. He unbuttoned his black suit jacket, revealing a plain white shirt, red power tie, and gun on his hip. He pulled a slim wallet from his inside pocket and flashed his badge. "I'm Detective Slate."

"Nice to meet you." That was a big fat lie, but I knew enough to be polite. "Can I help you with anything?"

Laurel Hammer grimaced. "You can tell us why you didn't see fit to inform us about your altercation with the victim last week."

I raised a brow. "That's easy. I didn't have an altercation with her."

"That isn't what she told her boyfriend," she said.

"I can't help that."

"She said you threatened her."

That stopped me. "What?"

"You heard me. What exactly did you threaten her with?"

"Nothing! This is ridiculous. I ran into Christy coming out of the bridal shop last week. She told me she was getting married to Michael St. James. And yes, I reacted."

"How?" Laurel asked.

"Michael was engaged to Adele last month." But threaten her? I was baffled.

"So you told her off," Laurel said.

"No. I might have been a bit of a broken record about him being engaged to someone else a month earlier. But I didn't threaten her, even if she did provoke me."

"Provoked you?" Detective Slate asked. "How?"

"She knew I was friends with Adele, and she was flaunting her engagement less than a month after she'd broken up Adele's. It annoyed me."

"Enough to kill her?" Laurel asked.

"Come on," I said.

She bridled. "I suggest you—"

"Tell us where Adele is," her partner interrupted. "We came here to speak with her."

"She left to have lunch with her lawyer. I don't know when or if she'll be back."

"Oh, don't you?" Laurel stepped closer, forcing me to look up.

"No, I don't. I can call her if you like. Or you can, since I assume as part of your investigation you collected her number."

"I think you're covering for her."

"Why would I do that?"

The bell above the door tinkled, and Adele blew into the room.

"Because she's right here," Laurel said.

Adele halted in the open door and tucked a strand of hair behind one ear. Straightening, she pasted on a polite smile. "May I help you?"

I bit my lip. I'm not the sort of person prone to bad feelings, but right now, a sense of badness was raging.

Laurel reached behind her back and pulled a pair of handcuffs from her belt. "You'll have to come with us. You're under arrest." She moved toward Adele and grabbed her wrist.

Adele blanched. Her green purse slipped from her free arm and thunked to the floor.

"What?" I said. "Wait! There was a man who was just in here. He said he heard Christy and a man arguing inside the museum around six o'clock on Thursday."

"Oh, that's convenient." Laurel twisted Adele's arm behind her back.

Detective Slate cocked his head. "What man?"

"He said his name was Herb. When I suggested he talk to you, he ran out the back door."

The detective pulled a notepad from his inside breast pocket. "Has this Herb got a last name?"

"He must." Mouth dry, I clawed a hand through my hair. This couldn't be happening. "But he didn't give it to me. He told me he was a collector for the museum. Adele, do you know him?"

She shook her head, eyes wide.

"You have the right to remain silent," Laurel said in a bored tone.

"A collector?" Slate asked. "If the museum has paid him, his name or contact information may be on your receipts."

"I'll look. Does this mean you won't arrest Adele?"

He lifted his hands and let them fall. "Sorry. But if you find his name, let us know. We'll follow up."

The handcuffs clicked shut.

EIGHT

"Do you really need to cuff her?" I babbled, following the two police detectives and Adele into the mid-day sun. It was deceptively bright on this chill winter day. I rubbed my arms.

Laurel reddened, whirling on me.

"That's okay." Adele's smile was tight. "You know silver is my color."

Silver was definitely not Adele's color. She wore gold. And maybe platinum.

Putting her hand on Adele's head, Laurel levered her into the police car.

"Just keep things running here—the remodel and the museum," Adele said. "And call my fa—"

Laurel shut the car door and glared at me, a vein pulsing in her jaw.

I retreated inside the museum and called Adele's father to tell him what happened. Terse, he thanked me and hung up.

Feeling helpless, I raked both hands through my hair. I had to do something. Herb. I needed to find Herb. There had to be a record of purchases from him with a telephone number or address.

Rummaging beneath the cash register, I found kitty litter and office supplies. But I'd seen boxes somewhere. Boxes with papers in them? I closed my eyes, struggling to remember.

"The Creepy Doll Room!" I opened my eyes. Two women in expensive track suits stood before me.

"We wanted to buy tickets?"

"Of course. That will be twenty dollars."

They handed me the money. I gave them their tickets and dashed for the Creepy Doll Room. Sliding back a cupboard door low in the wall, I pulled out a box and pried off its lid. It was packed tight with dusty manila folders stuffed with papers. Sneezing, I brought the box to the front counter.

Two hours later, I slammed the lid down on the cardboard box in disgust. I hadn't found a single receipt with Herb's name on it, and I'd gone through the box three times.

Sunlight slanted low through the windows, blinding, and I lowered the shade. Soon the sun would disappear behind the low mountains to the west.

From behind me came a low growl.

"Oh, what now?" I looked over my shoulder.

The cat hissed at me, back arching.

"Look, I'm sorry about the twenty bucks, okay? But Adele's in jail, and Herb might have information that can get her out."

"Adele's in jail?"

I started. "Agh!"

Dieter pulled a piece of the plastic sheeting aside.

Gulping, I pressed a hand to my chest. "The police arrested her a couple hours ago. Hey, that guy who ran out of here earlier—are you sure you haven't seen him before?"

Dieter shook his head, sawdust drifting to the floor. "Adele's really in jail? What are the cops thinking? She couldn't hurt a fly. Literally. When I find bugs in the building, she makes me catch them and put them outside."

"Yeah, at least she and Michael had that in common." Adele had motive and maybe she had opportunity, but a killer she was not.

Dieter slammed his fist into an exposed beam. "This is garbage." He clumped from the room, rubbing his knuckles.

———

"I can't believe they arrested her." Harper slumped in the booth, one arm on the damp table. The Bell and Brew's stained-glass lamp swayed gently above us, casting bars of red and gold light across Harper's fitted blue blazer.

The microbrewery was in full swing that Saturday night, the raucous atmosphere giving us a measure of privacy even if we did have to lean close and shout.

I finished the remnants of my third zinfandel. "I get that Adele's a suspect. The body was found in her building, and after the break-up, she was no fan of Christy's. But can the police have any real evidence? Isn't this all circumstantial?"

"Unless the police have something we don't know about."

"What could they possibly have?" I remembered Adele picking up that obelisk and groaned. "Her fingerprints on the murder weapon."

"What?"

"There was a replica of an Egyptian obelisk lying by Christy's body. Adele picked it up."

"How could she do something so stupid?"

"We were both pretty rattled," I said. "But I told the police I saw her grab it."

"All right. We both know she's innocent. Let's think." Harper stared at the ceiling, pursing her lips.

Our hunky waiter came by and slid the bill onto the table, his gaze fastening on Harper's full lips. "Whenever you're ready, ladies. No hurry."

Harper licked her lips, thoughtful, and his eyes filled with longing.

"Thanks," I said loudly.

"What? Oh. Yeah." The waiter bustled to another table.

Harper sighed. "We need to talk to Michael. The killer's usually the spouse."

"Christy and Michael weren't married."

"According to you, they were engaged, and that's close enough."

"He did know Christy best. If someone was out to get her, maybe he'd know who."

"Let's go!" Harper grabbed her briefcase off the seat.

"Now? It's nearly eleven."

"He'll be awake," she said uncertainly, replacing the briefcase.

"But I'm not." My head felt fuzzy. I looked at the bill and winced. "Ouch. Six glasses of wine really adds up."

Harper buried her head in her hands. "Six glasses? I know better than that." She looked up. "A bottle would have been cheaper."

"Ever the financial advisor."

"How much is it?"

"With the bread pudding and the bruschetta plate—"

"They make great bruschetta."

"Seventy-two dollars and seventeen cents."

She jerked upright, paling. "What? Seventeen cents?"

"Ye-es." More disturbed by the seventy-two dollars, I eyed her. I really needed to pay more attention to my spending. But Adele's arrest had knocked me for a loop.

"The number seventeen looks like a man on the gallows," Harper said.

"What does that even mean?"

"It's Italian, and it means terrible luck. We need to do something."

"When did you get superstitious?" I asked.

"Oh …" She waved her hand. "It's an Italian thing."

I eyed her. It might be an Italian thing, but I'd never remembered Harper giving evil eye signs and talking lucky numbers before. "You're drunk."

"You're right. Can you give me a ride home?"

"I've been drinking as much as you have," I pointed out. How was I going to get home? San Benedetto didn't have a taxi service. If my job hunt didn't pan out, maybe I could become a taxi driver?

"We should stay here and sober up." Harper lifted a finger and the waiter apparated to our table. "Another round of Haunted Vine zinfandel," she told him. "In honor of Adele!"

"Adele." I toasted.

The waiter scooped up our bill and hustled into the crowd.

"I can't believe they arrested her," Harper said mournfully.

I shook my head, feeling like we'd gotten caught in a loop.

The wine arrived, brought by the microbrewery's owner—first name Jim, last name unknown (to me at least). He was a blond with a beer gut and one of those cherubic faces that didn't seem to age, though I figured him for around fifty.

"Hi, Harper, Maddie. Where's Adele tonight?" He placed the glasses before us.

I twisted the paper napkin in my lap. "She couldn't make it." News would get out soon enough about Adele's arrest, but I didn't want to be the one to spread the story.

"So what are you two troublemakers up to?" he asked.

"We're trying to figure out who killed Christy Huntington," I said. *In vino veritas* and all that.

Jim slipped the round tray beneath his arm. "I'm putting money on the boyfriend."

"Why?" I asked.

"Because he and Christy had a big fight in here the other week. I had to ask them to leave. They were disturbing the customers."

A trio of bikers strolled past, helmets dangling from their meaty fingertips, a flaming skull on the back of their matching leather vests.

"This is a family place," Jim said.

Harper took a sip of her wine. "What were they arguing about?"

"I don't know, but there was a lot of yelling."

"Wait," I said, remembering Sam Leavitt. "Which boyfriend? Was she with Michael St. James?"

"Who?" Jim asked.

"Christy had more than one boyfriend?" Harper put down her glass with a clink.

"What did he look like?" I asked.

"Tall. Young. Well dressed. These young professionals all look alike."

"Did he have brown hair?" I asked. "Or sandy hair?"

"Yes," Jim said.

"Yes to which?"

"It was brown or sandy."

"Urgh." Harper dug her phone out of her leather briefcase, her fingers dancing across the keys. "Was it this guy?" She handed the phone to Jim.

"Yeah. That looks like him." He gave me the phone. Harper had pulled up a photo of Michael from a social media site.

"Have the police talked to you about this?" I asked.

"No. Do you think I should tell them? I hate to get involved."

"It might be a good idea," I said.

He shrugged. "If they ask me, I'll tell 'em. You two girls take care." Waving to a customer sandwiched between two cowboys at the bar, he headed in that direction.

"Amazing," Harper said. "You could be a private detective!"

"Huh." The way my job hunt was going, no options were off the table. I sipped my wine.

"What's wrong?"

"Sorry. I'm losing my sense of humor over my job hunt."

"You'll find something. Your company was stupid to let you go."

I rubbed a trace of my lip gloss off the glass. "They didn't actually let me go."

"What do you mean?"

My mid-section pooled with dread, heavy and thick. I cleared my throat. What the heck? I had to tell someone. "They sort of told me to leave."

Harper's brown eyes widened. "They fired you? What happened?"

"This government official was giving us problems over permitting. He let it be known he wanted to be bribed. When I explained to my boss about the hold-up, he told me to pay the guy off. I wouldn't, and they told me my services were no longer required."

"You're kidding! But why didn't you tell me this sooner?"

"Because I was fired." Corruption was the cause of endless misery in the developing countries where I'd worked. Only the poor went to jail—successful criminals had the funds to bribe their way out of prosecution. So I'd dug my heels in and lost.

"But you've never been fired. Every other employer you had wept tears of regret when you left. You've got nothing to be ashamed of. You did the right thing!"

But it still felt awful, more so since I was having such a hard time landing interviews.

Harper shook her fist. "I'd put a curse on them … if I was the sort of person to put curses on people," she finished quickly, flushing.

"The thing is, I wonder if the reason I've been having so much trouble finding work is because of them," I went on. "I can't exactly use anyone at that company as a reference, and it looks weird. The few interviews I've had went nowhere. I know they checked with my previous employers. They had to. What did they tell them?"

"You think they're blackballing you?"

"Maybe I'm imagining it. I do have an unusual resume, and I don't quite fit into the jobs I've applied for. Maybe that's the problem."

"You do have a big imagination." Harper belched delicately and signaled the waiter for the bill. "Don't worry, you'll find something. And I don't think Adele was kidding about you taking over the museum."

"I'm not taking over the museum." Though I had to admit, the work was intriguing.

The waiter dropped the bill on the table, and Harper snatched it up. "Eighty-eight dollars and thirteen cents!" She whooped. "Lucky thirteen!"

"Oh!" I slammed my palm on the table, shaking the glasses. "I've figured it out!"

"You know who killed Christy?"

"No." I stared into my half-empty wine glass, a garnet pool. "Poor Christy."

We meditated on that.

"So what did you solve?" Harper asked.

"I know how to get home. Shane can drive us!"

Marveling at my brilliance, I dug my phone out of the messenger bag on the seat beside me and called my brother.

"Hello?"

"Hi, Shane, it's Maddie. I've been drinking. Can you drive me home?" I winked at Harper.

"It's nearly midnight!"

"Did I wake you?"

"No, I was having a heart-to-heart with Mom—"

"Who's that?" my mother called faintly on the other end.

"It's Maddie," he said, his voice muffled. "She wants me to drive her home because she's drunk."

"Go get your sister. She's doing the responsible thing."

Shane growled. "Maddie? Where are you?"

"The Bell and Brew."

He blew out his breath. "Fine. I'll be there in fifteen minutes."

"Oh, and Harper needs a lift too."

Snarling, he hung up.

"Well?" Harper asked.

"He'll be here in fifteen minutes. He didn't want to come, but my mother made him. He sounded a little mad." I, however, was feeling good. Not only had I discovered another clue to help out Adele, but I was a responsible drinker. My chest swelled with virtue.

"He's angry? But we're being responsible!"

"I know!"

"And we found out about Michael's fight with Christy." Harper's eyes unfocused. "I hope it helps. I can't believe they arrested Adele."

And we looped around again.

NINE

THE NEXT MORNING, I opened the Paranormal Museum. Fog hung low on the streets, watery light filtering through the windows. My tongue felt like cotton, and my eyes burned from last night's drinking.

GD Cat trotted to me, meowing. When food was at issue, he seemed able to put aside his contempt. I poured kibble into his bowl and explored the museum. I'd already searched the obvious places for receipts or records that might have Herb's name on them and come up empty. But there were all sorts of cupboards and cubbies built into the lower part of the walls. I wondered if any records had been stored in non-obvious places.

I wrenched open a stuck cupboard, releasing a Vesuvius of dust, when someone knocked at the door. Sneezing, I shut the sliding door. The museum didn't open until ten o'clock, and whoever it was could wait.

Someone rattled the knob.

I stalked to the door. "All right, all right!" With two fingers, I pried the blinds over the door apart.

Harper stood outside, framed in the top glass panel. She shifted her weight, hugging herself in her puffy blue parka. Her long dark hair was knotted in a bun.

I opened the door, and she hurried inside. "Cold. Cold." Her teeth chattered. "My head is killing me. Please tell me you've got a coffeepot in here."

"Sorry." I sniffled.

She nodded. "Expect a housewarming gift. Or business-warming. Have you heard anything about Adele?"

"No. And since it's Sunday, there's no paper. I don't want to bother her family and ask."

"She didn't do it."

"I know."

"She couldn't have."

"I know."

But I read my own doubt written across her face. Could Adele have done it?

Harper looked around, and the tightness in her expression released. "This place really does have atmosphere."

"The stench of failure?"

Her green eyes grew thoughtful. "That bad?"

"No." I sighed. "I think the problems are fixable. But I'm not sure who's going to do the fixing."

"Are you kidding? This place was made for the Mad Kosloski touch. Besides, do you really want to work for someone else? You know you don't play well with others."

"Yes, but I didn't think you knew."

Harper snorted. "What are we going to do about Adele?"

"Find Herb. Like I told you the other night, he heard Christy arguing with a man inside the museum the night she was killed. But he ran off when the cops showed up. I've been going through our records, trying to find a receipt or invoice with his name on it, but so far haven't had any luck. I was just going to start looking through that wall cupboard for more files." I pointed.

She sighed. "Let's do it then."

We ransacked the shelves. I found an old Ouija board planchette, a broken doll, and a mummified mouse. The cat nudged it with his nose.

"Not for you," I said.

"What about this?" Harper dragged a dusty cardboard box from the shelf and unfolded the lid. "Ah ha! We've got paperwork."

She grabbed a fistful of folders and handed them to me, then sat cross-legged on the floor, flipping through those in the box. "You said his name was Herb?"

"You found him?"

"No. Someone named Harold. Sorry."

We reached the bottom of our respective stacks.

Harper blew her bangs out of her eyes. "And this guy Herb is the only lead that points away from Adele?"

"The only one I know of, but the police haven't exactly taken me into their confidence."

"And they've arrested Adele." Harper bit the inside of her cheek. "There's something I need to tell you."

Someone rattled the handle of the door.

I checked my watch. It wasn't even nine o'clock. "Why do people think it's okay to do that when the sign says 'closed'?"

Whoever it was banged on the door.

"Urgh." I hauled myself to my feet and stumbled. One foot was asleep. On pins and needles, I hobbled to the door and cracked it open. "The museum's not open for another hour."

A fat man in a stained hunting jacket peered at me through reddened eyes. "Is Dieter here?" he asked on a cloud of alcohol.

"No!" I slammed the door shut. "Dieter gets almost as many visitors as the museum. It's a plague of oddballs. Why is he so popular?"

"You haven't heard?" Gracefully, Harper unfolded herself and stood, brushing off the back of her jeans. "He's a bookie."

I eyed her askance. "No, I didn't know that. How did you?"

"One of my clients made twenty grand betting on the Christmas Cow two years back."

"People are taking bets on the Cow?" I asked. I couldn't imagine its odds for survival were high.

"He bet that the Cow would be destroyed by a means other than fire. That was the year it got hit by a runaway RV." Harper smiled wryly. "Not even Dieter predicted that."

"Have you ever placed a bet with him?"

"Are you kidding? I trust that guy as far as I can throw him."

"But isn't betting illegal?"

Harper stuffed the papers back inside the box on the floor. "Only if you get caught."

Fabulous. Dieter had turned the tea room into a part-time casino. Did Adele know? I dismissed the idea. She'd never allow gambling in her perfectly proper tea room. With Adele in jail, I'd have to deal with this, and I really didn't want to. My jaw tightened. "You said you wanted to tell me something about Adele?"

Harper busied herself straightening the papers in the box. "About Adele? No, not really. More about Christy. And it's confidential."

I frowned at that. "Too confidential to tell the police?"

"I was wrestling all last night with if I should tell you. A … client of mine told me something about Christy. She'd been"—Harper scrunched up her face—"not exactly *blackmailing* my client, but she was holding some information over her head."

"What sort of information?"

"I can't tell you that. But it might have damaged my client's business if it had gotten out."

"Which could be a motive for murder. Harper, you have to tell the police."

"My client's a woman. You said Herb heard Christy arguing with a man. I'm not going to blow my client's confidence for nothing."

"But if Christy made a habit of this sort of thing, she may have had other victims." Something gray whipped past me, and I swatted at the air. Why was Harper arguing about this?

"Look," she said. "Let's see how things go with Adele. She's got a good lawyer, and I can't believe the police have anything but circumstantial evidence against her. If things look like they're going badly, I'll talk to the police."

"Things are going badly. Adele is in jail."

"Just … let me think about it. Okay?"

"Think fast," I grumbled. I couldn't force Harper to call the cops. Besides, she and Adele went way back. I couldn't believe she'd let her best friend since fifth grade twist in the wind.

"We need to concentrate on this Herb guy," Harper said. "Look, I've got a client who's a private investigator. Let me ask his opinion. Maybe he can give us some tips on how to find him."

Still annoyed, I grunted my assent.

Harper handed me the box of papers and left. I prowled the museum looking for more hiding places, but didn't find any caches of hidden records.

At ten o'clock I opened the museum and was pleasantly surprised by the steady stream of customers. For a moment, I fantasized about making a go of the place. Could I make it work? I shook my head, banishing those thoughts as unrealistic. One busy Sunday did not a successful business make.

In spite of the crowd, there were gaps between selling tickets and answering questions. I couldn't do anything for Adele, so I called the San Benedetto Historical Association. The nice lady who answered the phone didn't know any more than I did about Cora McBride, but for a small donation offered to research the crime.

"But I have to warn you," she said. "If you're looking for court records from that era, they're kept at the police department."

"Not the courthouse?"

She sighed. "The police department had plans to open their own museum and took all the records. But the museum was never opened, so they're sitting in their archives, by which I mean their basement. Do you still want me to see what I can find here?"

I did, and I gave her the pertinent details and my credit card number. She promised to email anything she turned up.

Feeling virtuous, I opened a bag of pretzels and returned to the inventory.

Adele's family lawyer ambled through the door. Roger was out of his legal togs and wearing jeans and a black golf shirt. "Hey, ghost lady." He opened his arms wide. "How about a hug?"

"I don't do hugs." At least not with relative strangers.

"I had to try." Shrugging philosophically, he drew a folded piece of paper from his back pocket. "Adele asked me to give you this."

I took the paper and unfolded it. A to-do list: *Pick-up morning coffee (on order under my name) for Dieter (daily). Feed cat (daily). Collect spare keys from Wine and Visitors Bureau, etc. Oversee installation of marble counter on Wednesday* ... It was a long list, but I knew it was only a fraction of Adele's daily grind. How many other lists like this had gone out?

"You've seen Adele?" I asked Roger. "How is she?"

"I think she's more worried about what's going on out here now than about a future in jail. That's a good thing."

"But since you're not her criminal lawyer, how did you get in to see her?"

He quirked a brow. "I got myself on the list."

"Can I do that?"

"No. It's a very short list. So can I tell Adele you'll take care of that?" He tilted his head toward the to-do list on the counter.

Unenthusiastic, I reviewed it. "Sure." But with Adele behind bars, how could I say no? The museum was closed Mondays and Tuesdays, and I probably could get most of the stuff on the list done then.

"Thanks," Roger said. "I'll let her know. Is there anything else you'd like me to tell her?"

I thought of Dieter's betting operation. "Please tell her everything is okay with the museum, and I'll take care of her list. Do you know when she'll be released?"

He shook his head. "It's the weekend. She's stuck at least until her bail hearing on Monday. And who knows what they'll set bail at?"

I hesitated. "You're a lawyer."

"That's what they say."

"You know, I heard something that might bear on Adele's case."

"Oh?" Roger poked my open bag of pretzels. "Do you know what's in those things?"

"Pretzels?"

"Sodium and thiamine mononitrate! It can cause allergies."

"I seem to be doing okay."

He shook his head. "You only have one body."

"I heard Christy liked ferreting out secrets and using them against people," I said, trying to get the conversation back to Adele and away from my eating habits.

"Blackmail?"

"If it's true, there may be other people out there with reasons to kill Christy."

Roger raised his brows. "If it's true. Christy was a lawyer, and attorneys know lots of secrets. But we'd be out of jobs pretty quick if we held them over our clients."

"You worked with her. Was there ever any hint that she might have been doing this?"

He shook his head. "There is such a thing as professional ethics. You need to be careful who you share that gossip with."

I nodded, chastened. But the power of gossip was that it was frequently true. Christy hadn't been the nicest person. But Roger was right—it was a big leap from being unpleasant to being a blackmailer.

He opened his arms. "Come on. Hug?"

"Out." I pointed to the door.

Laughing, he left, the bell above the door jingling in his wake.

Sure, there were professional ethics. But it was Roger who'd told me everyone lied in court—including attorneys. And as an estate attorney, Christy would know where a family's proverbial bodies were buried.

I took another look at Adele's to-do list and frowned over the third item: *Collect spare keys from Wine and Visitors Bureau, etc.*

"*Etc*."? Did that mean there was more than one spare key outstanding? Dieter had one, but he needed it to get in and out of the building for the construction. Adele couldn't want me to confiscate his key. But if it wasn't Dieter, then who was the "etcetera?"

I growled beneath my breath, startling an elderly woman in khakis and a fisherman's hat. She jammed a dollar in the tip jar and scuttled out.

TEN

At lunch, I closed up the museum, putting a *We'll be back at…* sign on the door, and drove to the Wine and Visitors Bureau. Faded grape vines twined up its low brick walls, and a small "educational" vineyard stretched off to one side for visitors to explore.

I strolled past the wine barrel in the lobby and veered left at a placard advertising wine tasting classes: *Every Sunday at 3:00! Sponsored by the Ladies Aid Society!*

In the tasting area, a handful of tourists bellied up to the bar, swishing wine in their mouths.

A woman slid down the counter toward me. "Are you here for a tasting?"

Regretful, I shook my head. No drinking on the job. "No. I'm with the Paranormal Museum. I was told you had one of its spare keys?"

She pointed to an open door. "Ask at the office."

I nodded and wended my way past displays of T-shirts and corkscrews and purple wine goblets to the open office door.

A plump woman in a fuzzy gray sweater scowled at her computer screen. I rapped my knuckles on the door frame.

Her head jerked up, and then she smoothed her expression into a smile. "Can I help you?"

I edged past open boxes filled with posters for the upcoming wine festival. "I'm Maddie Kosloski, temporary manager of the Paranormal Museum. Adele said you had one of its spare keys?"

"Ah, yes." She rummaged through a desk drawer and lifted out a small key ring. "I'm a little sorry to hand it over, but I suppose it's for the best. Er, has Adele decided to keep the museum open?"

"For now. Why?"

She pried the key off its ring and leaned over the desk to hand it to me. "Oh, no reason. There does seem to be a strange synergy between your museum and the wineries. Chuck, the past owner, used to joke that after a round of spirits, tourists wanted to experience the real thing. I tried to explain that 'spirits' refers to distilled liquor, not wine, but he wouldn't let go of the joke."

I had noticed a high percentage of museum visitors with glowing cheeks and noses. Synergy indeed.

"Chuck was a faithful sponsor of our winery map." The woman tapped a stack of folded papers. "And the Paranormal Museum is on it as a result. I do hope Adele plans to maintain the tradition."

"Things are in flux right now, but I'll be sure to let the future owner know. That said, we are running low on maps at the museum."

She gave me a stack. "Take these. They're free for all our sponsors."

"Thanks for managing the museum during the interim. I know it wasn't your job."

She waved her hand, dismissing the idea. "Oh, it's our job. Like it or not, we have to stick together. People come to your museum and stop at the wineries, and vice versa. I know not everyone in town likes the museum, but I have to admit, I enjoyed it. Though several of our volunteers flat-out refused to work there again with all the weird stuff going on."

"Weird stuff?" Something fluttered in my mid-section.

She tugged her gold necklace. "Strange sounds. Cold drafts. Things moving around. Of course, there's no such thing as ghosts. I told them it was a combination of the construction next door and their imagination. But let's face it. You've got some strange exhibits. And if I did believe in demons, I'd swear that African mask has got one."

African mask? I tried to remember seeing one and failed.

"And now that Christy Huntington has been killed there, the museum's haunted reputation can only get worse. Not that I think a ghost killed her. But I can't say I'm all that surprised that someone did."

"Oh?" I put the maps in my messenger bag.

"That woman overcharged me on a trust. I guess someone had to pay for her designer clothes and fancy car. But my friend paid one thousand dollars for her trust, and I paid Christy six. It was criminal! I complained to her, and she basically challenged me to sue. At that moment, I wanted to …" She pressed her lips together.

"'Let's kill all the lawyers'?" I quoted.

"*Henry the Sixth*!" She clapped her hands together. "You know your Shakespeare. Though I suppose if every lawyer got killed for overcharging, we wouldn't have any left."

"Mmm." I had no idea what the going rate for a trust was, and guessed it depended on how complicated you wanted to make it. But six grand did seem like an awful lot.

The woman's eyes narrowed. "You know, we're looking for another actor for our Shakespeare in the Field series this summer. Are you …?"

"No, no. I can't act my way out of a paper bag." I backed out the door. Shakespeare in the cow pasture was more like it. It was a lovely pasture, and they'd built a little stage of sorts, but a cow pasture was still a cow pasture.

I thanked her and drove back toward the museum, stopping at a taqueria. Standing at the counter, I ordered a burrito and waited. That quiver in my stomach surely had been hunger, not unease. Ghosts in the museum. Ha!

I emerged from the restaurant, foil-wrapped veggie burrito in hand. A familiar figure passed me on the sidewalk, stopping me in my tracks.

"Herb?"

He glanced over the shoulder of his dingy beige windbreaker and broke into a run.

"Wait!" I chased him down the street, passing a dog walker. One of her shelties dodged in front of me, and I tangled the leash. She shouted at me. Ignoring her, I disentangled myself and plunged on, flattening against a brick wall to avoid a woman with a stroller.

Herb dodged around a cinderblock building, and I piled on the steam. I rounded the bend into an alley. Aside from a neat line of garbage bins, it was deserted. Herb had vanished.

Wheezing, I braced my hands on my thighs. Herb was skinny. He'd probably run track in school. I had not.

A battered yellow VW Bug blasted down the alley in front of me. I ran to the end of the block, but by the time I rounded the corner, the VW was a fading speck in the distance.

Something warm dripped down my fingers. I'd crushed my burrito into an hourglass shape. Green sauce oozed from the edges of the aluminum foil onto my hands.

Stomping back to my pickup, I swaddled my burrito in napkins to staunch the bleeding and drove back to the museum. I devoured it at the counter, ignoring the cat's hopeful looks.

"It's vegetarian," I said when his plaintive mews turned to yowls. "You wouldn't like it anyway."

GD sniffed and leapt onto the rocking chair, curling into a ball.

Tossing the foil into the waste bin, I busied myself with the inventory and a steady stream of visitors. Maybe the wine had lowered their resistance to the museum's high ticket prices. But even at ten dollars a ticket, I couldn't see how the museum could pay the rent and its owner's salary.

The bell over the door tinkled.

Detective Slate walked in, wearing a rumpled black blazer and an absentminded expression. He nodded vaguely, his deep brown eyes seeming to see past me, and came to a halt in the spot Christy's body had lain. I shivered, remembering that moment when it had felt like he'd looked inside me.

The cat raised his head, staring at the detective, fascinated.

He stood there a long time, looking at the floor, saying nothing. Then he paced in a slowly widening circle. GD sprang from the chair and stalked his black-loafered heels.

A pimply teenager emerged from the Fortune Telling Room. Wide-eyed, he tiptoed to my desk and whispered, "Is he a medium or something?"

"Or something," I said. "Best not to disturb him."

"Gotcha." The teenager leaned against the counter to watch.

The detective turned on his heel and disappeared into the tea room. With a sigh of disappointment, the teenager left.

I pretended to read my inventory binder, pencil poised above the paper as if on the verge of making a notation. We'd been cleared to open the museum and tea room. And I had tidied up, shifted things about since the murder. What was the detective searching for? I loosened my grip on the pencil and wiped my damp hands on my jeans.

Finally, detective and cat emerged from the tea room and came to stand in front of my counter. "Did you find Herb?" Slate asked.

"Not yet. I saw him in town earlier today, but he eluded me."

"Eluded?"

"He might drive a yellow VW Bug."

Slate raised an eyebrow. "Might?"

"I was chasing him down the street—"

"You were what?"

"And then I lost him and an old VW blasted past. I think it was Herb."

The detective shook his head. "I know Adele's your friend and you want to help her. But do me a favor and don't chase down any more suspects."

"But I can't find his name on any of the receipts. Oh, I heard that Michael St. James had a real fight with Christy last week at the Bell and Brew."

"Mmm."

"The owner, Jim, told me about it."

"Hmm."

"I don't suppose you can discuss Adele's case," I said.

"No."

Feeling foolish, I fumbled for something to say. "What about a closed case?"

His brows rose. "A closed case?"

"Cora McBride." I pulled the photograph from beneath the inventory book. "This portrait is an exhibit in the museum. She died in prison for the murder of her husband—a local crime."

"What year was the murder?"

"Herb told me 1899, though I haven't been able to confirm that yet. The photo was taken in the 1890s. Or is it a daguerreotype?" I really needed to learn more about these exhibits.

"It's a photo. Daguerreotypes were replaced with simpler processes during the Civil War."

"Oh. Are you a history buff?"

Slate shrugged. "A Civil War buff. One of my ancestors fought in the United States Colored Troops."

"You're kidding. So did one of mine." I shook my head. "I mean, not in a black regiment. In a Pennsylvania regiment. Though I don't know if he saw any action …" I trailed off. What had we been talking about? Oh yes, Cora. "Anyway, I'm trying to flesh out my exhibit card on Cora. The Historical Association told me the court records from that era were in your basement. In the police department's archives, I mean."

"The archives aren't available to the public."

That didn't seem fair, since the public paid for them. "Isn't there a way to get permission? Or find someone in the archives who can help me?"

Slate smiled crookedly. "I'll ask the clerk if there's anything on that case in the files. If there is, I'll let you know."

"Thanks."

The cat meowed at his feet.

"What's with your cat?"

"GD's either waiting for you to leave a tip, or he thinks you're haunted."

"GD?"

"Ghost Detecting."

Rolling his eyes, Slate left.

I liked him better than his partner, who seemed to have an irrational dislike of me. I rubbed the back of my neck. Surely she'd grown past her high school "issues" and was only being tough on us because it was her job.

I never could figure out why she'd chosen me as her high school punching bag. I'd been kind of nerdy as a kid—so had Adele and Harper, for that matter. We hadn't been part of the cool crowd or the jocks. And once high school was over, we'd fled for the farthest colleges that would accept us. I hadn't seen Laurel since.

The minute hand on the clock over the door edged closer to five o'clock. Near enough to quitting time, I decided. I shut the museum and aimed for home, driving beneath the cement arch that welcomed people to the downtown, past a residential section, and through the vineyards. The lowering sun set the gnarled vines on fire.

Shane sat on the steps to my garage apartment. The outside light made a halo of his golden hair. He huddled in his leather bomber jacket, his hands wrapped around a mug of coffee—from my aunt, I guessed.

Furtively, I looked around. Not seeing her, I got out of the car and approached my brother. "Hi, Shane. What's up?"

"I dropped by to see if you could come to dinner at Mom's tonight."

I imagined the scene—the dining room table laden with food from my mother's favorite restaurant and spiced with questions about my job hunt. "I told her I'd stop by next week," I hedged.

He shrugged. "She'll be disappointed, but I'll tell her you're busy."

Ah yes, I'd forgotten the lashings of guilt for dessert. "Next week isn't that far away."

"So what are you doing that's so important?"

"Tonight I'm researching an artifact."

"Is it possessed? Haunted? Demonic?"

"Just … interesting." I edged past him.

He rose, following me up the stairs. "By the way, I may have a lead on a job for you at San Francisco Airport. They're looking for someone to work the VIP circuit. You know, when VIPs arrive, help them get through in style while avoiding the press."

I couldn't imagine anything more vomitous than glad-handing a bunch of spoiled celebrities. My blood thrummed. "Thanks. But I'm not interested."

"Why not? You'd be great for it. You're worldly, sophisticated, can handle yourself. It would be interesting."

"Not to me. I hate airports. They smell funny." I jammed the key in the lock. "Did Mom put you up to this?"

"What?" He pressed his hand to his chest. "No. A friend of mine works at the airport and asked if I knew anyone. I wanted to give you the right of first refusal." It was an echo of Herb's words, and my irritation rose.

"Thanks for thinking of me, but I have to refuse."

"I don't see what you're so mad about, Mad."

"Why do you think I would want to go from managing my own projects to chasing after spoiled celebrities? I used to start up banks."

I guess that was my ego talking, but I liked having some independence and authority. Leaving the keys dangling in the lock, I turned and leaned against the door frame. I crossed my arms over my chest.

"Why would you want to go from managing millions to managing the local paranormal museum?"

"It's just temporary," I sputtered. "And what's wrong with the museum?" At least the museum would be mine. I'd be independent, self-sufficient, answering to no one.

If I bought the museum.

Which I wasn't going to do. But I was too aggravated to tell that to Shane, and I shouldn't have been. He was trying to help. "Why do you care?" I asked.

His blue eyes widened. "Your career is up to you. I'm just glad you're here, what with Mom being alone and all."

"Because you're not here?"

He stiffened. "What's that supposed to mean?"

"Nothing. Forget it." But I had the feeling that my presence in San Benedetto was relieving his guilt at not being around. And that was … annoying. Was I being unfair? Probably, but I'd sort that out later. "Besides, Mom's hardly helpless."

"I know that. She's doing great, all things considered. Look, I'm glad you're around, and if there's anything I can do, I want to help. Everyone knows that women are better at handling aging parents."

"So that *is* it! Shane, Mom's fine. Terrifying, actually. But if something happens, I'll be here for her. Not for your sake, for hers."

He turned and trotted down the stairs. "Look, do what you want. Be happy. I'm sure you'll make a success of whatever you do. But you can't avoid Mom forever."

"I'm coming to dinner next week," I shouted to his retreating back.

I went inside, kicking the door shut with my heel, and counted the reasons why he was being annoying and unreasonable. Then I ordered a pizza and got a hard cider out of the refrigerator. So I was having a little trouble figuring out my next career move. Moving home had been a big change. And if I was floundering a little, well, so what? It wasn't like I was mooching off my relatives…

I gazed around the kitchen of my cut-rate apartment, at the unopened boxes in the living area, the borrowed dishes on the counter. My heart sank. Okay, I was sort of mooching. True, I paid my aunt rent for the above-garage studio. But the rent was low, and it didn't exactly strike an independent-and-in-charge note.

I needed a job. A real job. But not, I told myself, at the airport chasing after VIPs and politicians. I shuddered. I still had standards.

Booting up my laptop, I checked my emails. Three thank-you-but-no-thank-you's from various potential employers. I told myself not to take the rejections personally. But when you're unemployed, every rejection is personal, every drop in your bank account a wrench to the gut. Another reason to knock off all the take-out food. Starting tomorrow. I stuck my thumb beneath the waistband of my jeans and hitched them over my muffin top.

Gnawing my lower lip, I returned my attention to my inbox. On the bright side, there were no emails at all from my first-choice financial services firm. I'd applied for an internationally flavored job there that I knew I'd be perfect for. Even better, their operations were in a mid-sized town on the Peninsula rather than the crowded streets of San Francisco.

I combed through various job websites. By the time the pizza arrived, I was thoroughly depressed, but the scent of spicy tomato sauce and pepperoni lifted my spirits. I picked off a pepperoni. Yes, I was emotional eating. But it really did make me feel better, and one should never job hunt morose.

I checked my email again and deleted a message assuring me I could make ten thousand dollars a month working from home.

In my last web search, I hadn't found anything about the murderous Cora McBride, but what about her victim, her husband? I typed his name into the search engine and finally found him in an article about a local feed mill that burned down in 1912. The mill, owned by Zane Donaldson, had previously belonged to "the infamous Martin McBride." Arson was suspected.

A search for Zane Donaldson rewarded me with a string of articles. He'd been a prominent businessman in the Victorian era, owner of the local paper and a member of the town council. A street was still named after him in downtown San Benedetto. The town had seized the mill in 1900 and Zane, then a councilman, had gained ownership. Convenient.

My cell phone rang, and I reached for it. "Hello?"

"It's Harper. I talked to that private investigator client of mine."

I straightened in my seat. "What did he say?"

"He said we need Herb's last name."

"If I had his last name, I wouldn't need an investigator."

"He also said that under similar circumstances, he'd stake out places the target frequented and try to follow him home. If we can get Herb's address, we should be able to learn his last name. My detective can also do a trace if we have a license plate or phone number."

I groaned. "I saw his car go by today but couldn't get his license plate. I'll keep looking through the files." I'd seen some nameless phone numbers scribbled on receipts like they'd been handy scratch pads. Maybe one of those numbers belonged to Herb. "Harper, I don't suppose your client would reconsider talking to the police about Christy's blackmail?"

"No. We need to find Herb."

"Oh, we'll find him," I said, grim.

I only hoped finding him would be enough.

ELEVEN

I STOOD IN LINE with half a dozen other caffeine addicts and waited to pick up Adele's standing coffee order. The scent of coffee and the whir of an espresso machine filled the air. Idly, I studied the flyers and business cards tacked to the nearby bulletin board. The local high school was doing *Oklahoma!* and there was a post-holiday discount on yoga classes. I knew I'd never get to either, but with nothing better to do while waiting, I read every word.

The man in front of me turned, and I was face (mine) to chest (his) with Detective Slate in a neat blue suit. He frowned, and my heart flipped over.

"Miss Kosloski. Good morning."

I yawned. "Is it?"

"Come here often?" His cheeks darkened. It had sounded like a bad pickup line, and I guess he knew it.

"I'm allergic to five-dollar coffees. But Adele always gets coffee for her contractor, and since you've put her in jail, I'm picking up the slack."

My jab bounced off his armor. "Speaking of which, did you find Herb's last name?" he asked.

"Not yet. Is Herb a suspect?"

"I can't even prove he exists."

"But you're trying? You believe me?"

"That was poorly worded. If you see this Herb again or find his contact information in your files, call me."

"Nakamoto?" The teenager behind the counter pushed a coffee carrier across the stained quartz. It held three paper cups: mochaccino for me, double espresso for Dieter, and a standard black.

"That's me," I said.

The clerk titled his head and stared. "You don't look like Adele."

"She asked me to pick up her standing order," I explained.

"Hmm," he said, looking skeptical.

I turned back to the detective. He was gone.

I added sugar to my mochaccino, trying to ignore the odd slide of disappointment I felt. Adjusting my grip on the coffee carrier, I strode onto the brick sidewalk.

A film of morning fog coated the sky. The Paranormal Museum was closed today, but I had cats and contractors to feed, and I still hadn't finished my inventory. It was taking longer than I'd expected, partly due to the poor quality of Chuck's record keeping and partly because the place was crammed to the rafters with exhibits. More shelves and a table in the main room would do wonders for freeing up space. Not that I had any intention of doing that. I would just manage the museum until Adele could find someone better to take it off her hands.

Assuming Adele got out of jail.

Gloomy, I dug the keys out of my messenger bag one-handed and unlocked the front door of the museum. Masculine shouts echoed off the walls. I nudged the door shut with my hip, locked it behind me, and laid my purse and the coffee carrier on the counter. Grabbing Dieter's espresso, I followed the raised voices through the tea room and down the short hallway to the open alley door.

Dieter and my next-door neighbor stood toe to toe, faces red, chests puffed out, their shouts overlapping and indecipherable.

Stomach churning, I eyed the men, who were both in jeans and battered T-shirts in spite of the morning chill. Dieter held a hammer in one hand. The motorcycle shop owner's fists were clenched. Tattoos swirled around his biceps.

"—taking bets," Motorcycle Man snarled.

"Coffee?" I handed Dieter the cup.

He didn't break eye contact with his opponent. "Maddie, this jackass—"

"I'm sorry." I turned to my neighbor. "As you might have heard, Adele, the building owner, was arrested over the weekend. I haven't had a chance for that discussion I promised. But she sent me a note through her lawyer asking me to manage things here while she's away, so you and I can discuss it. I've got coffee in the museum."

Without waiting for a response, I returned inside. After a moment, I heard the stomp of his motorcycle boots behind me, and the muscles in my neck relaxed. I held the plastic curtain for him, waving him into the museum.

"I hope black is okay," I said, handing him the cup. "I forgot to pick up any cream and sugar. Unless you'd prefer a mochaccino?"

"Black is fine."

"Good." I only liked coffee when it was diluted with copious amounts of milk, chocolate, and sugar. I took a sip, allowing myself to briefly revel in the zip of caffeine humming through my veins. "About the dumpster and circular saw … I'd like to work this out in a way that doesn't involve you breaking Adele's contractor. That would put her remodel behind schedule."

His lips quirked. "Dieter's a pain in the butt."

"But right now he's my pain in the butt. I'm Maddie Kosloski, by the way."

He nodded. "Mason Hjelm."

"What are the best and worst times for him to be using that saw?"

"Before noon is best."

"Then I'll make sure he's not using it after twelve. The dumpster's a bit trickier." There wasn't enough room in the alley for the dumpster without encroaching on some of the motorcycle shop's space. I outlined the problem. We dickered. And we finally agreed to shift the dumpster as far out of his space as we could, provided he could use the dumpster while it was there.

We shook on it, his calloused hand engulfing my own.

"Thanks," I said. "So what were you two arguing about?" It might have started with the saw, but Mason had definitely mentioned Dieter's bookmaking, and I wondered if he was a client.

"The usual."

At least Mason wasn't a tattletale. "Is there anything—?" A firm knock on the door silenced me. "Wait a second." I unlocked the front door and edged out.

A middle-aged woman in jeans and a pale blue pea coat stood on my step, her brown hair flooding from beneath a striped ski cap.

"I'm sorry," I said, "but we're closed on Mondays."

"I know." She stuck her hand out. "I'm Grace with the San Benedetto Ghost Hunters. I have an appointment with Chuck."

I stepped back and let her in. "Uh, Chuck sold the museum." San Benedetto had its own ghost hunting club?

"Oh." She cleared her throat, her brows drawing together. "We had an agreement that my group would have a ghost hunt here on Monday night, and then on the following Saturday. Is that still on?" She noticed my neighbor, his coffee in hand, and her brown eyes lit up. "Hi, Mason."

He nodded. "Grace."

She turned to me. "It would be awful if I had to cancel at the last minute. This is a small building, so we can only get in a few people at a time, and so many of our group want to experience the museum. And we already paid Chuck."

"Paid him?"

"Fifty dollars a person for the six of us."

Shaking an imaginary fist at Chuck, I stretched my lips into a smile. If they'd already paid, I was stuck. "Of course you can still have your hunt. What's your usual arrangement?"

"Chuck let us in at nine o'clock, so we could get organized, go over the rules with the participants, and set up. At one, when we're finished, Chuck would usually do a quick tour of the premises to make sure everything was okay, and close up."

I smothered a groan, watching my sleep time slip away, and all for three hundred dollars that I wouldn't see a penny of. "So you want me here from nine to one?"

"Oh no, not in here. You might taint the findings, and I assume you're not trained in ghost hunting. Chuck usually left us alone and then came back."

Wincing, I lowered my chin. "I suppose I could stay out of your way in the tea room." At night, the tea room's concrete floor would feel like a slab of ice.

"Great!" Grace pumped my hand. "I'm so glad you're open to this." She handed me a thin stack of papers. "Here are the liability waivers. Chuck insisted all the participants sign them in advance."

"Thanks." So that's what the forms were for. I'd seen them in the files I'd gone through, but I'd been clueless about why the museum needed waivers.

GD Cat wandered in, tail held high. Grace drew in her breath. "The cat. He'll be here tonight as well, won't he?"

"He pretty much goes where he wants," I said.

"Excellent. He usually joins us for the hunts. Of course, we have the latest in ghost hunting equipment, but the only thing that beats GD is our medium, and she won't be able to make it tonight."

The cat found a patch of sunlight and stretched, yawning.

"Such a character!" With a wave, Grace bustled out the door.

I locked it behind her and leaned against it.

Amusement lit Mason's blue eyes. He sipped his coffee. "Having fun yet?"

"Not really."

His chuckle was deep, rich. "You look like a kid who just heard someone canceled summer vacation. It's not so bad."

"You won't be huddling over a space heater in a concrete shell for four hours."

"You can always come up to my place. That's what Chuck used to do. We'd have some beers, then I'd go to bed and he'd watch TV on the couch until it was time to shut down the ghost busters."

I weighed the options. TV and a soft couch with a Viking who probably ran in a motorcycle gang, or three hours with the space heater. It was no contest.

"I'll bring the pizza," I said.

"I like pepperoni." Mason raised his coffee in farewell and ghosted through the plastic curtains into the tea shop.

I held my breath, half-expecting another explosion between Dieter and my neighbor, but heard nothing. I minced through the denuded tea room and followed a coil of orange extension cord out the back door.

Dieter plugged in his circular saw. "What happened?"

"We need to shift the dumpster as far onto Adele's property as we can." And by "we," I meant "he."

"There's no way I can move it fully onto Adele's property and still have room for my truck and space to work."

"I know. I told Mason he could use the dumpster in exchange for encroaching on some of his space. And could you limit the circular saw to before noon?"

Dieter blew out his breath. "Fine."

"And there's one more thing," I said. "You've been getting a lot of visitors."

"Sorry about that," Dieter said, not sounding at all sorry. "I've told them to come through the alley rather than bug you in the museum."

"If you get caught running an illegal bookmaking business on the property—and that part of the alley is Adele's property—she could be liable. You're going to have to tell your clients to make their bets after work hours."

"What?" he sputtered. "That's not always practical."

"Sorry, Dieter. You don't really want to risk getting Adele in more trouble?"

He flushed. "Fine. But just so you know, I do this for fun. It's not like I'm a professional."

I wondered if Christy had known what Dieter was doing. He had a key to the building. Had she threatened to expose him? And how big an operation did he really have going?

"Have you got odds on the Superbowl?" I asked. It was coming up in a week.

"The Superbowl?" Dieter sneered. "I only facilitate bets on out-of-the-ordinary events like the Fresno crab eating contest or the Christmas Cow."

"Or Adele's conviction?"

Dieter's hands clenched, his lips drawing into a white slash. "I said I did it for fun. Adele's arrest is no joke." He turned on the circular saw, killing further conversation.

I retreated into the building, stumbling to a halt as I neared the plastic barrier to the museum. Wailing echoed from the museum, an eerie accompaniment to the circular saw. The hair lifted on my scalp. *No such thing as ghosts.* There was definitely no such thing as ghosts.

Heart pounding, I sidled inside. The sound seemed to come from the Fortune Telling Room.

"Dieter?" I called, hoping for backup. But my voice was lost in the scream of the saw.

Movements stiff, I tiptoed across the checkerboard floor. The wailing grew louder. I pressed my elbows to my sides and slunk into the Fortune Telling Room.

The cat sat on the round table beside a crystal ball, his head arched back, an unearthly howl emanating from his throat.

"Are you kidding me?"

GD paused to look at me, threw back his head again, and wailed.

"All right, I'll feed you already!" I hurried to my counter and poured kibble into his bowl. The rattle of the dry food silenced the cat. He stalked into the room, tail quivering.

I set the bowl on the floor with a clatter. "All you had to do was ask." Which I guess he had.

I opened my inventory book and found where I'd left off. The spirit cabinet in the Fortune Telling Room. Even though the cat had been responsible for that unholy noise, I had to force myself back inside.

The spirit cabinet stood against one wall. It was about six feet high by six feet wide, and a little over two feet deep. Its three doors could be bolted from the inside. The center door had a diamond-shaped hole cut into it. And a bench with holes for ropes had been set into a side wall. What was this thing? I vowed to ask Herb. Right after I forced him to tell the police what he'd witnessed the night of Christy's murder.

But since Herb wasn't to be found, I returned to my computer to research spirit cabinets. Fortunately, P.T. Barnum had written a book debunking them. Spirit cabinets were used by mediums in séances to "prove" their powers were real. An assistant would tie up the medium inside the cabinet, and once he closed the doors, the spirits would go to work. Seemingly on their own, they'd rattle tambourines and wave ghostly hands through the diamond-shaped hole cut in the cabinet. But a good medium could untie herself before the doors finished closing.

I shook my head. In the 1850s, the general public hadn't been as exposed to stage magicians as we were today. But it was hard to imagine mediums getting away with it.

I checked my watch, hoping it was lunchtime. It wasn't. If I was going to have to spend the night at the museum, I had no intention of spending the rest of my day here. I could go home and clean my closets. Or job hunt.

An email from the Historical Association pinged into my inbox. I seized on it like a bridesmaid lunging for the bouquet. The nice lady at the Historical Association had sent newspaper articles: three on Cora's crime and an obituary on Martin. The print was old-fashioned, the pages stained by age. I had to enlarge the scanned articles to read them.

The first article reported the suicide of Martin McBride, who'd hanged himself from the second floor banister. His wife, Cora, discovered the body when she came down for breakfast in the morning.

Odd. I think I'd notice sooner if my husband hadn't come to bed. The sheriff must have thought it odd too, because the next article's headline was, *MURDER OR SUICIDE? LOCAL WOMAN TRIED FOR MURDER*. A neighbor testified he'd heard Cora and Martin arguing the night of Martin's death, and to Martin's violent temper. The sheriff testified that he'd found abrasions on Cora's hands when he was called to the site of the apparent suicide the next day. She claimed they were due to her attempts to get her husband's body down. The prosecutor argued murder.

I fished out the photo of the two. Cora was a slight woman, a good foot shorter than her bulky husband. How had she managed it?

The third article was short. The courtroom had been packed when the jury announced the guilty verdict. Cora proclaimed her innocence, and the judge sentenced her to life. I re-read the articles. There must have been evidence admitted that hadn't made it into the newspapers, because the case against Cora looked thin. Or there'd been other stories that the Historical Association hadn't managed to find.

"Cora, what did you do?"

GD Cat hopped onto the counter. Absently, I ruffled his fur.

He bit my hand.

"Ow!"

The cat leapt from the counter and bounded into the tea shop, setting the plastic fluttering in his wake.

TWELVE

Taking the cat's assault as a sign to leave, I shut down the computer and turned off the lights. I reached the sidewalk and was locking the door to the museum when a woman cleared her throat behind me.

Startled, I turned.

She dressed like my mother—expensively—in a cabernet-colored suit, pearls, and two-inch heels. Maybe that was why I felt a ping of familiarity. Graying hair mounted her head in marcelled waves. Her lips pinched. She stared at me like a hawk considering a slow-footed rabbit.

"Hello." I gripped my canvas messenger bag to my chest.

"Are you in charge of the museum?"

"Yes. I'm sorry, but we're closed on Mondays and Tuesdays."

"I am aware." She unsnapped the hook on her purse and handed me an envelope.

Automatically, I took it. "What's this?"

"A petition for the closure of the Paranormal Museum."

"Closure? Why?"

"It's in the petition." She turned on her heels and click-clacked down the sidewalk.

I tore open the envelope. It could have been worse. She could have been a process server.

Inside were two sheets of paper with columns of loopy, feminine signatures. At the top, it read: *We the undersigned do not want the Paranormal Museum within the city limits of San Benedetto. We stand with concerned citizens in opposition to an occult attraction that threatens the image of San Benedetto as a producer of world-class wines.*

"What?"

A woman pushing a stroller gave me a startled look and hurried past.

Muttering, I walked down the street to my truck and got inside. Cracking a window, I skimmed the list of names, sucking in my breath at the sight of a familiar signature.

I rummaged in my purse for my phone and called my mother.

"Madeline! We're still on for dinner next week, aren't we?"

"I wouldn't miss it for the world. Funny thing. Someone just handed me a petition to close the museum, and your name was on it."

There was a long moment. Then, "Oh, dear. I was afraid something like that would happen."

"What did you expect to happen when you signed a petition to shut down the museum?"

"I signed it weeks ago, before I knew you were going to take it over. And I told Mabel to take my name off. I will have words with the committee."

"The committee?" I slumped. There was a committee? Of women like my mother? I would have preferred a process server.

"It's part of the San Benedetto Ladies Aid Society."

"But … why? What do they have against the museum?"

"Some people think it's not the image we want to promote. Of course, now that I know you're in charge, I'm sure you'll take it in a new and more sophisticated direction."

My grip tightened on the phone. "I will do no such thing. And what's wrong with the image? The mayor's behind it. Mr. Nakamoto even changed the name of his wine label to fit the haunted theme."

My mother sighed. "And therein lies the problem. Not everyone approves of the mayor's ideas for economic development. And now that his best friend's daughter has been arrested, it's leverage against his development program."

A motorcycle rumbled past.

"This is a town of twenty thousand people," I said. "You're talking like this is a high-stakes political game."

"Don't you know that the smaller the stakes, the more vicious the infighting? Size is no guarantee against political shenanigans."

"For Pete's sake!" My gaze flicked upward to my pickup's fading red roof. "The dairy farmers build a stupid giant straw cow every Christmas."

"And we've been talking to the farmers about stopping. The larceny is becoming more of a draw than the cow. Do you know they put up live webcams in December? They said it was to prevent another incident, but the online video of the conflagration got over seventy thousand hits."

"If the dairy farmers can burn a giant cow," I said hotly, "I can have a paranormal museum." If I wasn't inside my truck, I'd have stomped my foot on the ground in a fit of petulance. Maybe it was a good thing I was in the pickup.

"I knew this would make you more stubborn."

"There's nothing wrong with that museum."

"Stick to your guns, darling, and don't worry about the petition. I know you'll be a huge occult … er, success, if that's what you want. I just don't want you to settle for something because it's there. Are you sure it's what you want to do?"

I thought I'd known what I wanted, but now I wasn't so sure. Why did I care so much about the museum? Was it simply because of Adele?

As if she'd read my mind, my mother asked, "How is Adele?"

"I don't know. She sent me a to-do list from jail."

"She's still in jail? I'd have thought she'd have made bail by now."

"So would I, but one of her lawyers told me they couldn't have the bail hearing until the weekday." It wasn't lunchtime yet. Maybe they'd had the bail hearing by now?

"Well, it wouldn't surprise me if she ended up running the place."

"She hates orange."

"Sensible of her. Now be nice to your brother." My mother hung up.

Baffled, I stared at the phone. When wasn't I nice to Shane? Even if I wasn't nice, it wasn't as if his ginormous ego would notice.

Shaking my head, I reapplied myself to the problem at hand. It was just a petition. It wasn't as if they could revoke my liquor license, since the museum didn't have one (if only). What could they do? Picket the museum? I tugged my jacket more firmly into place.

Starting my pickup, I aimed for home, determined not to think about Adele, or the petition, or the museum's finances. Instead I focused on the land. Even beneath iron-gray skies, and even denuded of leaves, the vineyards were magic, gnarled and dark. I felt the knots in my shoulders loosen.

At home, I made lunch, swallowed an aspirin, read a book. Monday was my day off, so I was going to enjoy it. But my mind kept wandering back to the murder and Adele.

The lighting dimmed, and I checked my watch. It was eight o'clock, and velvety blackness hung outside my windows. Had Adele made bail? I didn't want to call her family—if Adele hadn't gotten in touch with me, she probably wanted some alone time, assuming she was home. And if she wasn't home … that meant she hadn't made bail. How could I find out?

I checked the local newspaper on the Internet, but there was nothing new about Adele. My stomach rumbled. I called in an order for a large pepperoni pizza and drove through streets sunk in fog. The streetlights cut disembodied, glowing orbs in the swirling mist.

A man darted in front of my pickup. Heart in my throat, I slammed on the brakes, half-standing. Shoulders hunched and face obscured, he looked a bit like Herb. But by the time my heart returned to normal operations, the man had vanished, a phantom in the fog.

I picked up a couple of beers with the pizza and drove to the museum, parking in front. The lights were on inside the motorcycle shop, the chrome in its windows gleaming. I walked past, looking for a staircase that would lead me to Mason's upstairs apartment. Finding none, I balanced the pizza and beer on one hip and unlocked the museum.

"GD?"

The cat didn't respond.

I flipped on the lights. The plastic curtains billowed. I froze, rooted to the spot, then shook myself. It was the breeze from the front door closing, not a killer or a ghost. Suppressing a shiver, I hurried through the tea room to the back alley exit.

A narrow concrete staircase led me up to a studded metal security door, built to repel marauders. I rapped with my knuckles, the beer bottles balanced atop the pizza box. My knock echoed, clanging hollowly.

Sounds of bolts drawing back, chains rattling. My heart squeezed. Had this been the best idea? I barely knew Mason, and the fact that he looked like a tattooed Nordic god was no reason to split a pizza with him.

The door creaked open, and Mason's shaggy blond head emerged. "Hey. Come on in." He drew the door wide.

I skittered past, stumbling to a halt. A massive skylight soared above the studio's industrial-chic living area. A half moon glowed yellow through the fog above. The furniture was white, black, and modern, the walls bare brick, the floors distressed. Glass bricks divided a bedroom from the living area. The kitchen was open, stainless steel, and gleaming.

"Wow," I said.

He came to stand beside me, and I thought I could feel hot energy coiling from his body.

"Yeah," he said. "Nice night."

He took the pizza and beer from my hands and placed them on a glass coffee table. I gaped at the expensive-looking oriental rug, the big screen TV, the stone Buddha cross-legged in an alcove.

"Were you expecting a half-built motorcycle in my living room?" he asked.

"I didn't know what to expect. You're a mystery wrapped in an enigma. The loft is amazing. Did you build this?"

"Why pay someone else when you can do it yourself?" Mason grinned. "And avoid getting permits."

"Are you sure you want to reveal your criminal past?"

"Why? You're not going to narc on me, are you?"

"I'll leave you in suspense." I checked my watch and cleared my throat. "Speaking of which, the ghost hunters will be here any minute. You can start on the pizza. I've got to get down there."

"Hold on." He took the pizza to the kitchen and slid it onto a pizza stone, and then into the oven. "To keep it warm. I'll walk you down."

I thought of Christy and those billowing curtains. My inner feminista fled, cowering behind the black leather cushions on Mason's couch. "Thanks."

He followed me downstairs and through the darkened tea room. Its concrete floors and bare walls seemed to glow, chalky in the light streaming through the plastic drapes. I brushed through them into the Paranormal Museum. A woman's figure shifted behind the window, and I opened the door.

Grace hurried inside, her teeth chattering, a green knit scarf wrapped around her neck. "Whoo, it's cold out there."

It was cold enough inside the museum to see my own breath, and I offered to turn on the heater.

"No," she said, "you'd better leave it off. It'll create air currents and noise, and that will confuse our recordings."

It would also save on heating costs, so I nodded wisely.

GD Cat leapt onto the counter beside the cash register. Grace scratched his head.

There was a knock at the door and ghost hunters streamed inside, bundled in parkas and woolen hats.

Grace did a head count. "Eight. I think we're all here. Madelyn, is there anything we should be aware of?"

"The tea shop next door is under construction and off limits. I don't want anyone falling over equipment or stepping on a nail."

"Since it's never been part of the museum, that area isn't our target anyway," Grace said. "We'll stick to the main room, the Creepy Doll Room, and the Fortune Telling Room."

"Thanks," I said. "I'll pop down at eleven to make sure you're okay, and then when you're finished to close up. You've got my cell phone number if there are any problems. I'll be with Mason upstairs." Feeling suddenly awkward, I avoided Mason's gaze. My cheeks heated. That hadn't come out right.

A lanky, twenty-something woman raised her hand. "The woman who was killed here—where did that happen?"

The police hadn't told me to keep quiet about what I'd seen. But I also didn't want to encourage them to explore the tea room looking for Christy's ghost. I gave them an edited version. "Her body was found here, in the main room of the museum."

Mason frowned but said nothing.

Another woman, short and round, unzipped her parka, revealing a photographer's vest stuffed with electronic equipment. "Have you experienced anything unusual here?"

Aside from finding a dead body and discovering that the contractor was a bookie? "No, but I haven't worked here long."

She nodded.

"Thanks, Madelyn," Grace said, dismissing me. "We'll see you at midnight."

Mason and I escaped upstairs.

"I thought Christy was found in the tea room," he said as he opened the door and ushered me into his studio.

"You're half right." I watched him stride to the kitchen—his movements economical, fluid—and remove the pizza from the oven. The scent of melted cheese and pepperoni filled the room. "She was lying between the two, though from the position of the body, I'd guess she was hit in the museum and fell into the tea room. The mystery is why she was there at all."

Mason shrugged, muscles rippling. "She was a troublemaker."

"You knew her?"

"She had a bike. I saw her around."

"And when you say bike, I take it you don't mean a Schwinn." I tried to picture the uptight lawyer in leather, but failed.

"A Kawasaki. She'd come by the shop and hang out on weekends."

I'd noticed a lot of bikers hanging around his shop during the day. They took up all the street parking in front of his business but were careful not to infringe beyond that. "How did she cause trouble?"

"She was a flirt. Liked to get a rise out of the guys—or out of their girlfriends."

"I wouldn't have pictured Christy as a biker."

"Why not?" He dropped the pizza on the coffee table with a clatter. His Nordic-blue eyes hardened. "You think bikers are all anarchist thugs?"

Sheesh. Sensitive. "No. My father rode a motorcycle. I thought Christy wasn't the sort to mess up her hair with a helmet or wind."

Mason grunted and dropped onto a black leather lounge chair across from me, a slice of pizza in one hand. "What did your father ride?"

"A Harley."

"Wait … your father wasn't Fred Kosloski?"

"You knew him?"

He laughed. "Yeah, I knew him. He was a good guy. A straight shooter. I was sorry to hear about his passing."

I swallowed. Not a day went by that I didn't miss him.

"So what's your story?" Mason asked.

"I grew up here and couldn't wait to leave. Got an MBA with a specialization in international management. Went overseas for nearly a decade. Came home."

"Why'd you come home?"

"I was fired." I sank onto the couch, trying the admission on for size. I didn't like it. I'd suspected I'd get fired for the decision I made. But the truth shamed me, stinging my cheeks, forcing my gaze down to the plate in my lap. And that annoyed me.

"Downsized?" He bit into a slice of pizza.

"Something like that." I didn't regret refusing to pay that bribe. So why did I feel so small? "What about you?"

"Grew up in Fresno, couldn't wait to get out. Joined the Army at eighteen. Got a degree while I was in. Left the service ten years later and started building custom motorcycles. I still do, but most of my business now is selling bikes other people build."

"Why San Benedetto?" I sensed there was something important he'd omitted.

"It's affordable, and I like the vineyards. Are you really taking over the Paranormal Museum?"

"I don't know." And with a shock, I realized that was true. There was a possibility I might buy the place. Was I settling, as my mother had suggested?

I took a bite of the pizza and followed up with a slug of beer. "It feels good to be home," I said slowly. "And I can't get an internationally flavored job in San Benedetto. I'd have to work in a big city, like

San Francisco or Los Angeles or New York, and I'm not really a big city kind of girl."

The conversation was easy and relaxed, and more tension leaked from my shoulders. When we ran out of things to say, we watched old *Rockford Files* on TV. I fell into a semi-doze on the couch.

At eleven, Mason nudged me awake. "Time for you to check on the ghost hunters."

I stumbled downstairs, expecting to go on my own, but again, Mason accompanied me. Warmth at his chivalry warred with guilt. He surely hadn't played bodyguard to Chuck when he ran the museum.

Tensing, I stopped inside the darkened alleyway entrance to the tea room. It was black as pitch, silent as a tomb. When I'd left them, the lights had been on.

Mason prodded me in the back. "It's okay," he said in a low voice. "They keep the lights off for their hunts."

"Oh. Yeah." I tossed my hair and strode down the hallway, stumbling over a can of paint. It clanked to the floor.

The Paranormal Museum hadn't burned to the ground. No one had been sucked into another dimension by hungry poltergeists. So we retreated upstairs until one o'clock, when once again Mason saw me to the museum. This time, yawning, he left me inside the door, and I entered the museum alone.

Someone had flipped on the lights. Grace waited beside the front counter, fiddling with a digital recorder.

She looked up when I approached. "You missed the others, but I wanted to ask you to listen to something. An EVP we picked up."

"EVP?" And what had Herb been talking about? EMFs? I'd have to learn the ghost hunting acronyms if I was going to work here.

"Electronic voice phenomenon. We caught it on the tape recorder in this room. It sounds like a woman's, saying … Well, I'll let you hear it first. I don't want to taint your opinion."

The framed photo of Cora and her husband lay face-up on the counter. Forehead creasing, I picked it up. I thought I'd hung it back on the wall before I'd left for the day. Had the ghost hunters been messing with the museum exhibits? I hadn't told them not to touch anything.

I scanned the room. Everything else seemed in place.

She coughed. "Ready?"

On tiptoe, I hung the picture on the wall. "Yeah, sure."

Grace pressed play, and a burst of static erupted from the machine. Something creaked. "That was my chair," a voice said.

"We ask everyone to call out whenever they make a noise," Grace explained. "That way, later, we don't mistake the sounds for paranormal phenomenon."

"Makes sense." I edged closer to her, craning my neck toward the recorder.

There was another blare of static.

Grace looked up, her expression gleeful. "There! Hear it?"

All I'd heard was an earful of white noise. I shook my head.

She rewound the recording. "I'll turn it up." Static again, then something that sounded like a sigh.

"Was that a breath?" I asked.

"Listen again." She raised the recorder to my ear and clicked play.

Static blasted, and I winced.

A woman hissed, "*Innocent*."

The skin prickled on the back of my neck.

"Did you hear it?" Grace asked.

GD Cat sat beside my feet.

"Play it again," I said.

She fumbled in one of the pockets of her parka. Pulling out a pair of earbuds, she plugged them into the recorder. "Try it with these."

I examined them for cleanliness, and, finding them acceptable, stuck them in. The static was loud enough to make my teeth hurt. And then a breathy voice: "*I'm innocent.*"

GD Cat pawed at the cuff of my jeans. Adrenaline spiking, I yanked the earbuds free.

"Did you hear it?" Grace raked a hand through her long brown hair, her eyes sparkling with excitement.

"It sounded like a woman," I said, grudging. But there was so much feedback, it was hard to tell if I had imagined the words or not.

"It was Vincent! She said, *it was Vincent*! Do you know of a Vincent associated with any of the objects in this museum? Or maybe with the murder of that poor woman?"

I shook my head. "I can't think of any, but I'm in the middle of an inventory. If there's a record of a Vincent attached to an object, I'll let you know." Now I was sure we'd imagined the words. I'd heard "innocent," she'd heard "Vincent," and it was all probably just a bunch of random static.

"Do you mind if I post this online?" she asked.

"Go for it."

"And you'll let me know if you find anything?" Grace fingered the gold chain around the throat of her turtleneck.

"Of course." The museum could always use good press, and if I could dig up a creepy story on someone named Vincent, all the better.

"We got some great orbs as well, around your counter and around the entryway between the museum and the tea room. I'll send you copies."

Orbs between the museum and the tea room, where Christy had died? Weren't orbs supposed to be ghosts captured on film? I swallowed. "That's great news."

We agreed do it again on Saturday. Grace left, and I locked the door behind her. I took a quick tour through the museum, the cat at my heels, to see if anything else had been disturbed. The creepy dolls stared balefully from their shelves. My skin twitched, and I moved on to the Fortune Telling Room. It, too, appeared undisturbed. I gazed at the Ouija board on the table. A psychic had once told me to never, ever, ever bring a Ouija board into a home. As far as I was concerned, the board was just wood and paint. A game. But was there more?

A chill rippled up my spine. Two spots heated between my shoulders, burning.

I wasn't alone.

I whipped around. The cat startled into a crouch, teeth bared. He bounded from the room, tail low.

The feeling of being watched intensified, stripping my nerves. I yanked open the doors of the spirit cabinet.

Its wooden bench was empty. A spider crawled down its back.

There was no such thing as ghosts, and my only living company in the museum was the cat. I was imagining things. Perfectly normal when someone I'd known had been murdered here days before. But there was nothing to be afraid of. Nothing at all.

I returned to the main room, jingling the keys in my pocket. I stepped beside the cat, who was seated in the center of the checkerboard floor. He stared at me, emerald eyes unblinking.

"I'll need to do something about these drafts," I said.

Another chill prickled my scalp. It wasn't my imagination. Someone was watching, their gaze heating my skin. I turned. An apparition blurred in the darkened window.

I gasped, clutched my chest, then realized I'd caught my own reflection. I laughed, an uncertain sound. "Yes, GD, I really am afraid of my own reflection."

I looked over my shoulder. The cat had vanished.

THIRTEEN

Tightening my jacket around me, I scanned the museum for the cat. The overhead fluorescent lights flickered. GD really had vanished. He might as well have exited into another dimension.

I snatched my purse off the counter. Right. GD could take care of himself.

A thunderous banging sent me leaping skyward, a personal high-jump record. I whirled, clutching my bag to my chest. A face in the window, its mouth contorted, pinned me with its gaze.

My throat closed, stopping my breath. And then the face resolved itself—Herb.

Nostrils flaring, I wrenched open the door. "Herb! It's after one a.m.!"

He scuttled into the museum. "I am well aware of the time. I was passing and saw you inside."

"Passing or lurking?" Blood pounded in my head. How long had he been watching me?

He drew himself up, his barren skull gleaming beneath the fluorescent ceiling light. "I do not lurk. Given recent events at the museum, lights on after midnight seemed suspicious, and I came to investigate."

"I thought you were just passing."

"I came to investigate as I was passing."

"Whatever. Herb, you're the closest thing to a witness to Christy's murder, the only person who can say it was a man with Christy. My friend Adele is in jail, because the police think she did it. You need to let them know what you saw."

"I agree that in spite of my quite logical aversion to law enforcement, we do have a civic duty."

Blowing out my breath, I muttered a thank you to whatever higher power might be listening. "Fantastic. Detective Slate is in charge of the investigation, and he seems reasonable."

"Then you can tell him something else I've remembered—something the murdered woman said. 'You dug your own grave,' she said."

"You dug your own grave?" But Christy was the one who'd died. "You're sure? Did she say anything else?"

"I'm quite sure she did, but I didn't hear it. That's all I remember. Good evening." He sidled toward the door.

"Wait! Herb, it won't matter if I tell the police. They need to hear it from you."

"I don't see why." He grasped the door handle. "Information is information, and you appear to be a fairly reliable source, in spite of your bizarre employment."

"Because you're the one who heard Christy." Even I could hear the high whine of desperation in my voice. "You're the witness!"

"And I have told you everything I know. Please relay it to your lieutenant."

"At least tell me where I can get in touch with you if the police have more questions."

"I think not." He darted out the door.

Cursing Herb, the police, and myself for getting in the middle of this, I ran after him, slamming the door shut behind me. Its bang echoed down the fog-shrouded street, and my teeth clenched. This would not win me points with the Viking upstairs.

The fog swirled, leeching color from the street, pressing against the streetlamps. Some people find fog eerie. I find it comforting. It didn't bother me that I couldn't see Herb. I could hear him, his footsteps thudding ahead on the sidewalk. I took off in pursuit.

A car door slammed. An engine revved. Two red lights blinked on, blurs in the fog, illuminating the mud-spattered license plate of a yellow VW Bug. I made out the first number and letter—4G—and the car roared off.

Stumbling to a halt, I considered returning to my pickup and trying to follow. But my romance with fog does not extend to driving in it. In this gray soup, not even Dieter would give odds on me catching Herb. But at least I had the beginnings of a license plate. Add to that the make and model of the car, and the police should be able to track Herb down. Shouldn't they?

I walked back to the museum, careful not to trip over the sidewalk's cracks and crevasses. I passed a gleaming motorcycle in a shop window and turned back. I'd gone too far, missed the museum door.

The open museum door. A gust of wind caught it, and it swayed. My hand shot out, steadying it.

I'd closed that door.

My hand clenched. I knew I'd closed the front door. I remembered wincing as it banged shut.

Blood thrumming, I pushed the door wide and edged my head inside. The plastic curtains billowed … stirred by the breeze from the open door? Or had someone walked through them into the tea room?

"Hello?" My heart thudded against my ribs. Stupid. I was being stupid, imagining things.

A low, feline growl was my response.

My shoulders slumped. The cat. It had probably disturbed the curtains. But that didn't explain the open front door.

I bit my lower lip. Had I locked the alley door? The thought of checking left me cold, but I forced my leaden legs to move forward. I found the unopened bottle of Kahlua beneath the counter and grasped it around its neck like a weapon. The liquid gurgled as I tilted it upside down. The bottle was satisfyingly heavy.

I crept toward the plastic drapes. Of course it was just me and the cat. I paused beside the plastic sheets. How many times had I done this in my own home, half-afraid someone had broken in, only to find I was wrong?

Taking a breath, I burst through the curtains, bottle extended. Weak light from the street and the museum made monsters of the boxes and buckets in the tea room. The looming silhouettes might not be creatures of evil, but they made great hiding places for a human invader.

I was creeping myself out. I hurried to the electrical switch and flipped on the overhead lights. The fluorescents flickered to life, humming. Bare concrete. Boxes of wood flooring. Paint cans. A saw horse.

No one was inside.

A cold breeze stirred my hair, raised gooseflesh on my neck. I followed the draft through the short hallway, past the restrooms, to the alley door. It stood wide open. An overhead light gleamed off the dumpster outside.

Somehow, I'd messed up.

But I wasn't the sort of person to leave doors open willy-nilly. And I knew I hadn't now, not after a murder had been committed. That door had been closed. I might not have locked it when I came in, but I knew I'd shut it.

Someone had been inside the museum.

FOURTEEN

I brought the bottle home with me and poured myself a Kahlua and ginger ale to settle my nerves. It must have worked, because in spite of my tumbled thoughts, I drifted into sleep.

The ring of the phone woke me. I stumbled to the kitchen, blinking in the sunlight shining through the floral-print curtains.

"Hello?"

"Madelyn, it's your mother."

Of course it was. Only my mother would call me at seven a.m. on a day off. "Hi, Mom. What's up?"

"I wanted to let you know that I didn't learn about it until today. The ad went in before I had a chance to register my protest."

"What ad?"

"You haven't seen the morning paper then," she said flatly. "I don't understand how you can sleep so late on a weekday."

A muscle spasmed in my left eyelid. "Because I was up until two a.m. dealing with a ghost hunt at the museum, and I have today off. What ad?"

"You never were a morning person. Let's talk later." She hung up.

I looked at my bed, thinking of all the reasons I should return to it. Pinching the bridge of my nose, I squeezed my eyes shut. But I had to feed the cat and get Dieter his standing coffee order, and I really should call the police about Herb's latest revelations. And get the morning paper, apparently …

I stumbled to the closet and dressed in jeans and a soft cream-colored sweater. If I kept the museum, I could chuck my tailored slacks and business heels and wear jeans every day. Comfort clothes and a rocker T-shirt would be—as Adele might say—perfectly proper in a paranormal museum.

Mood improved, I tackled my morning errands. At the coffee shop, I caught myself looking for Detective Slate. I didn't see him, and my heart sank.

I drove to the museum with the coffee carrier balanced atop the local newspaper on the seat beside me. The sun was shining, the air was crisp, and last night's fears had vanished. Reluctantly, I faced facts. I must have left the tea room's back door open. How could I have been so stupid?

The whir of the circular saw assaulted my eardrums when I opened the museum's front door. I slammed it hard, and sure enough, it bounced back open. So I'd been the guilty party after all last night. Although that didn't explain the open alley door.

Locking the front door behind me, I dropped the paper on the counter and followed the shriek of the blades to the alley. Dieter hunched over the saw, feeding it a two-by-four. A section of lumber thunked to the pavement. He turned off the machine and pushed his safety goggles to the top of his shaggy head. Beneath his stained khaki-colored overalls, he wore a T-shirt advertising a local beer. His eyes were puffy, inflamed.

"Your double espresso." I placed the paper cup on a vacant sawhorse.

"Thanks. And thanks for getting your neighbor off my back. He was almost human this morning. You heard anything about Adele?"

"No, but I'll let you know if I do." I turned to leave.

"Did you move any of my tools around last night?" Dieter asked.

I stopped, faced him. "No. Why? Is anything missing?"

He scowled. "No, but I like to keep everything in its place so I can find what I need. If you need to borrow my tools, ask."

"I didn't touch your tools." My stomach knotted. It could have been some of the ghost hunters. I'd asked them to stay out of the tea room, but the temptation might have been too great. Or … I hadn't been imagining things. I hadn't been an idiot. And someone had taken advantage of the open front door to get inside the tea room, escaping out the back. "What exactly was moved?"

"Just little things. My toolbox was open and things were shifted around. The cable around my drill was unwound."

"There were some ghost hunters in the museum last night, and I left them unattended. Some may have wandered into the tea room." I didn't want to admit to the open doors.

"People shouldn't go in the tea room, especially at night. They could trip over something and hurt themselves."

"I know, and I told them to stay out. Did you notice anything else?" He shook his head.

"If you find anything else out of place, let me know. And Dieter …" I hesitated. "Did Christy ever place bets with you?"

"Is that your way of asking if she knew I was a bookie?"

"Did she?"

Turning his back on me, Dieter switched on the saw.

Figuring that for a yes, I returned to the museum and fed the cat.

I settled in behind the counter and opened the paper. The local high school students were being tested for college readiness. A serial car burglar had been arrested. And candidates had been nominated for San Benedetto's Person of the Year. Since I knew I wouldn't be on that list, I skipped that article and continued past the comics to the classifieds. No ad leaped out at me. And there was nothing about Adele's arrest.

I flipped the paper over and saw, bordered in black like a funeral announcement, *AWARD FOR TACKIEST MUSEUM IN SAN BENEDETTO—THE PARANORMAL MUSEUM.* Beneath the headline, in smaller print, was the petition to get rid of the museum and instructions on how to submit signatures. I clipped the award and folded it into my jacket pocket.

I ground my teeth. It may be that no publicity is bad publicity, but this made me mad. No pun intended.

"Why do people care?" I asked GD.

The cat brushed against my ankle.

"It's a perfectly innocent museum," I said. "Maybe a little silly, but what's wrong with that?"

The cat had no answers, so I grabbed the coffee carrier, locked up, and peered in the window of the motorcycle shop. The sign said *Closed*, but Mason sat behind the counter, glaring at a computer.

I knocked on the glass door.

Looking up, he stretched, muscles rippling beneath his black T-shirt. He ambled from behind the counter to the door and opened it. "Hey."

"I've got another spare coffee." I raised the carrier. "Want one?"

"Sure." He opened the door wider and stepped back.

I brushed past, trying not to notice the warmth radiating from his body. Giving him his coffee, I looked around. Motorcycles stood, chrome gleaming, atop the slate tile floor. I ran a hand over the buttery leather seat of a teal-colored Harley. Motorcycles terrified me, but I had to admit these had style. "These are works of art."

"Maybe not that one, but mine are."

"Are any of yours on the floor?"

Mason led me to an orange and black and chrome bike, low-slung to the ground and elongated like a great cat pouncing on its prey.

I whistled. "You made this?"

"Not one of my best efforts, but I expect to get fifteen grand for it. If you're interested in a chopper."

I laughed. "No. I do have fantasies of working up to a Vespa someday, but I doubt it'll become a reality. Some things are better as dreams."

He gazed at me, an invitation in the blue depths of his eyes. "Not always."

My cheeks warmed. I changed the subject. "I don't suppose you heard anything in the museum last night, after I left?" I took a sip of my mochaccino.

"The ghost, you mean?"

I coughed. "Ghost?"

He laughed, a low, rolling rumble. "I'm joking. No, I didn't hear anything, but I sleep hard. I doubt I'd hear anything short of a fire alarm or that damn saw. Why? Did something happen?"

I told him about Herb, and the open doors on my return. "I told myself I'd imagined it—that the front door bounced open after

I'd slammed it and I'd forgotten to shut the back. But Dieter just said someone messed with his tools last night."

"The ghost busters?"

"Maybe. But it wouldn't explain the open door to the alley. Because I wouldn't have left it open. Since Christy's murder, I'm paranoid."

"It could have been some kid. This is a quiet town, but we do have our share of teenage vandalism. Was anything taken?"

"Not that Dieter noticed." Had Christy's killer left something behind in the museum? But the police had searched the museum and tea room, and they'd been thorough. Hadn't they?

"Probably just a kid," Mason said, "getting his thrills in your museum."

———

I drove back to my loft. No relatives or murderers waited on the steps, so I went upstairs and dug Detective Slate's business card from my wallet.

He answered on the first ring. "Slate here."

"This is Madelyn Kosloski. You told me to call if I heard from Herb again."

"Where can we find him?"

"He stopped by the museum last night, and I got a partial license plate on his car, a yellow VW. It starts with 4G. And Herb told me he remembered something from Christy's argument. She said—and I quote—'you dug your own grave.'"

"Is that all?"

"What more do you want?" A headache stirred behind my brows. I willed my neck muscles to relax. "Herb wouldn't give me his address. I was lucky I caught any of his license plate."

"I only meant that I have to go, if that's all you've got."

"Oh. Yeah. It is."

He hung up.

I drummed my fingers on the linoleum kitchen counter. Okay, so it hadn't been much. But I'd hoped for a bit more enthusiasm. It *was* a clue. Should I have told him about the intruder in the museum last night? No, he'd think I was paranoid.

And he'd be right.

What *had* Herb been doing outside the museum after one a.m.? Had he lured me away so an accomplice could enter? Why? What was the connection? And what was I going to do for lunch?

I called Harper.

"Have you heard anything about Adele?" she asked.

I filled her in. "And the Ladies Aid Society has taken out a full page ad declaring the Paranormal Museum the tackiest museum in San Benedetto."

"You're not running against a very deep bench. Isn't it the only museum in San Benedetto?"

"That's not the point," I huffed.

"For someone who isn't sure about taking on the museum, you seem to care about this a lot."

"Because this campaign against the museum is ridiculous." The headache roared, and I went to the cupboard in search of aspirin. "Look, are you free for lunch later? I used to know what was going on in this town, but I'm back to being an outsider."

There was a long pause. "I'm trying not to eat out so much, and I brought my own sandwich."

"Ever the financial advisor. What about a picnic at Adele's winery?" I found the aspirin bottle behind a box of crackers and popped it open with one hand. "Noonish? And I'll bring my own sandwich."

"See you then." Harper hung up.

I spent the rest of the morning with a self-help book. At noon, I clicked off my e-reader. Meditation and ego-work was all well and good, but it would have to take a back seat to my problems at the museum.

Hauling myself off the couch, I went to the kitchen. Harper had the right idea about not eating out so much. I stuck my head in the refrigerator. Cider. Cheese. A yogurt past its sell-by date. No fruit. No sandwich makings. Ugh.

I drove to the deli for a roast-beef-and-swiss sandwich and a bag of tortilla chips, then drove west. Five minutes on wide, straight roads and I was in the fields, zipping past rows of bare vines dormant from the winter.

A sign alerted me to turn right for the Plot 42 Vineyard. I drove down the gravel road toward Adele's family winery. Plot 42 was a good name. I wondered why Adele's father had felt the need for the new Haunted Vine label. And I wondered where Adele was, if she'd gotten out on bail.

Harper had parked her BMW beneath a weeping willow. Nearby, the tasting room, a converted barn, stood shut.

I pulled in beside Harper's car. She sat atop a picnic table, her feet resting on the bench, and chatted on her phone. Her loose hair cascaded past the shoulders of her white blouse, which was rolled up to her elbows. She wore blue pinstriped wide-legged slacks.

I raised my paper-wrapped sandwich in greeting and walked across the damp grass.

She waggled her fingers at me. "Paris in March?" she said into the phone. "I'm sure I can clear my schedule." She murmured a goodbye and hung up, looking like the cat who'd swallowed the canary.

"Spring in Paris? I'm assuming that's not Paris, Texas."

"You assume correctly. A client wants me to do some planning for his mother in Paris. She's got assets here in the U.S. and finds our laws confusing." A sandwich in a plastic baggie and a tub of something lay on the table beside her, along with a bottle of water.

"And he'll pay for the ticket?" I asked.

"He's a she, and of course she'll pay," Harper said. "Why don't you come along? We can do some shopping."

Not on my current salary. I still had a stash in my savings account, but I didn't like seeing the balance moving in one direction—down. "Maybe next time."

Nodding, she slithered off the table onto the bench. "It turned out to be a nice day. This was a good idea."

I sat across from her and tilted my head back, enjoying the warmth of the sun on my face. The door to the barn/tasting room rolled back, and a man in khakis walked outside and set up a sandwich board. Scrawled across it in pink chalk were the words, *Yes, we're open!* Grapevines grew above the door, and yellow and pink and orange flowers I couldn't identify sprouted in clay pots around the brick path to the barn.

"I'd suggest getting a bottle of wine with our meal, but I suppose you've got to meet a client after lunch."

"You suspect correctly, but the client is Mr. Nakamoto." Harper reached into a canvas satchel near her feet and pulled out a bottle of Haunted Vine Cabernet and two glasses. "I don't think he'll mind. In fact, I'm sure he'll ask for a review of his latest vintage."

"He needs financial advice? About Adele's bail?"

"Her bail was set at two million dollars."

"Two million! That's crazy! She's no flight risk. But they only have to pay a bondsman ten percent, don't they?" But that was still two hundred thousand dollars, a huge sum. The Nakamotos had done well, but I doubted they had that sort of money in cash, especially after investing in their new wine label.

"I can't really talk about it," Harper said. "The bail is public knowledge. Everything else is confidential."

I sighed. "Consider the subject changed."

Uncorking the bottle, she poured the wine and set the glasses on the table. "I should have opened this sooner, but it's better to let it breathe in the glasses anyway. So, aside from your recent award, how are things going at the museum?"

"Never a dull moment."

"So you like it?"

I scratched my cheek. "It's a challenge, but I'm not sure if it'll be one that pays off even under the best of circumstances."

Harper took a sip of her wine. "And the paranormal side? How do you feel about that?"

I laughed. "I don't think the place is haunted, if that's what you mean."

"It wasn't." She watched me, her green eyes intent. "I meant the paranormal in general."

"It's fun to consider." I wasn't sure what my friend was getting at, but there seemed something behind her question. "If you're asking if I believe in ghosts, I guess I'm open to the idea. There's so much we don't know about the universe. It seems arrogant to assume they don't exist simply because science hasn't been able to prove it. It wasn't so long ago that we didn't know germs existed."

"Hmm." Harper played with the stem of her glass. "Rhetorical question: have you ever wondered how we all ended up here in San Benedetto? You, Adele, and I, I mean. Adele has a Harvard MBA; she could work pretty much anywhere, but she wants a tea room here. You were a high-powered international executive—"

I coughed. "I wouldn't say high powered."

"But you came back."

"Because I obviously wasn't that high powered. I couldn't find anything in San Francisco."

She arched a brow. "You couldn't find anything? Or you couldn't find anything you wanted?"

"I couldn't find anyone who'd hire me." I really didn't like this line of questioning. The more I tried to be sane and logical about the job hunt, the more frustrated and defensive I grew. So I turned it on her. "What about you? You've done well for yourself. Why are you here?"

"That's easy. My clients are here. Moving locations would mean losing clients, and I'm not willing to start over from scratch."

"And Adele?"

Harper shrugged. "Her family's here, and the vineyard. I don't believe for a minute that she's keeping the museum because her father's pressuring her. Her father's never pressured her in his life. She's doing it because he took a gamble on his Haunted Vine label and she wants to help him. But why did you come back? What do you want?"

It was a good question, but with Adele still on the hook, it wasn't something I felt like exploring. "The usual. Life, liberty, and the pursuit of happiness. Adele's only got one out of three. This doesn't seem like the time for navel gazing."

Harper sighed. "Fine. Back to the problem at hand. You said you wanted to tell me something more about Herb?"

I told her how he'd heard Christy say, "You dug your own grave." When I finished, Harper said, "It sounds like Christy was taunting the person."

"Blackmail?" I suggested. "Could she have known about Dieter's extracurricular activities as a bookie and threatened to go to the cops?"

"The contractor? Did Adele give him a key so he could let himself in to the tea shop?"

"Of course she did." Dieter could have gotten into the museum to kill Christy. But he didn't seem like the sort to get too fussed about the cops. How much trouble could he get into for bookmaking? In his mind, was it blackmail-worthy? "Another possibility is that she was telling off Michael. A lovers' quarrel."

"Michael?" Harper's brow furrowed. "I guess that could explain what she was doing in the museum. He might have a key."

"He wasn't on my key collection to-do list." Digging it from my pocket, I smoothed it on the rough table, and my heart plummeted. "Oh no." Why hadn't I figured it out sooner? "The 'etcetera.' I thought someone else might have a key. Could it be …?"

Harper met my gaze.

"Michael," we said together.

"It makes sense he'd have one," Harper said. "Adele considered the building both of theirs—until she caught him with Christy. But why not just write his name down on your list? Why 'etc.'?"

"Could Adele be protecting him? I overheard her tell the police that Dieter and the Visitors Bureau had keys. She didn't mention Michael."

"I suppose Dieter could be the 'etc.,'" Harper said. "Maybe Adele wants his key back?"

"I can't imagine why. He still needs to get in there every day for the remodel. And she didn't include 'let Dieter into the building' on my list. If he gave up his key, someone would need to let him inside."

Harper ran her gaze over the list. "This list is pretty thorough."

"But the police found a key with Christy," I said. "If that key was Michael's, Adele would have guessed that. She wouldn't have put it on the list."

"*If* it was Michael's. And are you sure Adele would have assumed Christy had Michael's key? She's been under a lot of stress."

"I need to talk to him," I said. Michael couldn't stand me—this was not going to be fun. But I pulled out my smart phone and did an online search for his office number. "Here goes nothing."

I dialed. To my surprise Michael, rather than a receptionist, picked up.

"Michael St. James here."

"Michael, it's Maddie, Adele's friend." I made a face at myself. He knew who I was. "She asked me to get the key to the museum and tea shop from you."

There was a long silence. "I don't have it."

"But did you have it?"

"I don't see that that's any of your business."

It wasn't a denial. I bit my bottom lip. "Do the police know you had a key?"

"I didn't … Look, I can't talk. I'm with someone." He hung up.

What did he say?" Harper asked.

"He didn't deny it, and he hung up on me."

"Guilty conscience?"

"He was with a client, so maybe not. But it's suspicious. If he had a key, he could have had just as much motive and opportunity as Adele. And we know he was in the area—he stopped by the Bell and Brew that night when we were there. It's a short walk to the museum from there."

A gray-haired Asian man walked out of the barn and waved to us. Mr. Nakamoto. Shrugging into a navy suit jacket, he strode across the lawn. "Madelyn. Harper, I'm glad I caught you. I'm sorry, but I have to cancel our appointment today. There's been a development in Adele's case."

I straightened. "A development?"

"The police have found new evidence." He paused and blinked rapidly. "It isn't in Adele's favor. I have a meeting with her lawyer. Harper, may we reschedule?"

"Of course," she said. "If there's anything we can do, please let us know. And please tell Adele we're here for her."

He nodded and hurried to a vanilla-colored Cadillac parked beside an outbuilding.

"That doesn't sound good." Brushing the crumbs from her slacks, Harper stood. "I should go with you."

"Go with me?"

"To talk to Michael. Let's face it. He's a Class A weasel. It'll take the two of us to get him to talk. And if he is a killer, best you don't go by yourself."

"Now?" I glanced at my watch. I didn't want to go at all.

"My after-lunch appointment canceled. You said Michael was in his office. If we leave now, we might catch him before he goes to lunch."

I lowered my head, studying her. "You know where he works?"

"He's a CPA. I'm a financial planner. We share clients. He's got a little office downtown."

In other words, not far from the museum. It was a small downtown. "Fine." I finished my wine, savoring the plum, tobacco, and black pepper flavors. Take *that*, Napa Valley! "I'll follow you."

We caravaned downtown. Harper led my truck into a rear parking lot behind a two-story brick building.

She stepped from her BMW and pointed. "Entrance in the back."

We trooped up a narrow flight of stairs to a glass door with Michael's name on it. Harper grasped the handle. It turned easily, and we entered a reception room. Watercolor prints of vineyards and fog-covered mountains decorated the cream-colored walls. The carpet was forest green, and the abandoned reception desk a dark, heavy walnut. A bouquet of wilted flowers drooped, dropping yellow and pink petals on the polished wood.

"The door's unlocked, so Michael must still be in the office." Harper cocked her head. "I don't hear anyone. Maybe his appointment has left."

I moved to one of the chairs lined up firing-squad style against the wall, expecting to settle in for a wait.

Harper took off down a hallway.

"Harper," I hissed, and trotted after her.

"Never underestimate the power of surprise," she said in a low voice, stopping in front of a wooden door. She knocked and pushed it open.

Michael sprawled on the rug. The wound in his head turned the green carpet black.

FIFTEEN

THE OFFICE TILTED, AND my brain scrambled to compensate. The blood, the body—it looked too much like Christy's murder. I shook myself, trying to order my thoughts. Basic first aid: assess the situation, ensure your own safety, call 911. What came after those three steps, I'd long forgotten.

Dropping to my knees in the thick green carpet, I felt for a pulse in Michael's neck. There was none. An egg-shaped glass paperweight lay on the floor by his head.

"Call the—" I started to say "police," but when I looked over my shoulder, Harper was dialing, her lips pinched together, grim.

"Is he …?"

"I think he's dead." I pressed my fingers deeper into the side of his still-warm neck, praying I was wrong, knowing I wasn't.

She nodded and stepped into the hall, as if to give us privacy.

I reached for the paperweight. Fingertips inches from what was no doubt the murder weapon, I mentally slapped myself. The glass egg was mesmerizing, with red and blue spirals floating inside it like smoke … and no blood, no hair. Had the killer cleaned it off? Assuming this was Michael's paperweight, the crime must have been spontaneous. I couldn't imagine someone bringing a heavy glass egg along as a weapon. The urge to pick it up was nearly overwhelming. I resisted and stood, jamming my hands in my pockets.

I glanced at the closed closet door to the left of Michael's desk, looked over my shoulder at the open door behind me, and licked my lips. The closed door seemed threatening. Outside, Harper's voice was a soft murmur. I didn't want to stay in that room alone, but it felt wrong to leave Michael.

Harper stuck her head inside, her face pale. "The police said not to touch anything, and to wait in the lobby."

I nodded and followed her into the waiting room. She gripped her phone in both hands, sitting with her feet firmly planted, legs apart, ready to launch.

I edged into the chair beside her. "When I called Michael, he was with someone. He didn't say if it was a man or woman."

"At least Adele's off the hook for this one."

"Yeah."

"But this is the second body you've found in a week," she said. "The police will have to wonder."

"Yeah." My lunch was doing unpleasant things in my stomach. I scrubbed a hand over my face. Was Harper wondering about me as well? And why shouldn't she? We'd been friends for years, yes, but we hadn't seen each other much in the last five. She'd changed. So had I. Bile rose in my throat. "At least we've been together since the time I spoke with him."

Her jaw set. "Unless you were pretending to talk to him."

I stared. She couldn't really think I was a killer?

She shook her head. "Sorry. Of course you didn't."

I swallowed. "No. It's logical. But there will be phone records, won't there? Of me calling and someone on this end picking up? The police will check, I'm sure."

But was I so sure? They'd arrested Adele, and my faith in law enforcement was eroding. They seemed to stop at the most obvious answer, looking no further for suspects. Someone had picked up on Michael's end, but not necessarily Michael. I could have called an accomplice who'd killed Michael earlier and then waited for a phone call, fudging the time of death. Would the police see it the same way?

"He told you he was meeting with a client?" Harper asked.

"No, he just said he was meeting with 'someone.' It might not have been a client."

"But you told me it was a client."

"My imagination was embroidering. He didn't specify."

Harper crossed her legs, bouncing one over her knee, lips pursed. "So we were wrong. Michael didn't kill Christy."

So who had? Michael had been an ideal suspect, particularly since he was so dislikable. He never denied having the key. In fact, he'd left me with the distinct impression that he'd had it at one point.

Footsteps pounded up the concrete stairs and the door flew open. Cops poured into the cramped waiting room—Detective Slate with a couple uniforms. Laurel Hammer followed, crisp in a white blouse and khakis, her expression tight.

Slate pointed at me. "Stay." He strode past us and down the hallway, the coattails of his black suit jacket flapping.

Laurel glanced at the uniformed cops and nodded to the front door. One positioned himself beside it, a sentry preventing our escape. Lip curling, I looked away. If we'd wanted to escape, we'd already have fled.

Paramedics jogged into the office. At a word from the cop by the door, they disappeared into the hallway. Five minutes later they returned to the waiting room. They leaned against a wall, speaking quietly.

So Michael didn't need medical help. I'd known this, but my throat tightened. I'd never been a Michael fan, but this … this would kill Adele.

The detectives emerged. Laurel crooked her finger at me.

I rose, feeling three hundred pounds heavier. She led me into the stairwell, her expression grim. Through the glass door, I saw Slate speaking with Harper, their voices muted.

"What happened?" Laurel rolled up a sleeve of her blouse, as if preparing to beat out a confession.

"Adele asked me to collect the keys to the museum that were floating around. I thought Michael might have one, so Harper and I came to collect it. When we got here, we found the door unlocked and Michael dead."

She rolled up her other sleeve, exposing a dark sliver of tattoo. "Why did you think Michael had a key?"

I glanced down the concrete stairwell. It strobed blue with reflected light from the emergency vehicles outside. "The building was a wedding present. I figured both Michael and Adele might have keys. When I called him around lunchtime, he didn't deny it. He said he was with someone and hung up on me. I was having lunch with Harper at the time, at the Plot 42 winery. Mr. Nakamoto saw us." The blue strobes were making me dizzy.

Laurel smiled, her gaze predatory. "So he didn't tell you he had a key. What time—exactly—did you call him?"

I pulled my cell phone from my jacket pocket. "Twelve forty-seven. The call lasted less than a minute or two."

"Did he say who he was meeting with?"

I shook my head. "But at least it's obvious Adele couldn't have done it, or killed Christy either."

She canted her head. "Obvious?"

"She's in jail. And the two killings must be connected. Michael and Christy were lovers, and now they've both been murdered with the same MO within days of each other. It must be the same killer."

"MO?" Laurel smirked. "You've been reading too many mystery novels. And right now the only common denominator between the killings is you."

"Me?" My voice went up an octave. I cleared my throat.

"You were on the scene when both bodies were found."

"But I was with Harper when I talked to Michael on the phone. We were together the whole time after that. Mr. Nakamoto saw us!"

"So you say."

"Check my phone!" I waved it at her.

She grabbed my wrist. In a flash I was on the ground, arm wrenched upward, face mashed into the cold cement, something hard—Laurel's knee?—wedged between my shoulder blades. Heat flushed through my body as memories of Laurel the high school bully flashed through my head. Gritting my teeth, I forced myself not to struggle, not to give her an excuse to snap my wrist. The pressure on it was unbearable.

"Now you're just overreacting," I gasped. I knew it would madden her, but I'd reverted to high school. Thoughtless.

She twisted. Pain sparked from my wrist to my shoulder. The phone clattered from my hand.

A pair of polished men's shoes came to stand before me. "What's going on?" Slate asked.

"She made an aggressive move toward me," Laurel said.

"I was showing you my—" Her knee pressed downward, flattening my lungs.

Slate picked up the phone I'd dropped. "Your phone? Why?"

"She claims she called the victim while she was with Ms. Caldarelli."

"That's what Ms. Caldarelli says as well. If you've finished the interview, I think you can let her up," he said mildly.

The pressure released.

I stumbled to my feet, brushing the dirt from my cheek.

"May I?" he asked, holding up my phone.

I nodded, rubbing my wrist.

He thumbed through my phone log. "I see a call from twelve forty seven to this number. It looks like it lasted less than a minute. Make a note of that, Detective."

Harper barreled into the stairwell, her chin high, her breath noisy. "What's going on?"

"Nothing," Laurel muttered.

"Don't leave town, Miss Kosloski, Miss Caldarelli," Slate said. "We may have more questions for you."

Taking my arm, Harper steered me down the stairs. "Well, you know where to find us," she tossed over her shoulder. When we were back in the parking lot, she said, "What happened? One minute you were talking to Laurel, and the next she was on top of you. What's with her?"

Muscles quivering, I rolled my shoulder and shook out my damaged wrist. "Laurel Hammer was responsible for the single most humiliating moment of my life," I said. "Ever. If anything, I should be the one who doesn't like her. And for the record, I don't."

"What made her snap today?"

"I was showing her my phone. She interpreted it as a threatening gesture."

Harper snorted. "If she finds you threatening, then she's not much of a cop."

That was what worried me.

SIXTEEN

MY SHOULDER BURNED THE next day. Sitting behind the counter of the Paranormal Museum, I rubbed the ache, plotting revenge I knew I'd never take. Laurel Hammer was a bad cop. She wasn't interested in finding out who the killer was unless it was Adele or Harper or myself. Helpless rage bubbled inside me, and it wasn't getting me anywhere. I blew out my breath. Enough.

Morning sunlight streamed across the faded pages of a Victorian-era book on dream interpretation. I was still working on the inventory, but had gotten distracted looking up symbols from last night's dream. Dreaming of attending school foretold advancement and good fortune; the book didn't say anything about being late and unable to find my class or my locker. Did they have lockers in 1862?

A middle-aged couple walked in and picked up a wine tasting map. We talked tasting rooms, and I told them which were free and which not.

"Thanks," the woman said, shooting a look at her … husband? Boyfriend? I decided I didn't care enough to puzzle it out and sold them two tickets.

"If you have any questions, feel free to ask," I called as they strolled into the Creepy Doll Room.

The bell above the door tinkled and a man walked in, his face hidden by the giant cardboard box he gripped in his bony hands. He wore rumpled khakis. All I could see of his head was the shock of sandy hair protruding over the top of the box. I imagined a scarecrow had stumbled out of the cornfields and into the museum.

"Can I help you?" I asked.

He made to put the box on the counter. Hastily, I shifted the cat's tip jar.

He lowered the box, panting. It was Mr. Average, the lawyer Sam Leavitt, Christy's ex. "Hello again," he said. "Remember me?"

"It's not every day I meet a squire. What are you doing back here?"

"I'm here about your macabre art gallery."

"I don't have a macabre art gallery."

"My taxidermy!" He opened the box and removed a squirrel wearing a straw hat. It held a miniature banjo.

"You … collect taxidermy?"

From the box he withdrew a creature that had the body of a hen, the head of a rabbit, horns, duck feet, and the tail feathers of a pheasant. "Collect it? No, I create it. I'm a taxidermist. It's just a hobby, but my works are highly sought after on eBay. One critic wrote they were charmingly odd and macabre, so it would be perfect for your gallery."

I picked up the rabbit-duck-pheasant-chicken-alope. It was kind of cute, in an oddball sort of way. Whimsical.

He sighed. "Christy never liked them. She said they was creepy."

"Not a match made in heaven then."

He gazed at me, stricken. "How can you say that now that she's dead?"

"I'm sorry. That was thoughtless."

His bony shoulders slumped. "No, you're not wrong. Still, it seems fitting that my first gallery showing should be here, where she died. She wouldn't have wanted to die in a paranormal museum, but she loved galleries."

If Christy hated the weird taxidermy, it seemed less a tribute than a "take that!" Still, the animals were unusual enough to intrigue without being grotesque. I liked the squirrel better than the creepy dolls.

"So what do you think?" He leaned forward, eyes glowing.

"I think it would definitely fit the gallery, but unfortunately, the gallery doesn't actually exist. Right now it's only an idea about moving the best dolls out of the Creepy Doll Room, building shelves for them in this room, and clearing out the rest." I wondered if anyone would want to buy a creepy broken doll. Or maybe I could give them away as prizes?

"Fantastic!" Sam grabbed the Frankenrabbit and hurried into the Creepy Doll Room. The banjo-playing squirrel stared at me, its ghost no doubt plucking a wistful tune. I put it back in the box.

Sam's gleeful reaction did not go hand-in-hand with just being turned down. I had turned him down, hadn't I?

A few more visitors trickled in, and I handed out tickets.

Sam emerged from the room. "It's perfect."

"It's not ready, and I don't know if it ever will be," I said.

Tenderly, he packed his rabbit creation into the box beside the squirrel. "Oh, don't worry about that."

Before I could respond, he hurried out the door.

I considered going after him, but it seemed like too much effort. I had bigger fish to fry. I needed to knuckle down on the job hunt. As much as I hated to admit it, my mother was right. I couldn't stay in San Benedetto to run a paranormal museum.

Feeling a burst of optimism, I checked my email. Still nothing on the finance job I really wanted. But there had to be other opportunities out there. Between ticket sales, I identified potential jobs and sent out resumes online.

A bulky Pacific Islander in painter's overalls walked into the museum. He chewed his fingernail, gaze darting about. "I was told to come here for the counter installation?"

"Right. This way." I led him through the tea room and to the alley, where Dieter was tearing open a bag of cement mix. Introducing the two, I left them to it. Adele's to-do list had me supervising the counter installation, but I figured Dieter was better equipped. Besides, I had tickets to sell and resumes to buff.

Around noon, Dieter popped his head in. "The counter guys are done. I'm going to get a sandwich. Want one?"

I dug some money out of my wallet and handed it to him. "Thanks. Roast beef and swiss, everything on it. And a diet cola, please." I might as well start my diet sometime.

Shifting his weight, he took the money. "You know, I could have cut and installed the counter. Adele didn't need to bring in those guys."

"I'm sure if she'd known you could have done it, she would have used you. It would have been more efficient."

His forehead wrinkled. "Have you heard anything about her? About the case?"

"No, but … Michael was killed yesterday. It's got to be related to Christy's death." I'd been kind of a jerk to Michael, and guilt tightened my chest. Another set of parents would be mourning their child.

Dieter jerked with surprise. "Killed? He was killed? How?"

"Hit on the head, I think. Did you know him well?"

"Not really," he said. "Hey—since Adele couldn't have committed that crime from jail, the police must be giving her case a second look. How's she handling it?"

"I don't know." Did Adele even know Michael was dead? Had anyone told her? In spite of everything, I suspected she still had feelings for him. You couldn't shut feelings off like a water faucet. "At least she has a good lawyer."

"Too bad Roger doesn't do criminal law anymore," Dieter said. "The guy's a genius."

"Oh?"

"He's semi-retired—makes more from his property than he does as a lawyer."

"But I thought he was a genius."

"Genius with money. He's got property all over San Benedetto. He's a wizard at financing. Did you know he's never taken a bank loan?"

He'd never taken a mortgage? Roger must have done really well as a lawyer to have those kinds of funds.

Dieter jammed his hands in the pockets of his overalls. "Adele's not … Is she seeing anyone?"

I angled my head, surprised. Dieter was interested in Adele? "Not in the city jail."

"Oh. Right." Dieter backed away. "Just wondering." He disappeared into the depths of the tea room. A few minutes later, I heard his truck roar to life out back.

He brought my sandwich and cola thirty minutes later, wordlessly dumping them on the counter. I wasn't sure about the etiquette of ticket-taking while noshing, but I didn't have anyone to cover for me.

Mason, resplendent in a tight black motorcycle tee and jeans, strode through my door and my heart did a little skip. "You didn't deliver my morning coffee," he said. "What gives?"

"I like to keep you guessing. Besides, I'm not your coffee wallah."

He laughed. "'Wallah'? I haven't heard that word since Afghanistan."

"I'm surprised you heard it there, since it's Indian."

Something behind his blue eyes shifted. "I interacted with ISAF. Those are the international forces there."

I'd said something to disturb him, though I didn't understand how or what. And that disturbed me. Without thinking, I asked, "Where were you based?"

His gaze turned arctic.

"Unless it's top secret," I said, "in which case, forget I asked. Especially since I know little about Afghan geography, so your answer won't mean much to me anyway."

"Near Kandahar."

I didn't know where that was, but I'd heard it in the news enough to know it was a rough place for American soldiers. I wondered what he'd done there, and decided not to ask.

"I read in the paper that there was another murder," he said. "I guess that's good news for your friend."

"I'm not sure she'll see it that way." I frowned, thinking of Adele's unwillingness to say that Michael had a key. She'd still cared for him in spite of everything.

"But at least she's in the clear."

"Assuming the same person killed both Christy and Michael."

"Is there a reason to think we've got two killers in San Benedetto?"

"No," I admitted. "And they were both bludgeoned to death." But what if it was a copycat? The papers had reported that Christy had died from a blow to the head—what if someone wanted to put her in the clear by killing Michael the same way? I shook my head. No, that was too complicated.

"What's wrong?" Mason asked.

"Just thinking."

"Well, don't give yourself a headache." He grinned and swaggered out the door.

I returned to the job hunt. Tourists wandered in and out, displaying increasing states of inebriation as the day went on. But they were all good-natured, seemingly happy to be relieved of their ticket money.

The bell over the door rang, and I pasted on a smile.

Adele clacked inside on her Jimmy Choos. Her black hair was coiled in a bun, not a strand out of place. But the skin around her eyes sagged, dull against her blazing white blouse and icy blue skirt. Smiling broadly, she held out her arms. "Mad!"

"You're free!" Quickly closing the computer windows on my job searches, I hurried around the counter and hugged her. She'd always been small compared to me, but today when her ribs pressed into mine, I thought I could lift her off the ground. I stepped back. "You've lost weight."

"The single benefit of jail. I ordered food in but had no appetite."

"You can order food in jail? And are you out on bail? What happened?"

"They dropped the charges after Michael ..." She turned her head, blinking, and swallowed.

"I'm sorry about Michael."

She nodded.

"But I'm relieved they've dropped the charges."

"How have things been at the museum? Is Dieter behaving himself?"

I was embarrassed that I still didn't know if I wanted to take over the museum. So I told her about my ideas instead: the macabre art gallery, a gift shop and online store, more detailed stories about the pieces.

"Brilliant! I love the gallery idea. It's in keeping with a museum next to a tea shop. I could even come up with a themed tea." She gazed at a couple wandering past giggling, obviously having come from a marathon at the local wineries. "People will need food to soak up the alcohol—perhaps a blood orange and cocoa tea served with scones. Scones aren't particularly paranormal, but everybody likes them. I could do a ghostly white chocolate scone with coconut flakes."

"I thought you weren't going to do any of the baking."

She waved aside my objection. "My baker is a genius. She can do anything. And clearly, so can you. Thank you for helping out with the museum. I know it's not your first choice and you probably haven't come to any decision, but you've been a lifesaver."

"Thanks. I'm enjoying it. But you're right, I haven't made up my mind yet. It's a big decision."

She lowered her head. "I heard you found Michael. Was it ...? Did he suffer?"

"I don't think so. It looked a lot like what had happened to Christy," I said. "Adele, I'm sorry."

She looked away. Neither of us said anything for a long time. I knew Adele would get through this, but I couldn't imagine what she was feeling.

"Did Michael have a key to this building?" I finally asked.

She gnawed her lower lip. "Yes."

"Why didn't you say anything to anyone?"

"Because I wanted him to come forward. It would have looked terrible for him if someone else told the police about the key."

But he hadn't come forward. Had he been scared? Guilty? Or protecting someone?

"Has the museum given you any problems?" Adele asked.

I thought of the Ladies Aid Society and shook my head. "Nothing I couldn't take care of." I still had no idea how to take care of that particular problem, or if it was even worth worrying about. But I couldn't drop it in Adele's lap. She had enough trouble.

Adele's cell phone rang and she put it to her ear. "Hello?"

Returning my attention to the computer, I tried to ignore Adele's side of the conversation. She hung up, frowning.

"What's wrong?" I asked.

"The arrest has put me behind schedule. I don't know how I'm going to get everything done tomorrow. Unless ..." She gave me a speculative look.

I crossed my arms over my chest, wary. "Unless?"

"Would you mind dropping a retainer check by my lawyer's office tomorrow morning? Fred's office is on your way to work. I'd take it over now but I'm already late for an appointment."

"Sure." Friends helped friends when they were wrongly accused of murder. And then I realized the deeper meaning of her request.

"Retainer? But that's for future work, isn't it? I thought the police dropped the charges against you."

"They have, but if they find new evidence, they can always change their minds."

"What sort of new evidence?"

"They shouldn't find any evidence that implicates me, since I'm innocent. But my ex and his girlfriend are dead. Even though I was in jail when Michael died, the police are convinced I've got motive. Besides, there's such a thing as killers for hire."

"They think you hired a hit man? That's ridiculous!"

She laughed hollowly. "I'm glad someone thinks so. Can you deliver the check?"

"Of course."

"Thanks." She dug a thin envelope out of her purse and wrote an address on it. "They open at eight."

I took the envelope.

She gave me a brief hug. "I can't wait until this is all over. Mother always told me to stay positive. But I can't help feeling like another shoe is about to drop."

A cloud passed before the sun, darkening the museum. I had the same feeling. This wouldn't be over until the killer was found.

SEVENTEEN

I STUMBLED DOWN MY apartment steps, yawning at the morning sun. My breath made little puffs in the air, and I turned up the collar of my gray pea coat. Digging my keys from my pocket, I hiked myself into the truck and drove to the lawyer's office.

Its parking lot abutted the creek, which was crashing and splashing against round stones darkened by the water. The grasses along its bank were white with frost. So were the poor geraniums in the building's window box. They drooped beneath the crust of white, and I wondered if they'd survive.

I jogged up the short flight of steps to the building, half-expecting the office's tinted double doors to be locked. But they opened at my touch. I walked inside, scanning the sign board for the suite belonging to Fred, Adele's criminal attorney. The name was easy to find, the firm taking up the entire second floor.

I trotted up the stairs. They opened onto a plush reception room, with a cheerful patterned carpet. Inoffensive watercolors of geometric shapes decorated the walls.

The gray-haired receptionist looked up and adjusted the pink cardigan around her shoulders. "May I help you?" An antique-looking broach sparkled at her breast.

"Adele Nakamoto asked me to drop this off," I said.

She rose. "Of course. I'll take that."

A door burst open down the hall. We both paused, hands outstretched.

Sam stopped in the hallway, gaping.

I stared, confused to see the lawyer/taxidermist here.

Straightening his blue blazer, he strode in our direction. "Miss Kosloski! What are you doing here? Is this about my showing at the gallery?"

"Uh, no," I said. "I came to drop this off for Adele Nakamoto."

"Please, this way." He motioned toward a windowed conference room, its blinds half drawn.

Feet dragging, I followed him. I really did need to set him straight about the gallery, which only existed in my head.

Closing the door behind us, he took the envelope and ripped it open, peered inside. "The retainer, I presume? I'll deposit this in the trust today."

"The trust? But I thought this was the office of her criminal attorney."

"We are. A trust is just a legal term for an account, but I can see how you'd be confused."

"I guess I still am." I eyed the closed door. "How is it that you're working on Adele's case when she's accused of murdering your ex-girlfriend?"

"I'm not even a junior partner in the firm. My boss is managing Adele's case."

"But you're a part of it, or you wouldn't have taken the check. And even if you're on the case's periphery, this must be difficult for you. Christy was once your girlfriend."

"I am quite certain Miss Nakamoto is not the guilty party," Sam said.

"I am too, but that's because we've been friends since high school. Adele considers any form of violence inelegant and unladylike. She refused to play soccer because of the risk of accidental kicking. Her mother had to send her to ballet and get her a special exemption from P.E." That was probably too much information, but Sam's legal persona had me rattled. It was a far cry from the weepy Sam who'd first entered the museum, or even taxidermy Sam. The difference in behavior was jarring.

I edged nearer to the door, wishing he hadn't closed it. "Why are you so sure Adele is innocent?"

"Because Miss Nakamoto is too short. Christy would have to bend over for a woman of Miss Nakamoto's stature to hit her on the head like that. The police tried to argue it was what happened, but Christy wouldn't have bowed to anyone."

That jibed with what little I knew about Christy. But I was having a hard time getting my head around Sam the legal eagle. Granted, we all have different aspects to our personalities. And the taxidermy—well, it wasn't my kind of hobby, but there was nothing inherently wrong with it. Yet Sam's personality change seemed borderline Norman Bates. I wondered where he got the animals he stuffed.

"Christy worked with Mr. Nakamoto's estate attorney, didn't she?" I asked.

The corners of Sam's mouth drew downward. "Yes. That firm does business and estate law. Trust work, wills, trademark licenses, that sort of thing."

"And that's how you met her?"

"It's a small town, and there tends to be overlap between clients."

"Did Christy have any trouble at her firm?" I asked, thinking of the woman at the Wine and Visitors Bureau complaining about her high-priced trust.

"Trouble? She was the top earner!"

"I thought she was a junior partner."

"Yes, but the old guys in her firm are semi-retired. Christy brought in the business. I told her she'd be better off on her own, but she liked the prestige of being with an old firm."

"So her firm did well?"

"*Christy* did well. The firm was on its last legs before she turned it around. So, what about March? Is that too soon?"

I blinked. "Too soon for what?"

"To promote my exhibition. I plan on dedicating it to Christy. Under the circumstances, March seems the right amount of time."

"Sam, I don't know when or if that gallery will exist."

"That's not a problem."

It was a problem for me, and I drew breath to object. There was a soft knock at the door, and the receptionist stuck her head in. "Your eight-thirty appointment is here."

"Thanks." Sam checked his watch. "Sorry, got to run. Thanks for dropping this check by."

"But—"

Waving Adele's envelope in farewell, he rushed from the room.

I shook my head. I'd worry about Sam's taxidermy exhibit later. Right now, I had a cat to feed and a museum to open.

———

GD was waiting at the door. He twined around my ankles and I stumbled, grabbing the counter. The cat's whiskers twitched with amusement.

"That's not funny." I poured a bowl of kibble and refilled his water, then checked the computer. An email from the Historical Association waited in my inbox. They'd sent an article on Cora's husband, Martin McBride:

IRATE SUBSCRIBER ATTACKS NEWSPAPERMAN

Bad Blood Between San Benedetto Businessmen
Mr. McBride Airs His Grievances with His Fists

Thursday afternoon, Mr. Martin McBride burst into the offices of the San Benedetto Tribune. Drunk and raving, he hurled epithets at staff and assaulted the owner. Police were called, but no charges were filed.

Nice guy, that Martin. I could see why Cora would have wanted to get rid of him. But would she have had the strength to hang him? I unhooked their photo from the wall. She was tiny compared to her husband.

Someone knocked at the door. It still wasn't opening time, but I plastered on a smile and opened it for a freckled man with a boyish face. He wore an earnest expression, jeans, and a button-up shirt beneath an open leather jacket.

"We're not open yet," I said, "but I'll sell you a ticket if you're willing to put up with the cold. The heater hasn't kicked in."

"I'm not here for a ticket." He reached into the front pocket of his shirt and handed me a business card.

"*The San Benedetto Daily*?" I stiffened. "Look, I can't comment on the murders. I don't know anything."

I started to close the door.

He jammed his foot in the gap. "I'm not here about the murders. That's another reporter's beat. I'm here about the petition to shut down the museum. Since we ran the ad from the Ladies Aid Society, my editor thought it would only be fair to get your side of the story."

"I'm not buying an ad."

His serious eyes widened. "Even if you were, that's the advertising department. I'm a reporter." He pulled a digital recorder from the pocket of his leather jacket. "Why do you think people feel antagonistic toward the museum?"

I gripped Cora's photo to my chest like it was armor plating. "I have no idea. It's a perfectly harmless museum. The ad placed by the Ladies Aid Society says it's tacky. To each his own."

He raised a brow. "But how do you feel about their petition? Isn't it a slap in the face?"

I shrugged. "I'm happier when I don't indulge in outrage." I may have been quoting the self-help book I'd been reading. But I wasn't about to let Ladies Aid know they'd gotten my proverbial goat.

"Still, it's your museum. You must have some feelings on the matter."

"Why? Why take myself or the museum so seriously? The Paranormal Museum is a reminder that life is short and often strange, and we should enjoy it while we can."

"But it's not really a museum, is it? More of an attraction."

GD Cat leapt onto the counter and rubbed against the tip jar. Coins rattled.

I grabbed the jar before it could fall. "Call it what you want, but there's some real local history here, even if it's told from an offbeat perspective."

He tilted his head. "Such as?"

"Such as …" My mind scrambled. Such as, such as, such as … what? The spirit cabinet wasn't exactly local history. I thrust the photo of Cora and Martin toward him. "Such as Cora McBride. She was the first woman convicted of murder in San Benedetto, but there's evidence that she was innocent." Okay, all I had was suspicion, not actual evidence. But the case was over 115 years old, and I wasn't concerned about libel.

"I doubt the Ladies Aid Society will find that has any educational value. Besides, aren't most of your visitors from out of town?"

"Even better that out-of-towners get a flavor of our local history." I told myself to stay cool, but my heart raced. Why did this silly interview feel so intense?

He returned the photo to me. "But you're not engaging the community, are you?"

"Of course we are," I lied. "I'm currently preparing a mock murder trial, so the community can review the evidence and determine if Cora was guilty or unjustly accused." What? Why did I say that?

His head jerked upward. "A mock murder trial? That's something I'd like to see."

"The owner of your old competitor, *The San Benedetto Tribune*, will figure prominently." Oh, geez, shut up, Maddie! But I couldn't stop. I was on a roll of panic.

"Who?"

I laid Cora's picture on the counter. "The ghost of the owner, Zane Donaldson. We'll be calling him as a witness."

"How?" The reporter's lips quirked. "In a séance?"

Ooh, a séance was a good idea. "How else? But as I'm no medium, we'll use actors to play the roles of the ghosts."

He chuckled. "That will give the Christmas Cow a run for its money. When's the trial?"

"I'm still gathering evidence, so we don't have a date set. But I'll let you know."

The reporter tapped the business card in my hand. "Please do."

He left, muttering into his recorder.

I sagged against the counter. A mock trial? What had I done? If this story appeared in the paper, I'd be committed to the project. I didn't know the first thing about mock trials. I'd never even served on a jury. Would the Historical Association let me use the old courtroom in their museum?

GD batted my sleeve.

"I don't care what you think. I had to say something."

He sneezed and stalked away.

A mock trial wasn't such a bad idea.

I whisked a feather duster over the exhibits. At nine, I flipped the *Closed* sign to *Open* and took my place on the high chair behind the counter. No one beat down the door to get inside. But at nine thirty the bell jingled over the door, and I closed the job search window on the computer.

My brother walked in with a model on his arm. At least, I assumed she was a model. She stood nearly six feet tall, and most of that was legs. Her glossy, chestnut-colored hair, faded jeans, and black turtleneck sweater shouted wealth. Shane was also dressed casually, but next to her, he didn't have quite the shine. And compared to them both I was a tarnished penny.

Straightening, I pressed my lips into a smile. "This is a surprise." I should have been happy to see Shane—he was trying to be supportive—but all I felt was failure. And I needed to get over it.

"Hey, Mad." He came around the counter and kissed me on the cheek. "This is Brittany."

Of course she was. I shook hands with her across the counter. Her manicure was flawless, her nails a soft pink. I hid my own chipped nails beneath the counter. "Welcome to the Paranormal Museum. What brings you to San Benedetto?"

"It's that obvious I'm not from around here?" she asked.

My brother picked up Cora's picture and studied it. "I talked Brittany into doing some wine tasting."

"Napa is passé." Brittany grinned. "Or at least that's what Shane's told me. I'm waiting to be impressed."

Shane held up the photo. "Who's this? They look grim."

"I'm still doing some research on them." I felt suddenly protective of Cora—amends, perhaps, for offering her up to the local paper.

Brittany peered over his shoulder. "She doesn't look grim. She looks sad. Who was she?"

"Cora McBride. She was convicted of murdering her husband, Martin, and died in prison." I re-hung the photo in its spot.

"Why?" Brittany asked.

Why did she die in prison? Why had she been convicted? Why did she do it? I settled on the latter. "The prosecutor argued she killed Martin because he was abusive."

Brittany shook her head. "So many stories here. If San Benedetto were more picturesque, my magazine could do a spread on it."

I bristled, looking to Shane for backup. Our downtown was charming. And San Benedetto couldn't help it if it was as flat as a mashed pancake. It's hard to be picturesque without rolling hills. But the town had character: brick sidewalks, nineteenth century buildings, and a creek flowing through its center. Plus, wineries!

"Brittany works for a fashion magazine," Shane said hastily. "She's used to more European landscapes."

"I never would have guessed," I said, my voice flat. "*Vogue*?"

Brittany's green eyes widened. "French *Vogue*. How did you know?"

I would not hate her simply because she worked for a fashion magazine in Europe, looked like a model, and dressed like Adele. I wasn't that petty. I was certain, however, that there were other good reasons to dislike her.

"She's home on vacation like me," Shane said. To Brittany: "Mad's done quite a bit of traveling. Eastern Europe was her old stomping ground before she quit."

"I love Eastern Europe," Brittany gushed. "They say Prague is over, but I love the place. And Romania!" She rambled on about spas and high-priced restaurants, and I nodded, smile frozen. Why did her dissertation on the best of Europe irritate me? I wasn't jealous (well, of her clothes and long legs, a little). My traveling days were over, and good riddance. I was sick of airplanes and hotels. But she was go-go-going, and I was stalled.

I really was that petty.

I clenched my jaw. I had to try harder, with both Shane and Brittany. She wasn't a green-eyed monster—I was.

"So now you run a paranormal museum." She looked around. "How quirky!"

"I'm just helping out a friend. I'm not sure what my next step is."

She placed a hand on my arm. "My advice is not to rush things. Life is too short to choose a dull job."

Easy advice from someone who traveled Europe for a fashion magazine. I leaned away from her. "There's nothing dull about the museum."

Shane pulled out his wallet. "And speaking of which. Two tickets, please."

I waved away the money. "Friends and family discount."

His smile was dazzling. "Thanks, Mad." He put an arm around Brittany's waist and guided her into the Creepy Doll Room.

I re-opened the windows I'd closed on my computer and bent my head to the job hunt. Options. What I needed were options. I couldn't take over the museum for lack of anything better to do. That would be an insult to me and to the museum.

A high-pitched giggle issued from the Creepy Doll Room. My brother and Brittany emerged and strolled into the Fortune Telling Room.

The front door banged open. Adele tottered inside on three-inch black-and-white Mary Janes, her face pale against her snowy St. John suit.

"Is it too early for a drink? Chuck kept a bottle of Kahlua behind the counter. Is it still there?"

"I took it home." Sheepish, I rubbed the back of my neck. "What's wrong?"

"I just returned from the library board meeting, or the part of it I was allowed to attend. They very politely insisted I take a leave of absence. And our annual fundraiser is in six weeks! Do you know what that means?"

That Adele was off the hook? I shook my head.

"The weeks leading up to a fundraiser are critical. It's all-hands-on-deck time. And they don't want me!"

Ouch. A library board meeting sounded tortuous to me, but for Adele, getting kicked off would sting. "They're idiots," I said. "But their loss could be your gain. You've got a lot on your plate with the tea room. Now you can focus on building your own business."

"They're not concerned about the tea room. They're concerned about the murder accusation. I'm being shunned."

I darted a glance at the Fortune Telling Room and pressed a finger to my lips in warning. "Once the police find Christy's real killer," I said in a low voice, "they'll be groveling for you to take them back."

"But what if they don't find her killer?" Adele whispered. "Crimes go unsolved all the time. This is a small police department. How much experience does Laurel have with murder?"

"Detective Slate seemed fairly intelligent."

"You're only saying that because he's tall, dark, and gorgeous."

I looked down at my fingernails. "I hadn't noticed."

"Oh, that's believable. Even I noticed, and I was the one he arrested."

Shane and Brittany exited the Fortune Telling Room and headed our way. Adele straightened and smiled, and I made introductions.

Adele gazed at Brittany's hips. "Tell me those are Earnest Sewn jeans."

"You have a good eye." She gestured toward Adele's suit. "And your St. John—classic."

"I had a board meeting." Adele waved one hand negligently.

"And those shoes. Are they …?"

"Vintage."

Shane drew me aside as Brittany and Adele swapped fashion tips. "Hey, is it okay that I brought her here?"

"Why wouldn't it be?"

"You seemed kind of … unpleasantly surprised."

"Sorry. It's me, not you. I don't know what I'm doing with my life. I used to have a glamorous career, and now I'm sitting behind the counter in a paranormal museum. I don't mean to take my frustration out on family. And Brittany seems nice," I fudged.

"She is." He grinned.

"Ugh. Go away. And be sure to take her to Adele's family winery."

He nodded to the two women. "I think Adele's got that covered."

"—it's not on the list," Adele was saying, "but tell them I insisted you taste the Haunted Vine Reserve."

Shane looked back at me. "Mad ... I'm sorry. You were right about the thing with Mom. I was using you to relieve my guilt. It wasn't fair."

"No, you were right," I said. "I want to be here, so there's no reason you shouldn't be happy in Moscow, or wherever they send you. And even though Mom's no invalid, I should be spending more time with her. You don't need to feel guilty about going back overseas. You love your job and you're great at it."

"How do you know I'm great at it?"

"Fishing for compliments? Get out of here."

My brother and his friend finally departed, and Adele disappeared into the tea room to supervise Dieter.

At least Dieter would be happy.

I returned to my job hunt. Between handing out tickets and answering questions, I tried to edit a resume for a project manager position. But my mind kept turning to the museum, to Adele, to the murders. Two murders in one week. That had to be a record for San Benedetto, and I wondered if Adele was right. Would the police be able to find the killer? The murders didn't seem random, or robberies, which meant the killer was someone who knew both victims. That should make it easier for the police, shouldn't it?

The bell over the door tinkled.

I was getting sick of that bell.

The attorney, Roger, ambled inside. His yellow polo shirt was untucked, and his khakis sagged around his hips.

"Hi, Madelyn. Is Adele here?"

I nodded toward the curtained-off tea shop. "She's in back with Dieter."

He blinked. "Great. Oh, by the way, I've got the contact info for that art agent I was telling you about." He pulled a wallet from his back pocket and handed me a wrinkled business card. "Just tell him what sort of macabre exhibits you're looking for."

"Thanks."

"You know, I've never toured the museum. Shame, since this is one of San Benedetto's biggest tourist attractions." He pointed over his shoulder with his thumb. "Do you mind?"

"Go right ahead." If I kept letting people in without tickets, I'd never turn a profit. But he was Adele's friend, and this was still Adele's building. It was more her museum than mine.

I watched him wander into the Fortune Telling Room, head bowed as if in thought. Two more visitors came in, and we chatted about the local wines before they disappeared into the Creepy Doll Room.

Dieter brushed through the curtains, running a hand through his tousled hair. "Hey, Maddie. Adele wants—"

Roger strode from the Fortune Telling Room, grinning. "Well, it's weird. I'll give you that." He went to Dieter and shook his hand, clapping him on the shoulder. "How's the work going?"

"Good." The contractor darted a glance at me. "Hey, Roger, you got a minute?"

"Looking for legal advice?"

"Something like that." Dieter drew the curtains back and jerked his chin toward the tea room.

With a lift of his eyebrows, Roger followed him inside.

In the other room, the men's voices were a low rumble. I grabbed the feather duster and wandered to the display of haunted objects on a shelf by the plastic curtains. Flicking the duster over a monkey skull, I practiced eavesdropping. It was an art I'd neglected, and one that requires regular cultivation.

"You're the one who recommended her to me," Dieter was saying.

"Actually, I recommended you to her."

"But I wouldn't have done Christy's kitchen if it hadn't been for you. That was six months ago. I need to get paid."

Roger chuckled. "Since when have you had trouble getting money from a woman?"

"Well, she's dead now. So who do I talk to about my bill?"

My hand clenched on the duster. Christy had owed Dieter money?

"Her trustee. A fellow named Sam Leavitt."

My feather duster paused over a dome clock. Sam Leavitt? But he was a criminal attorney. Why wouldn't Christy have used one of the estate attorneys at her own firm as a trustee?

"Thanks." Dieter coughed.

I beetled back to my spot behind the counter and whisked a fleck of dust from the top of the old-fashioned cash register. But neither Roger nor Dieter emerged, and I finally figured they must have escaped out the back.

EIGHTEEN

It was dark when I arrived home. Toeing off my shoes, I sprawled on the couch and unbuttoned the top snap on my jeans. I couldn't ignore my weight gain any longer.

The remote control on the coffee table was just out of reach. I stretched, unwilling to make the effort to sit up and grab it. Handing out tickets was surprisingly grueling.

My phone rang, and my fingers brushed the remote, knocking it to the floor. With a snarl, I got up and dug my cell from the pocket of my jacket, which I'd slung over a Mediterranean-blue chair.

"This is Maddie."

"It's Harper. Are you at home?"

"Yes."

"Have you eaten?"

"No."

"Good. I'm outside."

Before I could tell her I was in no mood to go out, she hung up. A pair of feet thundered up the steps.

I opened the door, and Harper handed me a warm pizza box fragrant with tomatoes, cheese, and mushrooms. She'd changed out of her work clothes into jeans and a tight olive-colored sweater under a tan leather jacket.

She knotted her long hair into a loose bun. "I presume you have alcohol."

"Wine or beer?" I nudged the door shut with my foot. In my prior life overseas, friends didn't casually drop by with pizzas. I'd moved around too much to develop relationships. This was … nice. Even if I was heading toward pizza overload.

"It's too cold for beer," she said. "I hear Cabernet works with pizza."

"Cabernet works with anything. Wine's in the rack in the kitchen." I set us up at my coffee table with plates and wine glasses, while Harper uncorked the wine—a Cabernet from Paso Robles.

She sat down in a wing chair and poured us glasses, then raised hers in a toast. "Cheers."

I took a sip, letting it roll over my tongue. Dry, with a faint hint of blackberry. Mmm. "So what brings you to my door?"

"I wanted a vegetarian pizza and didn't want to eat it by myself. What has Adele said to you? She told me they've dropped the charges, but she was pretty close-mouthed."

"I met a lawyer, Sam Leavitt, this morning when I dropped off a check for her criminal attorney. Sam said she was off the hook because she was too short—that the person who struck Christy had to be taller. And, of course, she was in jail when Michael was killed." I wrinkled my brow. "But Adele told me the police seem to think she could have had an accomplice. So she isn't in the clear."

I'd found the body with Adele. I'd been on the loose when Michael was killed, and had found his body. Could the police possibly think I was that accomplice? I gnawed my lower lip.

"Dammit." Harper put her glass on the table with a clatter. "It's so stupid. Anyone who knows Adele knows she couldn't have done it."

"There's something else that bothers me," I said. "This lawyer, Sam, used to date Christy. It seems like a conflict of interest for him to be working for the lawyer handling Adele's defense. When I asked him, he played it down. But it doesn't seem right."

A slice of bell pepper fell to Harper's plate. "That's the problem with living in a small town. For better or worse, if you want a local lawyer, you don't have a lot of options. I know about Sam dating Christy and it ending badly. Trust me, he's got no reason to mess with Adele's case."

"What do you mean?"

"After Sam and Christy broke up, he was kind of moping around her, hoping to get back together. I was at a Chamber of Commerce function—one of those wine-and-cheese things—and the two were there. Christy loudly told him to leave her alone, and insulted his, er, performance in the process. I felt bad for the guy."

"If it was such an ugly breakup, why is he the trustee of Christy's estate?"

Harper took a bite of the pizza and chewed. "The breakup was about six months ago. Maybe she hadn't gotten around to making the change?"

"And why isn't someone from her own firm the trustee? You'd think, with them being estate attorneys, that someone from her firm would be a logical choice."

"Maybe. But sometimes you want to keep your work and personal life separate, you know?"

"I'm starting to wonder if that's possible." I'd lied to that reporter when I'd said the petition against the museum hadn't bothered me. My ego was getting tangled in the museum, just like it had in my prior career. It was all personal.

"In a town this small," I continued, "all the relationships—even the professional ones—seem incestuous. Is there a lawyer or CPA in town you don't know?"

She laughed. "There'd better not be. My business depends on networking."

I turned the stem of my wine glass, my insides tensing. "Harper, were you the 'client' Christy was blackmailing?"

Her expression tightened. "You know I didn't kill Christy. Or Michael. Does it matter?"

I stared at the hole in my sock. She wasn't denying it.

"We're friends, and you deserve your privacy," I finally said. "I don't need to know what it was about. But the police do need to know if there's someone else out there who might have had a motive for murder. If you were her blackmail victim, then I'll drop it. But if there's actually a client out there who has a motive … Harper, you've got to tell the police. Adele is still in jeopardy."

Her jaw clenched. She looked past me, and I had my answer.

We sat in silence, sipping wine that turned to dust in my mouth. I wasn't sure where to go from there, so I said nothing. Adele would have thought of some adroit way to change the subject, but all I could think of was blackmail and murder.

"I don't need details," I said.

Abruptly, Harper stood. She walked to the window, her face reflected in the glass, blackened by the night. "You do. I should have told you years ago."

She didn't turn. Didn't say anything.

I couldn't believe Harper had done anything wrong. Maybe silly or embarrassing, but not wrong. Not Harper.

"Don't tell me," I said. "You're a serial killer. With a string of unpaid parking tickets. You never got a permit for your home remodel, did you?"

"No, you idiot." She turned to me, her lips twitching.

"Late library books? An embarrassing rash?"

"I'm a strega." She looked toward the kitchen.

"A what? Wait, is that one of those kinky—"

"A witch!" Harper fisted her hands and jammed them on her hips. "A witch from the Italian tradition. You know how my dad's mother raised me after my parents died? Well, when I was in college, she turned up a box of my mom's things when she was cleaning out the attic. We're still not sure how it got there. Once she realized they were my mom's, she stopped looking at them and handed the box off to me. That's what she says, at least. Underneath the clothing were books and talismans and my mother's notes. She was a strega. At first I started studying it because I was curious about her. At first it was academic. But then I began practicing. It made me feel closer to her. Now it's just what I do."

I shook my head, disbelieving. "Is that all?" Relief mingled with hurt as I sank into the couch. Harper had been doing this since college? Why hadn't she told me? "And Christy was blackmailing you over it? How did she know?" How had Christy known and I hadn't? My lungs constricted.

"I have to keep my work and my craft separate. This may be California, but how do you think my financial planning clients would feel if they knew I was a witch? They'd begin to suspect I was using magic to predict the stock market."

"Would you?"

"Of course not! As a financial planner, I know enough not to even try. You should base your investment choices on your goals and risk tolerance, not …" She laughed shakily. "Sorry about the financial lecture. It's become automatic."

"But why didn't you tell me?" That came out more plaintive than I'd intended. I wanted to ask if Adele knew, but pride held me back. Then: "Wait a minute. That business about the tea recipe you wouldn't give Adele … Was it a special strega tea?"

Harper hung her head.

So Adele didn't know. This made me feel better for all of five seconds. Then I realized what it meant. "You've got to tell her."

"Maddie, I can't!"

"She's going to find out, and then she's going to ask me if I knew, and I'm going to say yes, and then she'll be mad at me. Tell her. We've been friends for years. I still can't understand why you've kept it such a secret."

"At first it was about me and my mom, family business. And then I got so used to keeping that side of me private, it became a habit."

"How did Christy find out?"

"I'm not sure. For a short time, I was in a local coven. One of the women there may have told her."

A slice of pizza slid off my plate and into my lap. "There's a coven in San Benedetto?"

Beneath her olive sweater, Harper's shoulders tensed. "You say it like they're Satanists or something."

"I say it like I can't believe people are upset about the Paranormal Museum when we've got a coven practicing witchcraft! It's totally unfair!" I blotted pizza grease from my jeans.

Harper smirked. "Well, now you understand why I'm keeping my alter ego on the down-low. If the Ladies Aid Society is after your little museum, imagine what they'd do to me."

"Point taken," I grumbled. "Got any spells for increasing sales at the museum?"

"First, I think you need a spell for clarity on whether you want to buy the museum."

"Yes, please." I sat up straight and folded my hands in my lap. "Give me clarity."

"Are you having fun?"

"Fun?" I leaned back on the couch and stared at the ceiling. A tiny spider crawled across it. "You mean aside from riding herd on a bookie, and finding a body, and battling the Ladies Aid Society?"

"Aside from that."

I thought about Herb the "collector" and Sam's oddball taxidermy. "There've been some entertaining moments."

"Is it a challenge?"

"Figuring out how to turn a paranormal museum into a profitable business? I'll say."

"Do you like the area?"

I liked nodding at people I knew on the street. I liked friends dropping by just because they could. I liked the fog rolling over the vineyards, the neat rows of orchards, the Victorian houses. "It's good to be home," I said.

"Then I think you have your answer."

"There's more to it than that."

"Is there?"

I tried to summon a steely look and slid another slice of pizza onto my plate. "To recap: Christy had broken up with Sam and wasn't very nice about it. So he might not mind that she's dead. You're a strega, and there's a coven in San Benedetto. Anything else I should know?"

"Just one. Your museum is being haunted."

"It's haunted." I tilted my head, skeptical. "Let me guess. By the ghost of a brunette with deep-set eyes and a long nose, dressed in a gown from the nineteenth century and named Cora."

Harper's jaw dropped. "You can see her too?"

"Cut it out, Harper." One corner of my mouth twisted downward.

"Cut what out? You're a ghost whisperer? How long have you been able to see spirits?"

"Ghosts don't exist." This had stopped being funny. Was she also pulling my leg about being a strega?

"You're a ghost whisperer who doesn't believe in ghosts? That will be a challenge."

"Knock it off," I said sharply.

"Knock what off? I'm serious—you're being haunted by a woman like you described."

"I told you I was researching Cora McBride."

"Cora who?"

I must have told Harper about Cora. Hadn't I? Or if I hadn't, maybe she saw my research and her subconscious picked it up. "If you can see Cora, ask her what happened. I'd love to get the story from the horse's mouth."

"I can't talk to them, or even see them. I only get … impressions."

"Because you're a strega."

Harper lowered her head and chewed her bottom lip. "You don't believe me."

"I respect your beliefs," I said carefully.

"You just don't share them."

"No." I couldn't lie to Harper. Not to a friend.

Sighing, she shook her head. "You will."

We moved the conversation to lighter fare—a winery event, a trip to Tahoe next month, and whether the Dairy Association would build another Christmas Cow.

Harper left an hour later. Stuffed with wine and pizza, I returned to my sprawl on the couch and finished reading my self-help book. My self did not feel helped.

Maybe I should have started reading paranormal books instead? It made sense for the museum's theoretical gift shop to sell theoretical paranormal books. Grabbing my e-reader, I downloaded a book about a metaphysical detective in San Francisco and began reading.

The phone rang, startling me out of a high-tension scene in a pie shop. Struggling from the couch, I lunged for it. "Hello?"

"Mad, it's Shane."

"Shane. It's …" I checked my watch, rubbed my eyes. "After eleven. What's up?"

"I need a favor. Brittany lost one of her diamond studs and thinks it might have fallen off in your museum."

"No problem. I'll look for it tomorrow."

"Uh … could we look for it tonight? Brittany's got an early morning flight to New York."

I smothered a curse. "If I find it, I'll mail it to her."

"Sis, have a heart. It has sentimental value."

"Color me heartless. It's almost midnight!"

"It's eleven fifteen. And her father gave the earrings to her before he died."

I stared at the ceiling. The spider was gone, no doubt biding its time until I fell asleep to play tiddlywinks on my nose. Assuming I ever got to sleep tonight. "Fine. I'll meet you there in thirty minutes."

He breathed a sigh. "Thanks, Mad. But you still owe me one for picking you and your buddy up at midnight."

Muttering bad words, I jammed on a pair of tennis shoes and shrugged into a jacket. I stopped in front of the mirror before the door. I would not compare well to Brittany. My hair was mashed on one side from lying on the couch, my makeup worn thin. I grabbed a knitted hat from the coat tree and pulled it over my head. That solved the couch hair problem. The museum would be too dimly lit for her to notice my blotchy skin.

A heavy layer of fog hung low over the deserted city streets. I parked in front of the museum, then figured I might as well start the search inside rather than wait for my brother and Brittany. The sooner I found that earring, the sooner I could get home to bed.

Unlocking the door, I flipped on the overhead light and paused as one of the fluorescents flickered to life. The one above the counter remained dark. I frowned at it, willing it to blink on. It blinked erratically, washing the room in flickering, yellowish light. I cleared my throat, uneasy. More was off than the overhead light.

I held my breath, listening. As if expectant, the museum seemed to hold its breath with me.

Shaking off my overactive imagination, I closed the front door, locking it for good measure. Something moved at the edge of my vision. I spun toward it, hands extended like the boxer I wasn't.

The rocking chair swayed, empty. I gritted my teeth. Because there are no such things as ghosts, I forced myself to walk to it. Black cat hairs sprinkled the wooden seat. I blew out my breath, shoulders sagging. GD must have jumped from the chair when I'd let myself in. That was all. Ghosts. Ha! I'd almost half-believed the chair really was haunted. I'd told Harper I didn't share her beliefs, but when things went bump in the night, primitive superstition ran wild.

The plastic curtains separating the museum from the tea room rippled. My pulse quickened. Even though there was no such thing as ghosts, it wouldn't hurt to get a move on and find that diamond earring. I'd start where Brittany and Shane had stopped to talk to me—the front counter.

I explored the area around the counter. No diamond winked at me from the linoleum, but the wonky fluorescent above me was not a light to hunt diamonds by. Reaching over the counter, I grabbed for the flashlight. Its weight felt solid in my hand, comforting.

Cold rolled in on a wave of silence.

I went rigid. The cold was unnatural, the quiet uncanny. Eerie. Wrong.

No, I didn't believe in ghosts, but every primal instinct I had screamed at me to flee. My limbs rebelled. Fear locked them in place, frozen.

Imagination is not always a gift.

The atmosphere thickened, choking me. The quiet stretched, the only sound my own harsh breath, breath I could see in the air. It was a nails-on-a-chalkboard silence, a deep silence that tightened my throat and made me tremble.

Noiseless, a white sheet of paper drifted off the counter. It alighted on the checkerboard floor, making a slithery, rustling sound. I heard myself take an uneven breath, and the room warmed.

It was over.

Hand shaking, I stooped to grab the paper.

Something whooshed over my head, and pain exploded at the top of my skull.

NINETEEN

Gasping, I pitched sideways against the counter, curving inward like a pill bug, my hands protecting my head. Someone big moved past me. The door slammed.

I crouched there, shaking, heart slamming against my ribs. I knew I should move, should run, but my legs didn't want to obey my commands. My skull was splitting. Lights danced before my eyes.

Footsteps pounded toward me, and I fumbled for the flashlight I'd dropped. But I was clumsy, moving through molasses.

Two Masons crouched beside me, their azure eyes unblinking. "Are you okay?"

I nodded, and more sparks made merry in the museum. Someone had assaulted me, and anger and shock and fear waltzed through my head.

"Where did he go?"

"Front door."

Mason darted outside. I leaned my back against the counter and let my legs sprawl. The floor was cold. I didn't care.

I was small. Insignificant. Unimportant enough to hit over the head and throw away.

GD Cat stuck his head out of the Creepy Doll Room. He growled, reminding me that now was not the time to fall apart. I needed to cowgirl up.

"Hey, GD." I reached a hand toward him. It flopped awkwardly to my lap. So I'd just sit here some more. Cowgirl Maddie was going to have to get her wind back.

Belly low to the ground, the cat slunk toward me. He sniffed my sneakers and pawed the leg of my jeans. Satisfied, he crawled into my lap.

Mason returned, and I snapped myself back into reality enough to take a good look at him. His mane of blond hair was rumpled, as if he'd recently awakened. The top button of his jeans was undone and the bottom of his white T-shirt ruched up, exposing a blond arrow of hair on his washboard abs. His feet were bare. Normally, these details would interest me for all sorts of reasons. Tonight I just felt bad. Bad I'd woken him. Bad someone thought so little of me they'd tried to smash my head in. Bad I hadn't found that stupid earring.

"Whoever it was, he's long gone." Mason knelt beside me and took my chin in his hands. "Someone broke the lock on the back door to Adele's tea room."

I shuddered, closed my eyes.

"Hey," he said. "Look at me."

Purring, the cat kneaded my thigh with his paws. I opened my eyes, trying to focus. "I am looking at you."

He swore. "You've got a head injury."

"How can you tell?"

"Your hat is bleeding. You may have a concussion. I'm calling the paramedics."

"Get away from my sister!" Shane stood in the doorway, fists clenched. Brittany peered over his shoulder.

My hand flopped in a limp wave. "Hi Shane, Brittany. I didn't find the earring. This is Mason, my upstairs neighbor. Mason, this is my brother, Shane."

"What's going on?" Shane took a cautious step inside. Brittany stayed glued to his back, her manicured hands clutching the shoulders of his leather bomber jacket.

"There's been a break-in," Mason said. "Your sister's got a head wound. Her balance and coordination are off. It may be a concussion, but I'm no doctor. I was about to call 911 when you arrived."

Brittany squealed and edged around my brother. In her black turtleneck and yoga pants, she looked like a cat burglar. "A break-in?"

"I'll call." Shane pulled a cell phone from the pocket of his jacket.

"My hat is bleeding?" It was time I inserted myself into the conversation.

"Don't worry." Mason patted my knee and stood. "Head wounds bleed like crazy, but it's probably not that bad."

The cat worked his way up my stomach. I ruffled his fur. My arms and legs were working again.

Brittany sized up Mason, her eyes narrow, appraising. The corners of her lips tilted upward. I found myself liking her less and less.

Shane hung up the phone. "They're on the way. So what are you doing here?"

"I heard someone in the alley," Mason said. "At first I thought it was just a drunk, but then Maddie screamed."

"I screamed?" I didn't remember screaming.

Mason ignored me. "What are you two doing here?"

Brittany dimpled. "I lost a diamond stud earring, and the one place we haven't looked is the museum. Would you help me find it?"

Mason shook his head. "The cops will likely want to take fingerprints. We shouldn't mess around in here."

Brittany ran her gaze over Mason. In our family, taking a girl to the airport meant a serious relationship, so why was she making googly eyes at Mason? I hoped Shane wasn't too infatuated with her.

"With all the people who've been inside the museum," I said, "I doubt fingerprints will be much help."

Shane put his hands on his hips, a superhero in blue jeans. "He's right. We should wait."

I reached for the white paper that had fallen to the ground and turned it over. Cora and Martin stared out from their photo. I looked at the wall opposite and its row of haunted pictures. One frame hung empty. I'd shown the photo to the reporter that morning, and then Shane had looked at it. Had I left it on the counter? I couldn't remember, but in my brain-scrambled state, something seemed off.

"But what if someone steps on my earring?" Brittany asked.

I looked up. Beneath strands of her chestnut-colored hair, something glinted in her collar. "Not much danger of that," I said.

"Why not?"

"Because your earring is snagged in your collar."

"What?"

Shane peered at her neck. "She's right." He parted her hair and unsnagged the diamond stud from her knit turtleneck. "Mystery solved."

Brittany's hands fluttered about her. "What a relief." But her lips pressed tight, as if disappointed.

My butt was growing numb on the cold floor, so I shoved the cat off me and lumbered to my feet.

Insulted, the cat sneezed and stalked away, tail quivering.

"Steady." Mason chuckled, a low rumble. "You haven't got your sea legs yet."

"Good thing we're inland." But the floor rolled, and I leaned against the counter.

Someone rapped on the door. Without waiting for an answer, Detective Slate strode inside, his jaw darkened by a five o'clock shadow. Two uniformed cops fanned out behind him, hands on their holstered guns.

Stripping off his blue parka, the detective tossed it on the counter, covering the tip jar. He jammed up the sleeves of his navy V-neck sweater. "What happened?"

I opened my mouth to respond.

"Mad surprised an intruder." Shane draped a protective arm over my shoulders.

I glared at my big brother. It was my museum. I could speak for myself.

The detective arched a brow. "Mad?"

"My sister."

He looked at me, his chocolate-colored eyes unfathomable. "Then maybe she should tell me what happened."

"I got here around a quarter to midnight," I said. "Someone surprised me. I didn't see him." Lightly, I touched my hand to my head. The knit hat was damp, the spot tender.

"Him?"

"It could have been a her, I guess." The person had *felt* big, but I'd been cowering on the floor. Everyone's big from that angle.

"What were you doing here so late?" Slate asked.

Brittany stepped closer to Mason and shivered dramatically. "I lost an earring and thought it might have been dropped here. Since I've got an early morning flight tomorrow …" She checked her watch. "Oops, today, I mean. Maddie offered to let us search the museum for it tonight."

"Can you describe the assailant?"

My cheeks warmed. "No. My back was turned. He hit me with something, and I fell."

"What did he hit you with?"

I looked around, but I didn't see any potential bludgeons. Weird. The man who'd killed Christy and Michael had left the weapons behind. My teeth chattered. "By the time I knew what had happened, he was out the front door."

My brother draped his bomber jacket over my shoulders and rubbed my arms.

"How did he get in?" Slate asked.

"The back door was busted open." Mason pointed at the plastic drapes. "That's how I got in when I heard Maddie scream."

The detective nodded to the two uniforms. "See what you can find."

They disappeared through the plastic.

"You see him?" the detective asked Mason.

He shook his head. "By the time I arrived, he'd taken off. I went into the street but didn't see anyone, so I came back to check on Maddie."

"Anything taken?"

"I don't think so," I said. "The cash register didn't seem to be tampered with. But I'd have to look around."

"Later," Slate said.

A paramedics truck pulled up, illuminating the room with flashing blue. Two paramedics, a man and woman, hurried into the room, medical bags at their sides.

Detective Slate pointed at me. "Check her out."

Gently, each grasped me by the elbow and escorted me to the rocking chair. I started to sit, remembered it was haunted, and jerked upward.

"What's wrong?" the man asked me.

"Nothing." I sat.

They removed my hat, prodded my head with gloved hands, asked questions, shone lights in my eyes.

"You might have a mild concussion," the woman said.

Slate walked over. "What's the verdict?"

"She was lucky," the male paramedic said. "It was a glancing blow, and that knit hat gave her some cushion. It's a nasty bump and she'll need a few stitches. Possible concussion, but she'll be okay."

The photo had saved me. I must have brushed against it when I reached over the counter for the flashlight. A chill rippled through me—if the photo hadn't fallen from the counter at the right moment, I might not have been so lucky. I might have ended up like Christy and Michael.

"You feel up to taking a look around and letting me know if anything seems to be missing?" Slate asked.

I nodded.

He escorted me through the Creepy Doll Room, still creepy but clean. In the Fortune Telling Room, I flipped on the light. The cloth over the round display table in the center had been tugged to one side. "The tablecloth's been shifted." I pointed with Cora's photo to the spirit cabinet. "And that's been moved."

The detective knelt beside it. A black scrape in the linoleum marked the trail where the cabinet had been shifted away from the wall.

Slate rose and took the photograph from my hands. "Cora and Martin McBride? What does the photo have to do with this?"

"Nothing. It had fallen to the floor. I was reaching down for it when I got hit." I wobbled, dizzy.

Slate grasped my elbow and an electrical current seemed to ripple through me. He let go as if scalded.

He cleared his throat and dropped his gaze to the photo. "Interesting case."

I wasn't sure if he was talking about Cora or the Paranormal Museum.

We returned to the main room, where Mason and my brother joked with the paramedics. Brittany edged closer to Mason, her expression calculating. A blot of worry grew beneath my breastbone. Shane couldn't be serious about her. Could he? But he seemed oblivious to her admiration of my neighbor, too confident to see that anything was amiss.

"How're you feeling?" Mason asked me.

I grimaced. "Like someone hit me on the head."

The female paramedic packed up her case. "You'll need to go to the emergency room to get stitches."

I frowned, wondering how much that was going to cost.

"I'll take you," Mason said.

"Would you?" Shane asked. "I've got to get Brittany back to San Francisco for her flight."

"If your sister is hurt, we should all go." Brittany eyed Mason through lowered lashes.

"It's only some stitches," I said. "It's no big deal."

My brother was quick to agree, shuffling a reluctant Brittany through the front door.

Laurel Hammer edged past them as they left, catching one of her three-inch heels on the threshold. Her sequined silver mini-skirt barely covered her assets.

"Catch you on a night out?" Slate asked her.

She scowled at me. "Tomorrow's my day off. Of course I was out. What happened?"

"Break in and assault." Slate pointed at me with the eraser end of his pencil.

"And why aren't I surprised to find you in the middle of this?" Laurel asked me.

"Because it's my museum?"

She lowered her head, staring. "I thought you were just managing it for a friend."

I clapped my hand to my head and saw stars. Adele. The break-in was in her building. "I've got to tell Adele what happened."

"I'll let Ms. Nakamoto know about the break-in," Detective Slate said. "You go to the hospital and get your head examined."

Laurel snorted. "So what's this about, Kosloski? Who broke in?"

"How should she know?" Mason's Nordic brows drew together.

Laurel reddened. "Within one week she's been on the spot for two murders and a break-in. That strikes me as suspicious."

"Obviously," I said, "the killer returned to the scene of the crime."

She stepped closer, forcing me to crane my neck or get an eyeful of cleavage. "How do you know it was the killer?" she asked.

"Who else would it be?" Was she being willfully stupid or trying to goad me into some admission?

"Teenagers looking for a scare," she said. "A petty burglar. You."

"I hit myself on the head? Come on! The killer was here and knocked me down, just like he did to Michael and Christy."

"Not exactly," she said. "They died."

"I was lucky!" I jammed my hands into my pockets, fists clenched. "It had to have been the same person. It's too big a coincidence. And he came here for a reason, probably to look for something."

A pulse beat in her jaw. "If you're suggesting we missed something, think—"

"I'm suggesting there's more to this than a simple break-in!"

Mason draped his arm around my shoulders and gave me a warning squeeze.

I blew my breath out, struggling for calm.

"Are you certain your attacker was a man?" Detective Slate asked.

"It was a big person. I suppose it could have been a very tall woman," I said, reluctant.

"What's wrong?" Slate asked.

"I got a sense of … mass. I can't be one hundred percent sure it was a man, but I'm fairly certain it was."

He nodded. "Go to the hospital, Miss Kosloski."

"Come on, Maddie." Mason pulled me toward the door.

"But I've got to lock up. I can't just leave."

"They'll take care of it. Won't you?" Mason asked the lieutenant.

Slate grunted an assent and disappeared through the curtains into the tea room. Drilling me with a hard look, Laurel followed.

"Where's your car parked?" Mason led me onto the sidewalk. The fog had thickened. Eddies of white swirled around us, kissing my cheeks with chill and damp. A truck rumbled in the distance.

With my toe, I nudged the whitewall tire of my faded pickup, parked at the curb. "Here."

He gazed at it for a moment and shook his head. "Keys." He held out his hand.

I burrowed through my messenger bag and handed them to him. "How bad is the alley door?"

"An easy fix for Finkielkraut. I guess this lets him off the hook."

"What do you mean?"

"There's no reason for Adele's contractor to break in when he's got a key."

I mulled that over as we drove. My head throbbed. This recent attack would put Dieter out of the running. Unless he'd broken in to the museum to make it seem like it was someone else. Leaning my head against the cool window, I watched the streetlamps fade in and out of existence.

"This is some truck," he said. "A '58?"

"I inherited it."

He didn't ask me who I inherited it from, which was a good thing. I couldn't think of my dad right now. Tears were already too close to the surface. The attack had flattened me in more ways than one.

I needed to stop playing devil's advocate with myself. This wasn't an Agatha Christie novel, or a thriller with a byzantine double-cross. The killer so far had been pretty direct—a bash on the head and done. The break-in was likely as direct as the murders. The killer wanted something inside the museum. Something he'd dropped when he'd killed Christy? Something incriminating? Or was there something else about the museum that had brought the killer there the night of Christy's death? Had she been in the wrong place at the wrong time?

The idea opened up a world of new motives. But if that were true—that the killer had always been after something in the museum—then why kill Michael? And why had Christy been in the museum? Michael had said he didn't have the key … what if that had been a half truth, and he'd given the key to Christy? Perhaps to return to Adele because doing it himself was too painful? That explanation would be the simplest, and I was a big fan of Occam's Razor—the simplest explanation was likely correct.

TWENTY

Who doesn't hate hospitals? Aside from giving birth, there's no good reason to be inside one. We sat in the waiting room over an hour, Mason growling and pacing, before a nurse led us into a small examination room. Another forty minutes before a doctor stuck his head in and disappeared. More waiting. Finally, a nurse sewed three stitches into my scalp and ordered Mason to make sure I wasn't left alone that night.

Being alone with Mason sounded exciting. But the night was pretty much over, the sun lightening the horizon, by the time he drove me back to the museum. Adele waited for us outside, her fingers tapping the leather-lined steering wheel of her Mercedes.

"She shouldn't be alone tonight," Mason said.

"Got it." Adele saluted with two fingers. She drove me home, and I tumbled into bed.

I woke up and staggered to the kitchen. In her cream-colored silk pajamas, Adele was sipping a cup of tea at the round linoleum table.

She folded her legs beneath her on the sixties-era blue vinyl chair and flattened the morning paper beside her cereal bowl. "Hungry?"

I wasn't. But breakfast is the most important meal of the day, so I stuck a piece of sliced sourdough in the toaster. "Thanks for bringing me home," I said.

"It was the least I could do." She tapped a manicured finger on the newspaper. "You've been busy."

The toast popped up, and I smeared it with butter and peanut butter. "I try to stay active."

She wrinkled her nose. "I can't believe you're eating that. And the Ladies Aid Society will not be pleased by your quotes in this article about the museum."

"Oh. The paper quoted me? Gimme."

"Maddie—"

"Well, I'm not pleased they took out a full-page ad voting the Paranormal Museum the tackiest museum in San Benedetto."

She handed me the paper. "I hate to break it to you, but it is the tackiest museum in San Benedetto."

"Then I'm honestly not sure what I can do." I sat across from her. "Ladies Aid's reaction seems over the top."

"At Harvard I took a class on negotiating—it's one of the few classes I use on a regular basis. Have you heard the story of the orange?"

I sighed and propped my head on my fist. "I'm sure I'm about to."

"One orange, two sisters. Each wanted the orange for a dish they wanted to bake, and they squabbled over it. In the end, they discovered that one sister needed the rind, while the other needed the flesh. Problem solved."

"I'm certain there's a lesson in there somewhere." I scanned the article. They mentioned the mock trial. I wasn't sure how I felt about that, but I'd been the one to shoot off my big mouth.

Adele made a face. "I suggest you find out what Ladies Aid really wants. Does your very existence bother them, or is it something else?"

"Fine," I grumbled.

"So what were you really doing at the museum last night at midnight?" she asked.

"I was really helping my brother's girlfriend find her earring."

She stilled. "They're a couple? Are you sure?"

"Shane took her to the airport this morning. He's not that nice unless he's getting something out of it."

"He's not bad." Adele lined the paper up with the edge of the pale-blue place mat.

"No, not bad. But contrary to popular belief, he's not perfect either."

She arched a brow. "I do believe you're jealous of his success."

"I have a hangover-worthy headache that wasn't preceded by a wild night on the town. I'm irritated."

"Well, I like your idea of a re-creation of the McBride trial."

"Thanks. But as long as we're making confessions, there's something else about the museum I should tell you."

"Oh?"

"Dieter's a part-time bookie. He was using the alley behind the tea room for his business."

Adele put her tea cup down with a clatter. "What?"

"Did you know about the bookmaking?"

"Of course not! Wait—*was* using? He's not anymore?"

"I put the fear of you into him and told him to knock it off. And I think he has."

"Anything else?"

"Harper thinks the museum is haunted." And the more I thought about Cora's photo, the more I wondered if she might be right.

Adele laughed. "I'll hold off on calling an exorcist. Look, why don't you take the day off? I can manage the museum today."

A day free of the museum? And a Friday!? "That's … seriously?"

"Absolutely." Adele checked her watch. "I'm going to get dressed." Grabbing her overnight bag off my couch, she beelined for the bedroom.

It almost felt like I was playing hooky from school. But I couldn't slack off. I had to job hunt. And get dressed.

I took a quick shower. Pulling a white T-shirt over my head, I slipped into an old pair of faded jeans and waited for the computer on my unmade bed to boot up. When it did, I opened my email and slid my belt through the loops.

"Can I borrow your toothpaste?" Adele shouted from the bathroom.

"Uh, sure."

My heart stopped. An email from the financial firm I'd applied to. Holding my breath, I clicked it open. *Dear Applicant …*

I collapsed on the bed, and the laptop bounced on the rumpled sheets. Rejection. I hadn't even made it to an interview. I hadn't even made it to getting my name on the rejection letter.

What was wrong with me? I'd been … well, not a big deal, but I'd had a job with big responsibilities, managing operations for multiple countries. That should mean something. Shouldn't it?

I guessed it didn't. Maybe work overseas didn't translate to work in California. Or I was doing a rotten job of marketing myself? Or both?

What had happened to my life? Harper was a success. Adele was a success. My whole family was a success. And in nine months, I'd scored two lousy job interviews.

On one foot, Adele hopped to the door, slipping a strappy heeled shoe over her other foot. "Mad, you've been running my errands and holding my hand through this awful murder investigation. And you've really stepped up with the museum. But your mother's right. You're better than the tackiest museum in San Benedetto. Don't feel like you have to buy it because we're friends. I know you've got bigger and better things in front of you."

I blinked, swallowing the lump in my throat. "Don't be silly. I love the museum."

"You do? That's wonderful!" Adele did a little shimmy and hugged me. "I knew you'd come around. Do you think you might actually buy it?"

Awkwardly, I returned the hug. "I haven't decided yet." My gaze fell to the dusty boxes I'd never gotten around to unpacking. The bottom dropped out of my rib cage.

"That's not a no …"

No, it wasn't. Was I actually considering this?

I saw Adele out the door and turned to stare at my (temporary) nautical-themed apartment.

I needed to get out, get away. And the farther the better. Tahoe? Santa Cruz? Yosemite? Any destination would work, as long as it was elsewhere.

Grabbing my keys off the counter, I paused at the top of the stairs and breathed a curse. The driveway was empty, my pickup still at the museum. It wasn't a long walk, but I didn't want to run into anyone I knew.

I wiggled through a gap in my aunt's fence and cut through an apple orchard to a deserted road. Weeds silvered by frost sprouted along the shoulder. The sky was clear and bright, the morning air nippy. I pulled my soft olive-colored jacket more closely about me.

When I was a kid, I'd had my thinking place. It had been years since I'd gone to it, and I wasn't sure that a stroll down memory lane wouldn't make me morbid. But my legs seemed to move of their own accord, and soon I was pacing the wide rows of the Nakamotos' vineyard. The bare January vines were twisted miniatures of gnarled oaks, and I saw that they'd been recently pruned. Tall emerald grass and yellow wildflowers beaded with melting frost dampened the cuffs of my jeans. I headed toward the old water tower, near the edge of the property.

A small brown bird flew past, low to the ground, and my disappointment began to drain away. Some of these vines were over a hundred years old, and their grapes improved with age. They'd survived Prohibition, droughts, and unseasonable frosts. By comparison, I had it easy.

The shadow of the water tower fell across my path, and the temperature dropped. Shivering, I looked up. The ladder seemed taller, more rickety than I remembered. I grasped a metal rung and climbed.

Reaching the top, I edged to a wide platform and dangled my legs over the side. The rows of vines angled away from me, converging on the horizon. A puff of dirt rose from a distant road, kicked up by a passing farm truck.

I dug my cell phone from my pocket and called a recruiter friend of mine. Her specialty was non-profits—not my field—but she'd given good advice in the past.

"Hey, Mad! How's it going?"

"Pretty good. I'm still job hunting."

Her voice turned sympathetic. "Haven't been able to find anything yet? Well, the economy is weak. Give it time."

"In the last nine months, I've only had two interviews."

"Really? That surprises me." There was a long pause. "I'm sure your last job wouldn't say anything bad about you." But her tone echoed my uncertainty. "In today's litigious society, they'd be sued."

"But?"

"But if they only give out basic information about you—date of hire, etc.—it can be a tip-off that you were fired. During an interview, honesty is usually the best policy. But in your case, it does sort of clash with the rule that you should never badmouth an old employer. You can't tell anyone you were fired because you wouldn't pay a bribe."

So I was between a rock and a hard spot, damned if I did, damned if I didn't. I reached for a few more tired metaphors and came up empty. There was really nothing to say.

"Thanks," I said. Feeling I'd monopolized the conversation long enough, I turned it back to her. She regaled me with the antics of her toddlers, then rang off to take another call.

Bad economy plus career transition plus indications I'd been fired … It wasn't a recipe for job hunt success. I pocketed the phone, nodding to myself, and touched something paper. I pulled out the folded Tackiest Museum "award" and studied it.

Biting my lower lip, I gazed across the fields. A breeze rippled the grass and wildflowers, rapid waves of green and yellow flowing west. For a moment it seemed the gnarled vines anchored a sea of emerald and gold, and I flew above it all.

An ache swelled in my chest—not depression—love. I loved this broad land and the people who farmed it. I loved the fog that hung heavy over the vineyards on cold winter mornings. I loved launching myself from a tire into the swimming hole in the heat of summer. I even loved the stupid Christmas Cow.

San Benedetto was home. Carefully, I folded the clipping and returned it to my pocket.

Now I thought I understood why I'd landed so few interviews, and why the few I'd gotten had ended in failure.

I didn't want those high-powered Bay Area jobs, so I hadn't tried hard enough.

I wanted to be here.

"Hey," a masculine voice called from below.

I leaned forward and looked between my toes. Detective Slate peered up at me, shading his eyes with a manila folder.

"What are you doing?" he asked.

"Just thinking."

"Thinking about jumping?"

I laughed. "Not a chance."

"You don't feel dizzy from that concussion?"

"It was a mild concussion. They're not even sure I had one at all. And I have an excellent head for heights."

"Good." He climbed up, the folder tucked beneath the arm of his navy-blue blazer. The detective thunked onto the platform beside me, breathing lightly. He smelled of musk and wild grasses. "Nice view. You know you're not supposed to be up here?"

"No," I said. "I've been coming here for years, and the owner, Mr. Nakamoto, doesn't mind. What are you doing here?"

His face tightened. As a cop, I imagined he was unused to being contradicted or questioned. But he nodded. "Someone called and said a woman looked like she was going to jump from the tower."

"Not Mr. Nakamoto! He knows I come out here. He wouldn't mind."

"No, a passing motorist. I was nearby, on my way to the museum, so I took the call." He handed me the folder.

Our hands brushed, and a pleasant, electric tingle passed between us.

"Here," he said. "The clerk found this for me in the police department's archives. Photography was still new when McBride was killed, and the police were proud of their photos, so they kept them."

"Photos of the murder scene?" I flipped open the folder and winced at the headshot of Martin McBride. Even in sepia tones, the corpse looked gruesome.

"The local police weren't sophisticated enough back then to photograph the scene of the crime. But someone did take a shot of the body." He pointed to the bruise circling Martin's neck. "See anything strange?"

I studied it. I didn't know what a rope bruise would look like, but this dark line looked like one to me. "I'm no expert, but it does look like a mark made by a rope, going straight across his neck."

"And that's the problem. If the bruise had been caused by hanging, the mark would have been in more of a V-shape, not a straight line."

I rubbed my temple. "So … someone strangled him and then hanged him?" Martin had been murdered and Cora had been in the house. She was the logical suspect. But …

"I'm no coroner, but it looks that way," Slate said. "I'm not surprised the police at that time missed it. This was still the wild west.

And in a small town, they'd go for the most logical explanation, not necessarily one that fit the evidence."

"Like arresting Adele?"

He gave me a long look. "She's not under arrest anymore."

My jab might not have been fair, and I felt myself flush. But I wasn't convinced that apologizing was in order, so I changed the subject. "Would Cora have had the strength to strangle her husband?"

A gust of wind fluttered the lapel of Slate's jacket and carried the scent of wild thyme. "It's possible," he said. "Maybe if he was unconscious first."

I wrinkled my brow. "From what I've learned, he was a drinker. A neighbor testified that he'd heard them arguing the night of Martin's death. Maybe he was too drunk to know what was happening." Oh, Cora. What had happened?

"What's wrong?" Slate asked.

"It doesn't feel right."

"You just don't want to believe Cora was the killer."

"No, I guess I don't."

"Wanting to see the good in people isn't so bad."

"But I don't see the good. I'm hardened and cynical."

He laughed, displaying even, white teeth. "If you say so. You've certainly got my partner's dander up. What's between the two of you?"

"No idea." I offered him the photo, and he shook his head. I slipped it into my jacket pocket.

"Well, thanks for finding this for me," I said.

"Digging through the archives was interesting. Maybe it will help with your mock trial."

"You read about that?"

"Are you kidding? It's the talk of the town."

"Which shows how little we have to talk about."

He shrugged. "I kind of like it. That's small-town life."

"You spend much time in small towns?"

"I grew up in one. Later, I worked in New York City, but the body count got depressing. I'd catch violent offenders and the prosecutors would let them go. Not enough resources to deal with them."

"So you moved to San Benedetto?" It seemed a big jump from the mean streets of New York City.

"After my divorce I decided to change coasts. San Francisco looked a lot like more of the same problems I was trying to get away from. So I came here. No regrets."

"It's strange. When I was a kid, all I wanted to do was get out of here. Now, I'm not sure what I was trying to escape. The beach and the mountains are a two-hour drive away. The streets are clean. The people are friendly. There isn't much crime." I paused. "I hope that's not changing."

"You'll get no argument from me." He brushed off his navy slacks. "And on that note, I've got to get back to work. You coming down?"

"I guess I'd better, before I scare another motorist."

We clambered off the water tower. Slate gave me a ride in his blue sedan and stopped in front of the museum.

"Thanks for the lift," I said.

"Any time. And try and stay out of trouble."

I stared at the dark windows of the museum. Why did I feel like trouble had found me?

TWENTY-ONE

I BRIEFLY CONSIDERED GOING inside the museum. But Adele had given me a free pass for the day, and I wasn't about to let that treat go to waste. I unbuttoned my pea coat. It was too late for a drive to Tahoe and too cold for the beach.

So I drove to Old Town Sacramento and wandered its wood-plank sidewalks. Picking up a burger-to-go with extra napkins, I picnicked on a bench overlooking the Sacramento River. A riverboat parked in the water, its paddle still, its red-and-white sign advertising dinner tours.

Sacramento was the nearest big city to San Benedetto. I imagined Martin McBride leaning against the hitching post across the street, waiting for Cora while she shopped for dress fabric. I wondered if the murder trial had made any of the big city papers. Or what if—

"Kosloski!"

"Aah!" I levitated off the bench. The burger splatted on the ground.

Above me loomed Detective Laurel Hammer, a rhinestone cowgirl in a too-tight checkered blouse, denim cut-offs, boots, and a hat. "What are you doing here?" she said.

"Just … sitting and thinking, enjoying a day off." Or at least I had been. I bent to clean up the remains of my lunch. "Your day off too?"

Her eyes narrowed. "What do you care?"

"I don't. I mean, I don't mean to pry. You deserve downtime like anyone else. Being a police officer must be stressful." Ugh, I wished she'd go away. Trashy Cowgirl Laurel was even more alarming than Angry Cop Laurel.

"Detective." She stabbed a long finger at me. "I'm a detective. And I'm watching you and Finkielkraut."

"Me and … Dieter? Why?"

"Tell him I know what he did to the Christmas Cow. I may not be able to prove it yet, but I will. And whatever twisted partnership you two have is going to bring you down. So if you know anything, it's in your best interests to tell me now."

"Partnership? I barely know the man!"

She bared her teeth. "And yet every time the Christmas Cow has burned, you've been in San Benedetto."

"Well, of course. I always come home for the holidays," I said, baffled. "So do lots of people. You think I was involved in the cow burning? Is that why you've been so hostile?"

Her nostrils flared. "'Is that why' … Are you kidding me? After what you pulled when we were in school?"

"What I pulled? You stuffed me into a gym locker! If anyone should be holding a grudge, it's me."

"Unbelievable." She stalked off, her boots kicking up poofs of dust.

I tossed my wrappers into a wire garbage bin. Not only did Laurel apparently blame me for some unknown teen trauma, but she also thought I was Dieter's co-conspirator in the annual Christmas Cow arson. I could think of only one explanation: she was nuts.

Abstracted, I wandered through more tourist shops. Most myths are based on fact. Sure, I had nothing to do with the cow conflagrations, but what about Dieter? Most years, the cow went up in flames. As a bookie, Dieter had a stake in the cow's fate. Could he have had an incentive to make sure it burned? Was Dieter the arsonist? And did he have a female accessory to the crime? I had a hard time picturing Christy involved in the caper, but stranger things had happened over a bowl of Christmas eggnog.

I bought a half-pound of peanut butter fudge and tried on some steampunk-style top hats festooned with gears and black netting. The hats weren't my style, but I wouldn't be wearing the fudge well either and that hadn't stopped me. Regretfully, I replaced the hat on its stand. No frivolous purchases allowed until I figured out if I was buying the museum.

When I'd depleted the attractions of Old Town, I drove back to San Benedetto and stopped at a frame shop. They were able to cut a black mat to size and iron my award flat, and soon I was parked in front of the museum, humming along to an eighties tune.

Adele looked up as I strolled through the door, frame beneath my arm. She was overdressed for the museum in her designer suit. The gold buttons on her jacket gleamed against its vanilla-colored fabric. A couple of tourists examined the row of photos on the back wall.

"What are you doing here?" Adele asked.

"I wanted to hang this in the window." I passed the framed "award" from the Ladies Aid Society across the counter.

She burst into laughter. "It's eye catching. But you should be careful with the ladies of Ladies Aid. They're involved in just about everything in San Benedetto—even the Christmas Cow. They could make things difficult."

"I have a plan."

"Which is?"

"Begging my mother for help." I took the framed newspaper clipping and balanced it on the ledge in the front window. "Want me to close up?"

Adele checked her watch. "Are you sure? The museum doesn't close for another hour."

"I enjoyed the day off, but you must have other things to do."

Looking longingly out the window, Adele let out a breath. "I did want to get to the tile store before it closed."

"Then get out of here."

She snatched her purse from beneath the counter. "Done. See you tomorrow!" She swished out the door.

I filed the picture of Martin's body beneath the counter and went to find Dieter. He wasn't in the main tea room, but I heard shuffling noises in back. I grabbed a screwdriver from an overturned box and walked down the hallway.

He was working in the bathroom, smoothing concrete on the floor.

"Hi. Can I borrow one of your screwdrivers?"

He looked up. "Why?"

"There are two generally accepted uses for a screwdriver," I said. "Screwing and unscrewing. Now personally, I prefer—"

"Fine. Take it."

Grinning, I returned to the museum and dragged my stool from behind the counter. I stepped up and removed the bell over the door. It felt good.

I returned the screwdriver and took up my post behind the counter to work on the inventory. Two visitors came in five minutes before closing, delaying my escape. I sold them tickets, flipped the sign to *Closed*, and returned to my chair. Not wanting to restart the inventory, I stared out the window and let my mind wander. The woman giggled in the Creepy Doll Room. Why did people find that room so entertaining?

The phone on the wall jingled, startling me. It was the first time I'd heard it ring. Tentatively, I pressed the receiver to my ear. "Hello?"

"I've got what you want," a man said.

"Is this an obscene phone call?" Did men still make obscene calls?

"No! It's Herb. I hear you're putting on a mock trial of the McBride case. I've got Cora's journal."

"Oh. Cool!" Yes, I had to play it cool. Herb was an ear witness, and I needed the cops to hear what he had to say. "Wait. Where'd you get it?"

"Same place I got the photo."

"What are the dates?"

"1898 to 1899."

"1899—that was when her trial took place. Is there anything about her husband's death in the diary?"

"That's for you to find out."

"How much?"

"Two hundred and fifty dollars."

"I'll give you fifty."

He made a cry of outrage. "Two hundred."

"If there was a confession inside it, you would have told me. Seventy five." We dickered, finally agreeing on a hundred bucks. That was probably ninety-five dollars more than I should have paid, but Cora had me hooked. "Can you bring it by the museum?"

"Too many cops. Meet me on the corner of Thirty-fifth and Willow. Seven o'clock. Come alone." He hung up.

Come alone, my Aunt Fannie. By seven it would be dark, and Thirty-fifth Street was out in farm country, where it would be even darker. And lonelier. I excavated Detective Slate's business card from my wallet and called. It went to voicemail, and I left a message about the meet. Seven o'clock was less than two hours away. What if Slate didn't check his messages? I could try the station, get hold of his partner, She Who Must Not Be Named.

I shuddered. No way. I'd rather be caged with an angry gorilla than stuck with Laurel in a deserted orchard. Two hours was plenty of time for Slate to get my message. I'd be fine.

The visitors wandered out, GD Cat sniffing their heels. I shooed him away from the door and called in an order for sweet and sour chicken. After all the walking I'd done today in Sacramento, I deserved a treat. I was nearing the finish line on the inventory. Since I had nothing better to do until seven, I might as well try to cross it.

GD ignored me until the food arrived. I gave him a piece of chicken.

He wolfed it down and meowed, expression pitiful.

"Come off it. One piece is plenty." How big a stomach could a cat have?

GD hissed and stalked into the tea room.

I finished dinner and returned to the inventory. But I was antsy, unfocused, checking my watch every fifteen minutes. And at six thirty, I gave up. It was still too early to leave for my meeting, but arriving early might give me an element of surprise. Hoping I wouldn't need it, I locked up the museum and drove.

The night was moonless. Outside of town, I flipped on my high beams, casting long shadows across the misshapen vineyards. I blasted past Thirty-fifth Street and made a U-turn, parking in the dirt beside a barren orchard. I sat there for a moment, listening to the ticking sound of the truck's metal contracting, and then got out.

I checked my phone. Slate hadn't called me back. I dialed his number and left another message.

In a month or two, the rows of apricot trees would erupt in masses of white blossoms. But tonight, dried leaves crunched beneath my shoes. A small animal rustled in the weeds. I flinched, eyes straining in the darkness.

My hands were moist in spite of the snap in the air. Maybe arriving early hadn't been the best idea. What if someone was right behind me, waiting? I spun around, heart thudding. Trees loomed, skeletal shapes against a sky pinpricked by stars.

I released my breath. I was alone and letting my imagination run away with me. So what if the trees looked like groping hands? And sure, that low pile of rocks could be anything from a goblin to a rabid raccoon. Worse—a raccoon with bubonic plague. Okay, not the plague. That hadn't been reported in a while.

There were, however, coyotes. And tree rats the size of cats. The branches rustled above me. I leapt from beneath them, scanning the dark limbs in vain. My mother had frequently informed me that the local wildlife was more scared of me than I of it. I remained unconvinced.

A flashlight beam bobbed among the tree trunks. Herb? If he intended harm, he'd be more covert. On the other hand, he was early too, so maybe he figured I hadn't arrived yet and was setting up his own ambush. Imagining the worst was too easy. I forced my muscles to relax. Rabid raccoons. As if!

The flashlight nodded closer, and I heard the stealthy tread of feet. It had to be Herb, harmless if weird, bringing the journal for which I was doubtless overpaying. But my pulse accelerated.

On the road, twin cones of light approached, grew larger.

I ducked behind a tree. It was a futile gesture, since its trunk was a fraction of my size, and now I saw the flaw in arriving early. Slate wouldn't be here until seven o'clock, if he came at all. My impatience had made me vulnerable. I hated when that happened.

A man walked into the clearing.

The car whizzed past, spotlighting him, me.

Herb's jaw dropped.

I waved, shamefaced, and stepped from behind the tree. "Hi, Herb. Looks like we both arrived early."

"You …" He clutched his chest, the flashlight making a ghoul of his face, glinting off his thick glasses. "You nearly gave me a heart attack. What were you doing behind that tree?"

"Just resting. Leaning. Have you got the journal?"

"Have you got the money?" He turned the flashlight on me.

Blinded, I turned my head, reached into my pocket, and pulled out five twenties. Sheesh, I was in a bad gangster movie. All Herb needed was a trench coat and fedora to complete the image, but his head was bare. A windbreaker bagged about his hips.

"Put the light down," I said. "I can't see a thing."

"Oops. Sorry." He angled the beam toward the ground. "Wait. Did you come alone?"

"What does it look like? Of course I came alone. Come on, Herb. Do we really need the cloak and dagger?"

"I'm not armed."

"I was speaking metaphorically. Now show me the journal." I mentally berated myself. *Show me the journal?* This wasn't a hostage negotiation. What had come over me?

He reached into his jacket and pulled out a thin package. "Careful. It's fragile."

I walked toward him, money outstretched. He snatched the cash from me and handed me the package.

Unwrapping the thick paper, I watched him count the money. Inside my package was a slim notebook, with soft, rounded edges. "Can I borrow your flashlight?" I asked.

He gave it to me.

Carefully, so as not to damage the journal's delicate paper, I opened the faded brown cover. The flashlight illuminated lines of a woman's graceful handwriting, along with Cora's name and a date. I'd found her! Feeling more excited about this than was warranted, I re-wrapped the journal and returned the flashlight.

Light blazed around us. I squinted, disoriented.

"Hold it," a man's voice called, deep, authoritative.

My hands shot into the air, and I bit back a curse. This was exactly what I needed—to get busted for trespassing. Oh, God. What if whoever had found us thought this was a tryst? With Herb? I'd rather get arrested.

Dropping his flashlight, Herb clutched the money to his bow tie. The light rolled on the ground, casting crazy shadows. "What is this? You said you came alone!"

"I did come alone!"

Herb raised his trembling chin. "Identify yourself!"

"San Benedetto PD." Detective Slate shifted the light so that it illuminated only Herb. "Are you Herb Linden?"

"Who wants to know?"

I lowered my hands, my knees going wobbly. The detective had gotten my messages after all. Wait—Herb's last name was Linden? Now I thought I understood the strange notations in the museum binder: *b.f.h.l.* stood for *Bought From Herb Linden*. Stupid acronyms.

"I'd like you to come down to the station and answer some questions," the detective was saying.

"I will not," Herb said. "You have no right."

"I can ticket you both for loitering, and take you in for trespass."

"Both?" I yelped.

Raising his brows, the detective gave me a glassy stare. He turned to Herb. "Or you can come along and tell me what you heard at the Paranormal Museum the night of Christy Huntington's death."

Herb glared at me. "You told!"

"Of course I told," I snarled. "You told me to tell."

"You violated my trust. You said you'd come alone."

"She did come alone." Slate said. "And I can't believe you were stupid enough to do that, Maddie."

"But … I called you. I left messages on your cell phone," I bleated.

"The battery died this afternoon." One corner of his mouth twisted. "You should have called the station and talked to my partner. She's on duty tonight."

"Call Laurel?!" He had to have noticed she hated my guts. She'd practically accused me of inventing Herb.

"Detective Hammer," he snapped.

A car drove toward us. Slowing, its lights illuminated the three of us, standing beneath the trees like the three witches in *Macbeth*. It sped up and moved on.

I changed the subject. "If you didn't hear my message, how did you find us?"

"I was following up on your lead about Herb's yellow VW," Slate said. "It's owned by his mother. She lives nearby. I was going to see her when I saw you lurking on the side of the road."

"I wasn't lurking."

"What exactly were you doing?"

I clutched the diary against my green jacket. "Buying Cora McBride's journal."

Slate tilted his head, his dark gaze drilling into me. "And that was worth a meet-up on the side of a dark, deserted road?" When he put it that way, it didn't sound that bright. But I'd thought he'd get my message. What kind of detective let his phone battery run out of juice? Sure, mine was frequently DOA, but I neither protected nor served.

"I need the journal for my mock trial," I said. "It might provide important insights." Ugh. I sounded as batty as Herb.

The detective shook his head. "Right. Where's your truck?"

"Across the street," I muttered.

"Come on Herb," he said. "Let's walk her to her truck."

Grumbling, Herb followed us to my pickup. Slate waited until I got inside, then slammed the door behind me. Without so much as a goodbye wave, he led Herb away. Since I'd been the one who'd put

Slate on Herb's trail, this seemed a little churlish. But at least I wasn't being taken to the station in handcuffs.

Okay, so I should have called the station about the meet with Herb. But if I had, I doubted Laurel would have passed on the message.

Since Slate was headed in another direction and the possibility of me getting a ticket was, therefore, reduced, I sped home, racing up the steps to my garage apartment. Throwing myself onto the couch, I flipped on the reading light and opened the journal in the middle.

Martin fell on an icy rail going to help Jared's horse and broke his left leg near the ankle. It was a terrible fright. Martin was roaring with pain…

Ouch. What sort of medical care had Martin received in 1898 San Benedetto? I skimmed forward. As there was nothing further about Martin and his ankle, I assumed it had healed. The journal was filled with other reports of injuries of various neighbors and relatives. Farm country in the 1890s was a high-risk place and time.

The journal was thin, the penmanship excellent, and I finished reading in less than an hour. I tapped its spine on my chin. Cora's observations about her neighbors were penetrating and lively; she'd described one pompous lady at an elegant tea in terms that had left me snorting with mirth. But there was not a word about Martin's abuse. Perhaps she'd been too ashamed to admit to it, even in the privacy of her own journal. But for an unhappy woman, Cora seemed awfully cheerful. She delighted in the rhythm of nature, writing detailed descriptions of the froth of blossoms in the spring. Her tales of the wicked little animals who dared raids on the chicken coop were Beatrix Potter–like. Her references to her husband were casual and reported with no air of fear, sadness, or regret. At least not until the final entries.

I reopened the faded notebook:

God, dear God. My Martin is dead. How can he have left me?

And then the final entry:

God Almighty, control Thou our lives, that through the vicissitudes of life we may yet win the goal—heaven. Grant we, each one and all, may find our places in the vineyard to serve Thee with cheerful hearts and so fulfill our mission.

Sighing, I laid the book on the coffee table. Cora didn't sound like a killer. Was she?

TWENTY-TWO

MURDER ON MY BRAIN, I should have felt wired. But that night, lying on the overstuffed gray couch, Cora's journal in hand, my lids sank to half-mast. When the phone rang, it startled me. I dropped Cora's journal onto the coffee table and staggered to the kitchen to grab the phone.

"Hello?"

"Madelyn, this is your mother."

"Hi, Mom. I was about to call you."

"You were?" She sounded pleased, and I felt a twinge of guilt. Shane had been right—I'd been avoiding her. And what had she done that was so awful? Nothing.

I settled on the couch, adjusting the waistband of my jeans. Seriously, no more junk food. "It's about the Ladies Aid Society," I said. "Adele said something to me that made sense—I should figure out what they really care about. And I'm having a hard time believing that they really care that much about the tackiness of the Paranormal

Museum, especially when they help the Dairy Association with their stupid Christmas Cow."

"The Christmas Cow is hardly stupid," my mother huffed. "Straw animals at Christmastime is an old Scandinavian tradition. The cow has become a big tourist attraction. I just wish it wouldn't get set on fire so often."

"Mom. That's the only reason why the cow is a tourist attraction. So why is your organization involved with it?"

"For the money, of course."

"There's money in it?" That surprised me. I had no idea how much straw cost, but the cow was two stories high. Considering the permit fees and the annual payoffs to the fire department, I figured the cow was lucky to break even.

"Oh, yes. The live webcam is popular, and we sell ads on the webpage. And we get half the profits on the sale of the merchandise. It's a terrific fundraiser."

I shifted Cora's journal away from an open bottle of cider. "I'm surprised the Dairy Association is willing to share."

"They're willing to split the work. Setting up that blasted cow is a huge endeavor. And marketing the cow is another kettle of fish. They're quite happy to let us do that work and get a share of the profits and publicity."

"I noticed Ladies Aid was hosting a wine tasting class at the Wine and Visitors Bureau. Is it the same sort of deal?" I picked at the label on the bottle.

"Of course. The Visitors Bureau gets half the profits, and they provide the space. We provide the marketing and the wine expert. It's win-win. We're involved with the Historical Association as well."

"Why not the Paranormal Museum?

"Because, darling, the prior owner, Chuck, wasn't interested in co-sponsoring fundraising events, or in Ladies Aid. I suspect he considered us a bunch of uptight snobs."

"What a crazy idea," I said. "I can't imagine where he got that impression." I was getting an idea of my own. "Is there any chance you could help me get a meeting with the head of Ladies Aid?"

"What are your intentions?"

"I'm going to make her a deal she can't refuse."

There was a long pause, then a chuckle. "I see. A meeting shouldn't be a problem. When?"

"As soon as possible."

"Done. I'll call you back when I've set an appointment for us. Or, er, do you want a private meeting?"

"Actually, I'd love it if you were there."

Twenty two and a half minutes later, my mother called back. She'd arranged a meeting with the president of the Ladies Aid Society, Mrs. Gale, on Sunday. I thanked my mother, wondering if Mrs. Gale was the battle-axe who'd presented me with the petition. No matter—I'd charmed corrupt Armenian cops. I could handle one small-town society matron.

I hoped.

No sooner had I hung up then the phone rang again.

"Hello?"

"Mad, this is Mason." His voice rumbled over a background track of AC/DC.

"What's wrong? Has there been another break-in? The museum hasn't burned down, has it?"

There was a long pause. "You sound almost hopeful, but no. Why would you think it burned down?"

Because Adele's contractor was a possible arsonist? I laughed weakly. "No reason. So what's up?"

"A local motorcycle club had their event space cancelled, so I'm letting them use my shop tonight. I thought you might enjoy getting out, meeting some new people."

I don't really like big parties. I'd just taken off my bra. It was late. All good reasons not to go. But my social circle in San Benedetto was limited to Harper and Adele. I needed to meet more people, though I wasn't sure a motorcycle club was the place to start. On the other hand, there was my hunky work neighbor.

Enough said.

"What's the dress code?" I asked.

"Jeans and a T-shirt will do. Leathers are optional."

"Then … sure! Thanks for the invite. Or are you inviting all the neighbors so you won't get noise complaints?"

His chuckle was rich, masculine. "Since you wouldn't have known about the noise if I hadn't called, I think you know the answer. See you when you get here."

It was just a casual thing. I didn't have to impress anyone. But I took a quick shower, touched up my makeup, and fluffed my hair into a tousled it's-just-a-casual-thing-and-I-don't-need-to-impress-anyone look. It went well with my faded jeans, white T-shirt, and cowgirl boots. I hoped they were an acceptable substitute for motorcycle boots, even if blue flowers twined up their sides.

I frowned at my reflection. My hair needed highlights. Since I wasn't going to get them tonight, I turned the frown into a pucker, slicked on some lipstick, and headed out the door, cash and credit cards tucked into my back pocket. I hate carrying a purse to a party.

The street in front of the museum was packed with motorcycles. I drove around back and parked in the alley, then walked through the museum to the street. Clubbers spilled onto the brick sidewalk. A heavy beat thrummed the air. Mason's motorcycle shop was standing room only.

Feeling awkward, I edged through the crowd, an upscale mix of men and women. A few wore leather pants. They all wore leather jackets or no jacket at all. Women's fashion consisted of tank tops and gold chains. In comparison, I looked like an insurance salesperson in my brown leather blazer.

Guests faced each other in little groupings, their backs like walls that kept strangers from trespassing on their conversations. This had been a bad idea. I considered leaving.

Someone laid a hand on my shoulder. "Mad."

I turned. Mason pulled me into a hug. A rough, manly, hard-muscled hug scented with motorcycle oil and pine that sent my heart thumping. His hands slid up my back and brushed my neck. I shivered. He stepped back, gripping my upper arms and smiling broadly. "You made it," he shouted over the din, his gaze sliding to my mouth. "I wasn't sure you'd come."

I felt pathetically relieved to have found him in the crowd. Then I wondered what Mason looked like beneath his T-shirt and jeans. Bad Maddie. But it had been a long time since a man had made my blood race or looked at me that way. "Did you think I'd chicken out?"

"Never." He jerked his head. "Come on, let me introduce you to some friends."

His broad hand on my lower back, he guided me through the crowd. We stopped near an impromptu bar—a wide strip of wood set upon two sawhorses. They looked suspiciously like Dieter's.

Mason clapped a gray-haired man on the back of his red leather jacket.

The man turned, pulling an elegant blonde in black leather pants with him. Discreet threads of silver hair and faint lines around her cornflower-blue eyes belied her age.

"Hey, Doug, Sarah," Mason said. "There's someone I'd like to meet. This is Maddie. She runs the Paranormal Museum next door."

Sarah grasped my hand, pulling me close for an air kiss. She smelled of cigarettes and roses and beer. "The Paranormal Museum? This is why I love San Benedetto. It's crazy! The Christmas Cow, the no-fuss wine tasting, and, of course, the best motorcycle shop in Central California."

"Aww, go on." Mason grinned.

"You are a godsend," she said, and then turned to me. "We thought we'd rented a bar for the evening and this morning discovered we hadn't. Mason saved our skin."

"My skin, you mean." Doug raked a hand through his wavy hair. "It's our club's twenty-fifth anniversary. We're a good group, but you do not want to get a motorcycle club angry."

"So what do you do when you're not biking?" I asked.

"Sarah's a software engineer. I'm a coroner in Sacramento."

I might have squealed. "A coroner? Really?"

"That usually doesn't get women so excited," Doug said.

"No, you can … I've been looking into a nineteenth-century murder. A photo of the supposed murderess and her victim are in my museum. She was said to have hanged him."

He raised his brows. "Hanged him? It's rare but not impossible. In most homicides by hanging—and let me say, that's one of the least common forms of murder—the killer is male. It would be difficult for a woman to manage it unless the victim was somehow incapacitated first—drunk, for example."

"I've got a photo of the corpse," I said. "Could I get your professional opinion?"

He shrugged. "I'm not sure what I'll be able to tell you from a photo, but sure."

"I'll be right back."

"After what happened last night," Mason said, "I'll go with you."

"What happened last night?" Sarah asked.

"Just a break-in," I said. "It's been a strange week."

"Well, you do run a paranormal museum," she drawled. "And I'd love to see it at night. I'm coming too."

Doug laughed, a thin, reedy sound. "Count me in. I could use some air."

We trooped over to the museum. Wary, I unlocked the front door.

Mason drew me aside. "Allow me." He grasped the door handle and strode inside, stopping dead about two feet in.

I hovered on the threshold, the coroner and the engineer pressed behind me. "What's wrong?" I asked.

"Where's the light switch?"

I reached around the door and flipped it on. No criminals leapt at us from the shadows. We walked inside, and I scooted behind the counter.

GD Cat slunk from the Fortune Telling Room, yawned and stretched, then sat in front of Sarah, waiting to be admired. She obliged him, scratching between his ears. They swiveled like antennae.

"Mind if I check out the Creepy Doll Room?" she asked me.

"Be my guest."

Mason went with her, a protective hand at the small of her back. Well, okay, so I wasn't the only woman he was touchy-feeling with. It had been a simple, meaningless hug. I found the photo of Martin beneath the counter and slid it across to Doug.

He studied it, frowning. "You say a woman did this?"

"That's what the prosecutor in 1899 said. The jury agreed."

"Strange. You see these ligature marks? They're straight rather than V-shaped, which indicates he was strangled rather than hanged. But the man's neck is clearly broken, which indicates hanging."

So Slate had been right. "She may have strangled him first, then strung him up to make it look like suicide," I said. "Can you tell me anything else?"

"Well, you'd need a drop of at least six feet to break his neck. Where was he hanged from?"

"From the interior second floor banister."

Doug pursed his lips. "He looks like a big fellow. Whoever did it would have had to lift his dead weight over the banister. How big was his wife?"

"Cora was a lot smaller than Martin."

"You say you have a photo of them both?"

I pointed to their picture hanging on the wall.

He shook his head. "I'd question her ability to pull this off. Under other circumstances, I'd be willing to believe she used a rope and pulley system to string him up. But he clearly dropped from a height. It's odd that she was convicted, but they didn't have the sort of crime-scene analysis in the nineteenth century that we do today. I'm assuming there was other evidence against her. Could she have had an accomplice?"

Yes, she could have.

But I didn't believe it.

Sarah emerged, giggling, from the Creepy Doll Room.

"I hate those dolls," Mason said.

"Me too, but they're a strangely popular exhibit," I said. And I wished I could get rid of them.

Something clanged from the back of the building. We all froze, staring at each other.

"Wait here." Mason brushed through the plastic curtains and into the tea room.

"Maybe it's a ghost." Sarah's laugh was brittle, uncertain.

"If only." I hurried after my neighbor, fumbling for the light switch in the tea room.

From down the hall echoed another clang, a metallic rattle, and a curse.

I found the switch, flooding the main tea room with light. The hallway to the alley remained dark. A metal door slammed shut.

"Mason?"

No response.

I hurried down the hall, the shadows lengthening the deeper I went until I was fumbling my way. I kicked something metal and it rattled against the wall. I moved more slowly and my fingertips brushed cold metal—the closed door. I fumbled for the latch and pushed it open.

Beneath the yellowish outdoor light, Mason scowled, hands on his hips.

I braced the door open and joined him. "What's wrong?"

"I'm not sure." He swung around and strode back to the door, then squatted beside it, examining the latch. There were scratch marks in the metal. "Someone was trying to get in. They must have heard me when I kicked over that bucket in the hall. You shouldn't leave stuff out like that."

"I didn't."

His expression twisted. "Of course. Dieter." He looked down the alley. "I could have sworn I saw someone by the corner, but they disappeared."

Sarah and Doug walked to the door.

"Disappeared?" she asked. "Like a ghost?"

"No," Mason and I said in unison. "There's no such thing as ghosts," Mason growled.

A ghost wouldn't need to break open the door. Still, I was starting to wish one had. Someone wanted inside the museum, badly. And I had an inkling about who.

I just didn't know what I was going to do about it.

TWENTY-THREE

I SLEPT LATE THE next morning, barely making it to the museum before opening time. No line of tourists waited for me, pockets full of money.

I grasped the knob, jamming the key in the lock.

My stomach turned to ice.

The door was open.

I swore. I'd definitely locked it last night. After the scare at the back door, Mason had watched me lock up, rattling the knob to satisfy himself that it was shut fast. I remembered this because it had annoyed me. Maybe Dieter had opened the front door for some reason? But why would he need to go inside the museum?

Dreading what I'd find, I pushed the door open.

Men's voices emanated from the Creepy Doll Room. My shock evaporated, transforming to irritation.

Dieter!

I stormed inside, colliding with Sam the squire. His scarecrow arms clasped a baker's dozen of dolls.

"What are you doing?" Blood pounded an angry drumbeat against my skull.

Dieter sauntered up behind Sam, further clotting the doorway. He also carried an armful of antique dolls. White splatters flecked his biceps. Paint? Spackle? Ectoplasm?

Sam straightened. "We're getting started on transforming the doll room into a gallery space. Of course, we'll build new shelves for the dolls in the main room. I told you I'd take care of it."

I took deep breaths. Calm, I would stay calm. "You can't just remodel the museum without telling me."

"Why not?"

"Because … because it's Saturday, one of the museum's biggest days, and people are expecting to see creepy dolls in the Creepy Doll Room." My voice had taken on a serrated edge.

The lawyer tilted his head. "So Monday then?"

I grabbed the dolls. "Out! Get out!"

Sam skittered from the museum.

Smirking, Dieter tumbled his dolls onto an empty shelf in the doll room and left me to sort them out. Part of me wished Sam *would* take them away, but there was a principle involved. People couldn't move exhibits around the museum willy-nilly. That was my job.

I replaced the dolls and checked my messages. Grace from the ghost hunters group had called to remind me about the hunt tonight. I groaned. Did I *have* to be here to let them in and see them out?

I gazed at the plastic curtains, imagined Dieter's mess of tools and supplies in the tea room. Yes, I had to be here. Too many weird things were going on at the museum. There would be no rest for the wicked or, apparently, for the Paranormal Museum's manager.

Straightening my shoulders, I strode into the tea room.

Dieter stood on a ladder, patching a hole in a wall. "So do you want me to turn that room into a gallery or not?" he asked. "It wouldn't take much—just clear the place out, install new flooring, and spruce up the walls. And installing a few more shelves in the main room is a snap. I could do it over a weekend, if I brought in help."

"I'm still thinking about it." I paused. "I ran into Detective Hammer yesterday."

He twisted, bracing his elbows on the top of the ladder. "And?"

"She suggested you might have been responsible for the Christmas Cow arson."

He scratched his face, leaving a smear of white. "Well, that wasn't very neighborly."

"She also implied that you had help—from a woman."

"I get it. You think it might have been Christy."

I raised my hands in a pacifying gesture. "Hey, I'm only telling you what she said." This might not have been the best time to pick a fight with him. Not with so many blunt instruments lying around. I eyed the hammer balanced across a paint-splattered plastic bucket.

"Thanks for the heads-up." Dieter grunted and turned his back on me, scraping a metal spatula across the bare wall.

Since I couldn't figure out a subtle way to push the issue, I retreated to the museum side of the building. Back at my counter, I pulled out a yellow pad. What if I really did turn the Creepy Doll Room into a gallery? I began figuring cost per square foot and sales, handing out tickets between calculations. I wasn't convinced a gallery would be enough to justify the space, but if I also used a corner of that room as a miniature museum shop …

Something tapped the top of my sneakers. I looked down.

GD Cat batted my shoe laces with a stealthy paw.

I returned to my deep thoughts. Unlike the museum, a gallery with rotating exhibits would bring in repeat business.

The cat nipped my ankle and streaked into the Fortune Telling Room.

Someone rapped on the counter.

I jerked my head up, startled.

Grinning, Mason draped his muscular arms over the top of the cash register. "What are you working on?"

"Some back-of-the-envelope budgeting." The sight of the big blond with the old-fashioned register was almost too much. I cleared my throat. "What are you doing here?"

"You've got another ghost hunt tonight. I came by to see if you wanted to stay at my place again."

And how. But I remembered his hand on Sarah's back last night. Mason was a friendly guy. I wasn't sure if this was a pity invite or ... well, I wasn't sure what it was. "I don't want to inconvenience you."

"As long as you're bringing dinner, we're good. By the way, I feel like Chinese tonight."

I pushed the yellow pad across the counter. "Place your order here."

He pulled a pen from the back pocket of his jeans and scribbled on the paper. "And don't forget the beer."

"I'm not a complete rube."

"Sarah and Coroner Doug couldn't stop talking about you and the museum."

"That's nice. Have you known Sarah long?"

"Since we were kids. She's my cousin. Why? Are you jealous?"

The phone beside the counter rang, and I lunged for it.

"I'll wait," Mason said.

"Hello?" I asked.

"Maddie, it's Sam. I wanted to apologize for my behavior this morning. I thought we were okay with the taxidermy exhibit, but now I realize I'd heard what I wanted to hear. I'm sorry."

GD wandered up to Mason and rubbed against his black jeans. Mason bent and ruffled the cat's fur.

"It's okay," I said to Sam. "I was just startled."

"Then will you think about the exhibit? I've been talking to some people, and I think I could get a good crowd."

"I'm running some numbers on the space now. Let me get back to you."

We said our goodbyes, and I hung up.

"Another scheme?"

"Please. I don't scheme. I plan."

"Tell me all about it tonight." Mason winked, sending my pulse into overdrive. He strolled out the front door, and I tried not to stare at his departing butt. He was only being a friendly neighbor.

I returned to my budgeting, calculating three different scenarios: optimistic, average, and pessimistic. I preferred the first, but who knew what the actual result would be? If I made an offer for the museum to Adele, any way I played this would be a risk. The spirit cabinet was worth a lot of money, and there were some other high ticket items in the Fortune Telling Room. I'd have to pay Adele fair market value for the collection, invest in some upgrades, and figure out a solution to the missing bathroom. My stomach fluttered, and I couldn't tell if it was nerves or excitement. Was I crazy?

At five o'clock, I flipped the sign on the door to *Closed* and returned to my spot in front of the computer. GD Cat leapt onto the rocking chair and curled into a ball, his green eyes fixed on me.

Packing away my budget, I fooled around on the Internet. It made little sense to go home when the ghost hunters would be here at nine o'clock.

The light faded.

I shifted on my stool, crossing and uncrossing my ankles, hating the fluorescents with their yellowish, flickering light.

The plastic curtains rustled.

I swiveled in my seat.

Dieter stuck his head through. "I'm headed home. See you Monday."

"Great. Enjoy your weekend." I sketched a wave, and he disappeared into the tea room. A few minutes later the back door slammed shut, followed by the metallic clicks of the door locking.

I looked at the cat. "Guess it's just you and me."

GD yawned.

I browsed my favorite news sites. Nothing good was happening in the world. Staying informed could be a real downer. Hoping for lighter fare, I checked the local paper. The Paranormal Museum's planned courtroom re-creation headlined the Internet version of the paper as well.

There was a metallic clatter from the tea room.

I froze.

GD stared at the plastic curtains, his ears swiveling.

"It's probably nothing." My voice echoed in the deserted museum.

The cat sneezed, contemptuous.

"Fine. I'll go check, if it will put your mind at ease."

GD stared, his emerald eyes daring me.

"I said I'd go." Sliding off the stool, I sidled along the wall to the curtained entry to the tea room, straining my ears.

Outside, a car hummed past, its lights sending shadows flitting across the exhibits.

I swallowed. I was being ridiculous. No one could be inside the tea room. Dieter had left. He'd locked the door behind him. And if someone had broken in, surely I'd have heard it. I was only scaring myself.

I wrenched back the curtains. No one barreled out of the darkness, axe swinging. I reached around the wall, fumbled for the light, and switched it on. The overhead fluorescents flickered, steadied.

The room was empty.

Of course it was empty. I walked inside, and my foot caught. Something clanked on the cement floor. A hammer. I picked it up. It must have fallen from the top of the upside-down bucket nearby. I returned it to its place and walked back into the museum.

GD looked up in expectation.

"See? No one there. Sometimes things just fall over."

His whiskers twitched.

There's no reasoning with cats, so I returned to the computer.

The room chilled. The drop in temperature was probably due to the setting sun, my pebbling skin a result of the icy atmosphere. But I couldn't shake my unease.

GD hissed. He rose, arching his back, the fur standing on end, and stared at the entrance to the Creepy Doll Room.

Right. Time to go. I almost felt guilty leaving GD inside, but I knew better than to try to tuck him under my arm. He'd shred my skin with those long claws.

I scurried out the door, leaving the light on so I wouldn't have to fumble around in the dark when I returned.

I walked down the street to the Book Cellar, a combo wine bar (in the basement) and bookstore (upstairs). Its carpeted aisles were devoid of bibliophiles. I ran my fingers along the books' colorful spines. I loved my e-reader, but I felt we were losing something to technology: a slower pace, true leisure, the scent of paper and ink.

I bought a mystery novel, took it downstairs, and ordered a glass of local zin. Tucking myself into a quiet corner, I was soon engrossed in the travails of an English village with a shockingly high body count.

Forty minutes before my "date" with Mason, I walked to the Wok and Bowl and shouted my order over the clatter of falling bowling pins and 1950s rock. The cashier took my money and spun to the kitchen window, her poodle skirt flaring. Taking my receipt, I sat down to wait.

I didn't see anyone I knew at the Wok and Bowl. What would it be like to run into friends on the street, to get to know the local business owners? I could be part of a community rather than just passing through. There was nothing stopping me from that but my own laziness.

I picked up my order and walked down the street. The bag of Chinese food was fragrant, warm against my chest. A bag holding two bottles of Tsingtao beer swung at my side.

I walked past the museum. GD Cat sat backlit in the window, his whiskers twitching.

Ignoring him, I walked around the block to the alley and trotted up the steps to Mason's apartment. He opened the door as I raised my hand to knock.

"Get in," he said. "I've been thinking about general chicken all day."

"Flatterer." I handed him the food.

He set the bags on the dining table and strode into the kitchen, his movements fluid. "How's Adele doing lately?"

"I'm not sure." I realized I hadn't seen her today, which was strange given the construction work at her future tea room. "I thought Michael's death would clear her. She was in jail when he was murdered, after all. But she says the cops suspect she might have had an accomplice."

Mason emerged with plates in one hand. "That doesn't seem likely."

"No. There are better suspects than Adele. And why is someone so interested in the Paranormal Museum?" I walked to the back window and angled my head. Past the dumpster, the alley door to the tea room was barely visible.

An idea bloomed in my mind. "I've disturbed one intruder. And it seemed like someone was trying to break in the other night. Plus, Dieter said he thought someone had moved his tools when he wasn't there. It's too much of a coincidence. The break-in at the museum and Christy's murder have to be connected."

"You're thinking there might be something inside that the killer wants?"

"That's exactly what I'm thinking." Laurel hadn't much liked this theory. Detective Slate hadn't said much, but he was a hard guy to read. I thought he'd blown off my lead on Herb, but he'd followed up on it after all.

"What you need is motive. Not for the break-in—that could be anything. For Christy's death."

"But nearly everyone had a motive," I said. Crossing the living area, I peered out the front window and checked for the ghost hunters. The wide sidewalk in front of the museum was empty, lit by the glow of a streetlamp. "Christy humiliated Sam, her ex-boyfriend. And she might have been blackmailing Dieter over the …" I was about to say the Christmas Cow, but it didn't seem right to throw Laurel's suspicions around. "Over his side gig as a bookie. Plus I heard that Christy liked holding information over people. Who knows how many people she blackmailed?"

"Yeah, but how did she get inside the museum? And why was she there?"

"I suspect she let herself inside. Michael had a key. She could have gotten it from him—who knows why? They were a couple at the time and Christy said they were engaged. Maybe he gave her the key to return to Adele, or maybe Dieter let her in."

Mason grunted. "My advice? Stick to your nineteenth-century murder and let the cops take care of this one."

"But one of the cops in charge blames me for ruining her youth and is out for payback. They already arrested Adele once. The police are looking for the easy answer, not the correct one."

Below me, a woman with a large orange duffel bag approached on the sidewalk.

"There's Grace," I said. "I'll be right back."

I hurried down the stairs and let her inside the museum. We went over the ground rules, which hadn't changed (stay out of the tea room), and I returned upstairs. Mason sat on his black leather couch, his bare feet on the coffee table, a plate of general chicken and white rice on his lap.

He took a swig of Tsingtao from the bottle. "The spring rolls were a nice touch."

"You didn't eat them all?" I did a double take, scanning the pile of white boxes for the spring rolls. I love spring rolls.

He chuckled. "Don't get your panties in a bunch. I stuck to my share."

"Good." I piled my plate with food. Cracking apart a pair of wooden chopsticks, I joined him on the couch.

"So, Nancy Drew, what's next in your investigation?"

"You've given me an idea. I think … I've figured out how to set a trap for the killer."

He sat up. "I meant what was next in the nineteenth-century investigation. You can't seriously—"

"I'm serious as a heart attack. It will be perfectly safe."

I had no idea how wrong I would be.

TWENTY-FOUR

Sleepy-eyed, yawning, I dragged myself from my bed. Keeping me awake when I want to go to sleep is the quickest way to infuriate me, and last night's ghost hunt had been punishing. I felt torn. The extra cash wasn't really worth it, but Grace's group promoted the hunts, and that meant PR for the museum.

I stumbled around the kitchen, squinting at the sunlight sparkling off the appliances. As Mason had pointed out last night, another murder (mine) at the museum would also be good PR, but that didn't make it a good idea. But when I fleshed out my plan, he admitted he couldn't see the harm as long as there was a free meal in it for him.

He was humoring me.

I didn't care. My plan was brilliant.

I slipped into jeans and a soft sweater and left for the Paranormal Museum.

GD sat by the door, meowing. It was breakfast he wanted, not my company, but guilt stabbed me for abandoning him last night. I poured cat food into his metal bowl and freshened his water. Rubbing my hands, I turned on the heat.

Last night I'd checked to make sure the ghost hunters had left things in good condition. But I speedwalked through the museum anyway, checking for anything out of place. The creepy dolls didn't look any less ghoulish in daylight. The Fortune Telling Room appeared undisturbed.

I aimed the planchette on the Ouija board to YES and headed for the main room. In the doorway, a wall of cold struck me. My feet stumbled and dragged to a halt.

The cat looked up from his bowl.

A blanket of quiet fell, smothering the outside sounds of cars, pedestrians, birds. The silence buckled my knees, thickened the air. The museum seemed to fold inward, listening, waiting.

It was happening again. What "it" was I didn't know, but I wasn't scared. Whatever was happening felt cold, yes, but also desperate, desolate. A woman sobbed, and I wasn't sure if the sound had come from within me or without.

Something slipped from the top of the counter, and sounds rushed back. A bicycle bell. A shout. The swish of car tires. The paper fluttered to the floor.

Trudging across the room, I stooped, picked it up, knowing what it would be. Cora and Martin McBride stared grimly from their portrait. The frame on the opposite wall hung empty.

"I believe you didn't kill Martin," I said in a low voice. "But I don't know what you want me to *do* about it."

GD buried his head in the bowl, and the sound of his needlelike teeth breaking kibble resumed.

I glanced out the window to make sure that reality outside was proceeding as usual. Two women huddled on the sidewalk, looking hopefully at the museum door.

Feeling a sudden need for human company, I opened early and sold them tickets. I reviewed my inventory. It was complete. With the exception of some of the antiques in the Fortune Telling Room—and they were big exceptions—the other objects held little financial value. I could afford to buy the museum.

And yes, I wanted to.

I didn't want to work for someone else again. When I'd been overseas, I'd been far enough away from HQ to have some measure of autonomy, independence. I wanted that back. I wanted to live here, in my hometown. I wanted a business of my own.

Adele swished through the door. Her pink alligator-skin heels clicked on the checkerboard tiles. A cream-colored tulip skirt fluttered about her bare legs. She buttoned her Jackie Kennedy–style jacket. "Brrr. It's cold in here!"

"I think it's the concrete floors from the tea room—they're a natural icebox."

"Dieter said he'd get started on the flooring next week," Adele said. "Soon they'll be covered in bamboo and throw rugs."

"Have you given any thought to the bathroom issue we talked about?" I asked.

"Some."

Roger nudged open the door behind her, a box filled with tiny cans of paint in his arms. He grunted. "Where do you want this?"

"Just put it on the counter for now," Adele said.

"You've got your lawyer acting as a bellhop?" I asked. "Is he charging by the hour?"

Roger wiped his palms on his slacks. "I was passing by and wanted to see how the remodel was going. What can I say? I'm nosy."

"Roger owns a slew of commercial properties," Adele said. "His advice has been invaluable. And he recommended Dieter."

"About Dieter," I said. "I was wondering if I could buy his services on Monday and Tuesday? He said two days is all it would take to convert the Creepy Doll Room into a gallery space and do some work in here as well. I've even got an exhibit lined up. I know it would be taking time away from your remodel, but of course I'll—"

Adele waved away my concerns. "He's yours. He's finished the bathrooms, and there's been a delay in shipping some of the supplies, so it's going to be a light week for him anyway."

"Thanks. I'm going to do a complete clear-out of the doll room and reorganize the rest of the space."

She eyed me hopefully. "Does that mean—?"

A young couple walked through the door. Relieved, I turned to deal with them. Scheduling Dieter's work on the gallery had little to do with my future plans for the museum, and everything to do with my plans to catch a killer. What can I say? I'm a multitasker.

By the time I'd finished answering the visitors' questions, Roger and Adele had disappeared into the tea room with the paint.

I called Dieter.

"Yeah?"

"Adele has said it's okay for you to work on the museum Monday and Tuesday," I said. "Are you still up for it?"

"Yeah."

"Bill me directly."

"Okay."

Hanging up, I called Sam to give him the news, hoping for more enthusiasm. I got it.

"Really?" he said. "We can? That's terrific!"

I moved the receiver away from my ear. "I'm looking forward to it too."

"Can I help?"

If he helped, it would ruin my plan to catch the killer. "Aren't Monday and Tuesday workdays for you?"

"Oh. Yeah. You're right." Then Sam's voice brightened. "I can come over today to help with the pre-remodel clean out."

"No, but thanks."

"But—"

"No." My cunning plan depended on my suspect not having access to the museum until I was ready.

Like I said—brilliant.

"Oh well," Sam said. "That's still great news. Hey, I've got to go, but let's talk promotion for my showing soon!" He clicked off.

I was marinating in smugness when Harper strolled through the door.

She gave me a cheery wave. "Hey, girl! Adele asked me to drop by and give her my opinion on paint colors."

Why hadn't Adele asked my opinion on the paint colors? I pointed with my pencil toward the tea room. "She's still in there with Roger."

"Thanks." Harper tilted her head to the side. "Something's different."

"Not really."

"Can't you feel it? That sense of … I don't know. Waiting for something to happen."

I shifted on my seat. It creaked beneath me. "That's strange. I was thinking the same thing when I opened the place up this morning."

"Then you feel it too?"

I shrugged. "I thought I did, but not anymore."

"Maybe you've just gotten used to it. Has something changed?"

"Not yet, but Dieter and I are going to turn the Creepy Doll Room into a gallery space on Monday and Tuesday, and do some work here in the main room as well."

She knit her brows. "A renovation can disturb spirits." She shook her head. "But you haven't done anything here yet, so that can't be what's caused the change."

"Harper? Is that you?" Adele shouted from next door.

"Duty calls." Harper flashed a grin and disappeared into the tea room.

Rummaging in the drawer beneath the register, I found a piece of faded yellow construction paper. In thick, black felt pen, I wrote, *Closed for Renovations, Monday & Tuesday*. Even though the museum was always closed on Mondays and Tuesdays, the sign was part of my plan.

I taped it in the window beside my tackiest museum "award."

Roger wandered out of the tea room, a pained expression on his face. "This is why I hire people for this sort of work." He gave an approving nod to the apple on my desk. "An apple a day keeps the doctor away." Sketching a wave, he left.

I wished I had some nachos.

Adele and Harper sauntered into the museum.

I swiveled toward Adele. "Why don't you want my opinion about the paint colors?"

She rolled her eyes. "You run a paranormal museum."

"That doesn't mean all my taste is in my mouth."

"Harper and I thought we'd have lunch here," Adele said, "and give you a break. Unless you'd like to stay for lunch, in which case, we're ordering Thai."

I grabbed my purse before they could change their minds. "Thanks. I've got an errand to run."

"That meeting with Ladies Aid?" Adele said.

"Why are you meeting with Ladies Aid?" Harper asked.

"I'm not. I mean, I am, but not right now. Enjoy your lunch!" I hustled out the door and down the street.

The Historical Association was in a white-painted Victorian at the edge of San Benedetto's version of Old Town. I walked up the porch steps and into a cool hallway. Sunlight from the window above the door glinted off wood floors, and the scent of lemon polish hung heavy in the air. To the right was a closed wooden door marked *Office*.

I knocked.

"Come in," a woman trilled.

I went inside.

A white-haired woman looked up and smiled. She wore a tight fuchsia sweater, which had an embroidered spray of lilacs over her left breast pointing toward her heart. "What can I do for you?"

I extended my hand. "My name is Madelyn Kosloski. I think we spoke on the phone."

"Miss Kosloski! Thank you so much for your donation. I'm Harriet Jones, and I enjoyed the research. I'm sorry I wasn't able to turn up more."

"Is your library open to the public today?" I asked. "I was thinking of broadening my search to get a better sense of what was happening in San Benedetto during that period."

She rose and walked around the desk. "I'd be happy to help you find what you're looking for." She took me down the hall to a room with bay windows that overlooked a lush garden. Bookshelves and wooden filing cabinets lined the walls. A plain walnut table anchored a floral rug in the center of the room. The room smelled, oddly enough, of cherry pipe tobacco, the same kind my father had smoked, and the memory walumphed me in the gut.

"Most of our materials are organized by date," she said.

"Oh? Yes." I struggled to reorganize my thoughts. Part of me wished ghosts did exist and I could see them. I'd give anything to speak to my father again. But I didn't like thinking of him as a dis-embodied spirit floating aimlessly through the world. If anyone deserved to go straight on to a better place, he did.

Harriet gave me a quizzical look. "Let me show you our archives." She led me to a wooden case with labeled drawers. A phone rang in the distance. "Oh! Excuse me!" She bustled from the room.

I pulled open a drawer labeled *1895–1900*. I wasn't sure what I was looking for, but soon I was sucked in by black-and-white pho-tographs of old San Benedetto. Dirt roads and wagons. Men (and a few women) on horseback. Most of the pictures from the 1890s were of buildings rather than people. I squinted at a picture of what ap-peared to be a large wooden warehouse.

"How are you doing, dear?" Harriet asked over my shoulder.

I jerked, startled. Her breath smelled like peppermint schnapps. "I was trying to make out the name on this warehouse."

"Oh, that's no warehouse. That's the Donaldson feed mill."

I flipped the photograph over. The date read 1902. "The old Mc-Bride mill?"

"Yes. As you know, Martin died in 1899. Zane Donaldson took over the mill after Cora's death."

Right. He'd gotten it when the town council seized the land. "He owned a newspaper, didn't he?"

"Yes. He owned several businesses and was a town councilman." Harriet snapped her fingers. "I know what you might enjoy." She toddled to a bookcase and ran a gnarled finger along the spines. "Would you like to see some maps of old San Benedetto? I believe the feed mill is in here."

She drew out an oversized book with a red leather binding, laid it on the table, and opened it. "This is from 1890. A bit earlier than the trial, but I don't think the town changed much between then and 1899."

I came to stand beside her, watching her flip the pages of maps inked in soft pastels.

My new friend pointed to a pink square by a line of railroad tracks. "There's the mill."

I bent for a better look, read the neat print. "That says 'McBride-Donaldson Mill.' They were partners?" I hadn't known there was a close relationship between the two men.

"Yes, and then they had a falling out in … around 1895, I think."

That might explain why Martin had gotten drunk and attacked Donaldson in his office. Bad blood.

"Wait." Harriet raised a crooked finger and pulled open another file cabinet. She thumbed through it and drew out a binder, which she opened on the table. "I thought so! Oh, I should have found this for you sooner."

She tapped a yellowed, type-written page. "Years ago a genealogist did some research on the Donaldson family. There's an interesting little write-up on Zane. He was quite the rogue. According to the story, Martin bought Zane out of his share of the partnership, all according to the contract. But Zane didn't want to be bought out. He wanted the mill, and he brought in a group of men to physically take it. It didn't work, and his men were driven off."

"You're kidding. How could Zane have believed that would work?"

"It might have. The sheriff wasn't likely to interfere with a town councilman. If Zane had gotten control of the mill, well, possession is nine tenths of the law." She pointed to the open map in front of me. "There's Cora's house."

I stared at the square of yellow, neatly labeled *McBride House*. It was on the edge of town surrounded by fields, and … "You're kidding."

"What's wrong, dear?"

"The McBride house. The nearest home to it is the Zane Donaldson house."

"Well, they were business partners once."

"Zane Donaldson must have been the neighbor who testified he heard them fighting the night of Martin's death. He's the only neighbor anywhere near the McBrides."

Adjusting her spectacles, Harriet peered at the map. "That must have been quite an argument. The houses are a good distance apart."

"Yes, but the Donaldson house is still the closest to the McBrides'. The witness had to be Zane." I wondered how even he could have heard the supposed fight. How far did sound carry from inside a Victorian house across silent fields? He lived close enough to watch for an opportunity … to sneak over one night?

"Zane had means, motive, and opportunity to kill Martin Mc-Bride," I said. If Zane had lied about hearing the fight, could he have lied about other things? Cora had opportunity to kill her husband, but neither means nor any motive that I'd found. "Could Zane have done it?"

Harriet blinked owlishly. "Zane Donaldson?"

"I spoke to a coroner and showed him a post-mortem photo of Martin. He told me it was unlikely a woman had inflicted those wounds, and that it was most likely Martin had been strangled first and then dropped from the second floor and hanged. But I can't see Cora hauling his dead weight over the banister. Zane had motive—he wanted and got that mill. I've read Cora's journal—there's no evidence in it of an abusive relationship. The only testimony we have to that came from Zane. What if he killed Martin?"

But if I was right, there was more than one victim. This was a double murder, with Zane relying on the force of the law to kill Cora.

Harriet shook her head. "I think you're stretching. You'll need more evidence for your mock trial." She smiled at my reaction. "I do read the papers, dear. And I think the trial is an excellent idea. People pay no attention to history. They think it's dull. I can't think of anything more fascinating. And a trial is just the thing to get the community involved. Though I'm not sure how successful you'll be calling your ghost witnesses."

"I was hoping to get actors for that. And a better venue." I nodded toward the opposite door and the courtroom I knew lay beyond it. "Would it be possible to use the old courtroom?"

Harriet smiled. "With a donation, anything is possible."

She named a figure.

I flinched. For a bunch of sweet-looking old ladies, the senior citizens of San Benedetto were sharks. But I nodded. "I'll be in touch."

I'd left Adele and Harper taking tickets for well over an hour. Jogging back to work, I puffed into the museum. Adele sat behind the counter, frowning at a sheaf of fabric swatches.

"Where's Harper?" I asked.

Adele didn't look up. "She had to go."

"Sorry I'm late. But I don't think Cora killed her husband!"

"Who's Cora?"

"The alleged killer in my mock trial, remember? And thanks for watching the museum."

"You're welcome. But I don't think chintz sets the right tone. I need elegance, not country kitsch."

"Mmm hmm." I stared at her, baffled.

Adele left, muttering to herself about patterns and color. I was starting not to feel so bad about talking to imaginary ghosts.

My stomach rumbled. I ordered a tuna sandwich from a nearby deli and got back to work.

At three o'clock, my mother walked through the door, resplendent in a crisp white blouse and slim faded jeans. Turquoise earrings dangled from her ears, and a silver cornflower necklace encircled her neck. It shimmered like the threads of silver in her pixie-cut hair.

She sniffed. "Why does this place smell like fish?"

I shoved the trash bin deeper into the recesses beneath the counter. "Oh, that darn cat. And hello mother. You look nice today."

"Thank you, so do you. And I try to look nice every day. I hope you have a strategy for managing Cora."

I blinked. "My ghost?"

"What ghost? I was talking about Cora Gale, president of the Ladies Aid Society."

The door swung open and the battle-ax steamed in. Striding to the desk, she slapped a white-gloved hand on the counter. "We need to talk."

"Cora?" I gaped. The long nose, the deep set eyes. Cora Gale was older than my Cora from the portrait, her lines harder, coarser. But the resemblance was undeniable. I couldn't believe I hadn't seen it before. Could Cora and Martin have had children? I thought back over the journal. When she'd written about Martin... could there have been a Martin junior?

Mrs. Gale's face spasmed. "You've found me out. I suppose it was too much to hope you wouldn't splash my murderous ancestress all over town. Chuck threatened it often enough. But you actually did it. And I attended your baby shower!"

I reared backward. "What? I've never been pregnant."

"Your mother's shower," she said. "What will it take for you to call off the mock trial?"

"But I don't think Cora was a murderer." I waved the portrait in the air. "She was framed. No pun intended."

Mrs. Gale's lips parted. She blinked. "Framed?"

I laid out the evidence. "And Zane Donaldson had means, motive, and opportunity," I finished. "Cora doesn't make sense as a murderess."

"But... what about Martin's hot temper?"

"The only real evidence we have of his hot temper is his run-in with Zane at the newspaper office. There was no mention of it in Cora's journal, and no other witnesses to it aside from Zane Donaldson. I don't have enough proof yet, but I'll bet if we dig deeper we can find some. I think there's a real case to be made that Cora's hanging was a miscarriage of justice. But …" I took a deep breath. "I had no idea you were related to Cora. If you want me to stop the mock trial, I will."

"Innocent?" Cora Gale took a deep breath. "Could it be possible? Perhaps you think I'm silly, caring about something that happened to a long-dead ancestress. My mother always considered it a source of shame and made me swear never to speak of it."

"But she named you after her?" I asked. No wonder today's Cora had issues.

"She named me after a different Cora. And I never believed the murder had any bearing on my own place in the community, but I honored my mother's wishes."

My mother laid a slim hand on Cora's arm. "Then perhaps it's time we laid this ghost to rest. As you said, you have nothing to feel ashamed of. The murder"—she shot an inquiring glance at me—"is part of San Benedetto's history. But that's all it is: history."

"The Historical Association has said we can use the old courtroom for the trial," I said. "It could be a wonderful fundraiser for them, and for the Ladies Aid Society if your organization would like to help. The fact is, you're right. The museum is a bit tacky. I think it's part of our charm, but I also believe it can be improved."

Cora swallowed. "A retrial. I must admit that I've already heard positive buzz about your newspaper article. As president of the Ladies Aid Society, I cannot in good conscience say no for personal reasons." She nodded to herself. "Let me talk it over with the board. I can't make the decision unilaterally." She turned on her heel and walked out the door.

My mother stared at me, her blue eyes wide. "Cora's ancestress was a killer? What have you been up to?"

I threaded my arm through hers. "Let me give you a tour of my museum, and I'll tell you."

TWENTY-FIVE

"Have you called the cops yet?" Mason leaned against the counter, biceps bulging, brow thunderous.

I handed a ticket to a visitor and turned to him. "I haven't had a chance. Dieter's been pestering me about paint colors for the Creepy Doll Room. The museum's been crazy busy. And I keep getting calls from the Ladies Aid Society about the mock trial. They want to help, but the whole thing is getting out of control."

He tapped his watch. "It's four o'clock. The cops. Unless this is all an excuse to get into my pants."

I burst out laughing. "Would that work?"

He leaned closer, his blue eyes darkening. "A girl who can arrange a stakeout and knows how to fill out a pair of jeans? That's someone I wouldn't mind getting to know better."

"How much better?" I murmured, my heart hammering. He was close, so close. Another inch and our lips would touch. Mine burned with anticipation.

He grinned wolfishly.

I sighed. "I'm calling the cops."

Mason groaned.

Turning my back on him, I grabbed my phone off the counter. Stupid, stupid, stupid! Why did I just turn him down? He was hot, chivalrous, intelligent.

And I was chicken.

I punched in Detective Slate's cell phone number. It went to voicemail. Grimacing at Mason, I left a message, then called the police station and asked for him there.

"Just one moment," the receptionist said.

There was a ring, and then: "This is Detective Hammer."

Looking to Mason for fortitude, I pasted on a smile. "Hi, Detective Hammer, this is Madelyn Kosloski."

She sighed. "What do you want?"

"It's about Thursday's break-in at the museum."

"We haven't found the guy."

"I guessed. Look, someone wants inside the museum. I'm guessing it's the same person who killed Christy and Michael. I've let it be known that we're doing a clean-out and renovation of the museum on Monday and Tuesday—"

"Have you got a permit?"

I ground my teeth. Laurel wasn't in the city planning department. "No, because it's just a clean out and a paint job. Tonight is the killer's last chance to get in and find whatever it is he's looking for before he thinks we tear the museum apart."

"And so you figured it was *Hammer time*?"

I scrunched my forehead, confused. "What's an eighties song got to do with anything? I thought you …"

And then I remembered. Ninth grade. Laurel had informed us Mondays were push-a-freshman day, and like ninnies, most of the kids believed it. Even after we'd figured out she'd made it up, it made no difference. We still got shoved, usually into something unpleasant like an open locker or garbage can.

It had been a balmy spring Monday. Laurel, eyes glinting, headed toward Harper and me. And I'd blurted out: "Oh hell, it's Hammer time."

Other kids heard, and soon "Hammer time" became a punch line whenever Laurel appeared. It took some of the sting out of her bullying. It's harder to be afraid of someone you're laughing at. The bullying had pretty much come to an end after that—until the gym locker incident.

I seethed. "Hammer time? You're holding a grudge over Hammer time?"

"You made my life a living hell. Do you have any idea what teenage boys will do with something like that?"

"You were a bully. Have you forgotten push-a-freshman Mondays?"

"I was kidding around! I never hurt anyone."

"You were a year ahead of us and a foot taller!"

"Oh for … You're a grown woman. Get over it."

"You get over it! And I'll be staking out the museum tonight to see if the killer tries to break in."

Mason mouthed, "*We'll* be staking it out."

I nodded at him.

Laurel hung up.

Just kidding around, my Aunt Fannie. If Laurel really thought she was the victim in all this …

"So?" Mason asked.

"Told 'em. No problem." Laurel might hate me, but she was still a cop. She'd come. I hoped. Possibly to arrest me for interfering with an investigation.

Mason straightened off the counter. "Great. See you tonight." He winked and strode out the door to the admiring stares of two slim young women in sorority sweatshirts. When they stopped drooling, one asked me, "May we have two tickets?"

"Right. Sure." I fumbled around and gave them their tickets.

Had I really blighted Laurel's school life? I hadn't intended to, but guilt prickled the inside of my chest.

———

I pressed my head against the cool glass of Mason's darkened window and stared into the alley. He hadn't said anything about our conversation that afternoon. I wasn't sure if I felt relieved or disappointed.

In spite of the thick black turtleneck I wore, I shivered. The alley below was deserted. Lights mounted on the exterior walls illuminated two saw horses tilted against the brick wall. Adele's dumpster squatted in its proper place on the tea-room side of the property line.

Mason sat on the opposite side of his living room, watching the front entrance to the museum. The slim computer in his lap lit his rugged face glacier blue. He scratched his chest, tugging the fabric of his white T-shirt sideways, and yawned.

A fingernail moon shone through the skylight, beyond twisting specters of fog.

"I can't believe you talked me into this," he said.

"You're too easy to bribe." I wadded up my burrito wrapper. Walking to the kitchen, I dropped it in the bin beneath his sink. "Besides, when's the last time you've been on a stakeout?"

"Never. I was in the military, not the police."

"It's an adventure."

"We've been sitting here for three hours, and I still only have a four percent win rate on this solitaire game."

I returned to my position by the rear window. "That is tragic."

He folded the laptop shut and laid it on the glass coffee table, eyeing me speculatively. "There are other things we could do."

"I don't think you're taking my stakeout seriously."

He rose and prowled toward me. "I'm taking this very seriously."

"Oh." My legs trembled, and I gripped the window ledge for support. His eyes seemed to glow, and I shivered with want. I'm no saint. I can get swept away as easily as the next woman. And this was exactly the sort of situation where I could lose control. This was, in fact, why I avoided these types of situations.

I wrenched my focus away, to the window. A dark shape peeled away from the dumpster. It took me a couple of seconds to move, then I flattened against the brick wall. But I could still see the person below creeping toward the tea room. "Someone's back here."

"Mmm. Probably a drunk." Mason pressed his hands against the wall, trapping me between his arms. He leaned forward.

My body heated. Mason smelled so good. Clean, like soil in a vineyard after a rain. My brain started dissolving, as it always does at moments like these. I tore my attention from him, back toward the window.

The figure darted toward the tea room door. Something large and boxy swung from one fist, and from the other what looked like a crowbar.

"No." I swallowed. "He's going for the tea room."

Mason shoved me aside and peered out the window. "What's he carrying?"

"I can't tell." Stumbling to the couch, I shook my head and tried to get my bearings. There was a stage two to my plan. And it involved … I couldn't remember what it involved.

"Damn he's fast. He's got the door open." Mason cursed. "He's got a gas can. He's going to burn it." He darted for the door.

Stage two: call the police! I grabbed my bag, digging for my cell phone. "Where are you going?"

"He's going to burn the building, and I live next door. Where do you think I'm going? Call 911!" He vanished through the door.

Hands trembling, I dialed 911 and told the dispatcher what was happening.

"Stay right where you are," she said. "Police and fire are on their way."

"I can't." I jogged down the steps, panting. "Mason went after him. He might need help."

"Stay where you are," she bleated.

I raced into the alley. The door to the tea room stood open, its lock bent and fractured on the damp pavement. The hallway that led past the bathrooms and into the tea shop yawned before me, dark as pitch.

Holding up my cell phone, I illuminated a thin section of the hallway with its bluish light. I tiptoed inside, ears straining. All I heard were the dispatcher's faint squawks.

I angled my phone toward the floor and hoped I wasn't giving away my position. Where was Mason? Why was it so quiet?

I crept deeper inside, into the body of the tea room, and my foot brushed the upside-down bucket. It scraped against the cement floor. I flinched at the sound. The hammer still lay on top of it. I picked it up.

Ahead of me, the plastic curtains swayed, glowing translucent from a light in the museum. I edged along the bare wall and parted the curtains with the claw of the hammer. Light poured out of the Creepy Doll Room, along with the sound of splashing. Mason lay on his back across its threshold, his lower half in the doll room, his muscular torso in the main room.

"Mason's on the museum floor," I whispered into the phone. I prayed he was unconscious and not dead. "He needs an ambulance."

I'd gotten him into this. What had I done?

Something low and dark streaked along the floor. I gasped and clutched my chest, nearly striking myself in the chin with the hammer.

GD Cat leapt onto Mason's back. He sniffed at a dark spot over Mason's left ear.

Tiptoeing to Mason, I made a shooing motion.

The cat slunk off Mason and sat beside him, staring at me.

I dropped to my knees, pressed my shaking hand to Mason's neck, and found a pulse. I sagged. He was alive.

The scent of gasoline flooded the room, burned my nostrils.

My muscles quivered, anger boiling up inside me. I rose, my hand tightening on the hammer. He wasn't going to get away with this—with hurting Mason, framing Adele, the murders.

Bringing the phone to my lips, I stepped over Mason's body into the Creepy Doll Room.

A large figure in black sloshed gasoline over the dolls.

"Roger is inside the museum," I said to the dispatcher in my out-door voice. "He's splashing gasoline on the walls."

Roger spun around, tossing the gas can to the floor. "What the hell?"

"Roger who?" the dispatcher asked. "Are you still in there?"

"Roger …" I'd never gotten his last name. "Roger the lawyer." My voice steadied. "He's the Nakamotos' family lawyer. He assaulted Mason, and he killed Christy Huntington and Michael St. James."

"Shut up," Roger roared. Fumbling in the pocket of his black jacket, he pulled out a lighter. With a snick, a flame leapt from its top. "Drop the phone."

I lowered the phone to my side. "That was 911, Roger. They know you're here. They know everything. There's no benefit to setting the museum on fire."

"There's not much downside either."

"It was a trust, wasn't it?" I asked loudly, hoping the operator could still hear me. "Christy was overheard shouting at you, before she died, about 'trust.' And you work with trusts all the time, don't you? What happened? Did she catch you embezzling from the trusts? Did you need extra money for all those properties you've bought?"

He launched himself at me.

Blindly, I swung the hammer, connected.

He howled, and the lighter flew from his hand. We froze, watching its slow-motion arc. It struck the linoleum floor, flame guttering, and skittered to a stop.

I breathed. It hadn't ignited the gasoline.

GD Cat pounced, batting the lighter sideways.

The floor exploded in flames.

GD yowled and streaked out of the room.

Roger bounced me against the wall and ran. The front door slammed. Flames raced up the shelving, the dolls' dry, antique dresses catching fire.

I turned and jumped over Mason, grabbed his wrists, and tugged him toward the door.

He moved an inch. Two.

Smoke cauterized my throat, my eyes.

"Come on, Mason." I yanked, heart thundering. He slid another six inches. I threw my weight backward. Why wasn't he moving? How much did the god of thunder weigh?

The door banged open, carrying with it a burst of cool air.

Laurel Hammer, my high school nemesis, grabbed his other wrist. "Come on!"

Coughing, we dragged Mason outside, onto the sidewalk.

"Roger—"

"I've got him." Laurel jerked her head toward Roger. He was lying face down on the sidewalk, hands cuffed behind his back.

"GD!" I raced inside the museum and grabbed the fire extinguisher by the front door. "GD!"

Laurel put me in a headlock and dragged me backward.

"No! My cat! My museum!"

"Dammit." Releasing me, she ran toward the doll room. She kicked its door closed, containing the flames. "Where's the cat?"

"GD!" I rubbed my neck, aching from the headlock.

An answering yowl echoed from the tea room.

Together, we raced inside.

GD crouched beneath a paint-stained table, his inky fur standing on end.

"This is going to hurt." I grabbed him.

GD thrashed, clawing me. Later, I would find thick lines of scarlet down my arms. Now, they felt like streaks of fire.

"Come on!" Laurel wrenched open the tea room's front door.

Cat writhing in my arms, I followed her onto the street. I dropped GD on the sidewalk. He streaked away, past the fire trucks that wailed to a halt in front of the museum. Two police cars and an ambulance followed.

"Laurel, you came. Thanks." Then an awful smell assaulted my nostrils. "What's that?"

"What's what?" She looked up the street.

I gasped. Strands of her ponytail smoldered like lit fuses. "Hair! Your hair! Fire!" Complete sentences eluded me.

Reaching up, she raked her fingers through her hair, extinguishing the sparks.

"Oh," I said.

She folded her arms over her chest. "I really hate you."

TWENTY-SIX

HARPER HUGGED ME, THE sequins in her black tank top stabbing through my Paranormal Museum T-shirt. I didn't mind.

"You've done good," she said.

"Thanks." I looked around the old courtroom. Women in spring hats gossiped and clinked champagne glasses. Mason and his friend Doug, who'd been our star witness, chatted with Detective Slate, neat in a blue suit and tie.

Mason winked at me. I remembered our almost-kisses and my face warmed. I wasn't sure how he felt about being rescued by a woman.

So I'd told him Laurel did it. We had a real date planned for next week. (Okay, I'm a slow mover.)

Detective Slate turned his soulful brown eyes on me and shook his head.

"I think you'll have to take down her photo," Harper said.

I scratched my cheek. "Who's photo?"

"Cora and Martin's. She's at peace now. The photo's not haunted anymore. Can you feel it?"

I watched Cora Gale, president of the Ladies Aid Society, laughing with my mother. At least the great-granddaughter of Cora McBride could breathe a little easier. The mock trial had been a success. After some crack detective work by Detective Slate and a surprisingly witty defense by Sam the squire, Cora McBride had been acquitted. The living Cora looked relaxed and happy. As for the dead Cora? Unless the Ouija board in my museum got us a different result, I was calling that case "solved."

Adele pushed through the crowd, waving. "Congratulations, Mad. It's the event of the year! Or at least it will be until my tea room opens next week. Getting the Ladies Aid Society to co-host the trial was a stroke of genius. And they've asked about using the tea room as a venue for their next meeting!" Adele squealed. "I'm no longer a social pariah. Have you heard? Roger's taken a plea deal. He's confessed, and I am officially, one hundred percent, innocent."

"You were always innocent," Harper said.

A waiter glided past holding a silver tray aloft, and Adele snagged a mini-quiche. I passed. My jeans were still too snug.

"But not *officially* innocent," Adele said. "Or at least, not according to the town rumor mill, which is all that counts." She shuddered. "It's been a long six weeks. I still can't believe my own family's lawyer did it. Did you have any idea it was Roger?" she asked me. "Or were you just waiting to see who turned up?"

"I suspected," I said. "He was hanging around the museum too much. And he'd told me he'd never explored it, but he knew all about the spirit cabinet, which is in one of the back rooms."

"He's been a friend of our family for years. I still don't know why he did it."

"According to the legal rumor mill," Harper said, "which I hope is more accurate than the town's, Roger embezzled from some of his elderly clients' living trusts. He used the money to finance his property purchases. He said he was just 'borrowing' the money, and it seemed like he did always pay it back. But it's still criminal. Christy found out."

"But why were they in the museum?" Adele asked.

"I doubt we'll ever know Christy's motivation," I said. "But Roger apparently followed her there and watched her let herself inside. He saw the opportunity to get her alone, and he took it."

"She was up to no good," Adele said. "Accusing you of threatening her when you hadn't, cheating with Michael … but she didn't deserve to die. I'm just glad you didn't, Mad."

Roger had claimed he was only trying to scare me when he'd hit me over the head. I didn't believe him. If I hadn't moved at the last moment, reaching for that fallen photo of Cora …

Adele's arms hung at her sides, slack. "But why did he attack Michael?"

I glanced at Detective Slate. Roger had confessed, so I didn't think it would hurt if I told them what Slate had told me. "Christy had hinted to Michael what Roger was up to. When Michael figured it out, he confronted Roger about everything—the trusts, Christy—and Roger killed him."

We were silent for a moment. Then Harper took another sip of her champagne. "Too bad you weren't able to hold this event at the PM."

"Oh, no," I said. "No acronyms. It's the Paranormal Museum, not the PM."

"Acronyms are hot," Adele said. "In marketing terms, at least."

"I don't care. And I wouldn't have held the trial at the museum in any case." Thanks to Laurel's quick thinking, the fire had been confined to the Creepy Doll Room. The damage in there had been extensive, but the room would open next month as a gallery. "The museum would have been too small, and the courtroom made more sense."

After the fire, Detective Slate found what Roger had been looking for—a monogrammed business card case. The lawyer had dropped it during his argument with Christy, and when he couldn't find it later, he decided to burn the museum to destroy the evidence. Slate discovered the card case beneath a rolling shelf in the main room. The case was weighty, and I couldn't figure out how it had managed to fall under the shelf. I suspected GD Cat.

The cat was back in residence at the museum. Seemingly, he had forgiven me for dragging him from the fire. But there's no accounting for cats.

I handed Adele an envelope.

"What's this?"

"Open it."

She opened it and pulled out the check, her brow wrinkling. "What's this for?"

"The museum," I said. "The value of the contents, plus present-value estimates of the first year's income flow."

"Why? You already paid me."

"One dollar isn't a fair price. This is."

"But—"

"Just take it," I said.

"Then I guess I can tell you," Adele said. "I've solved your bathroom problem."

"Oh?"

"A secret door—a revolving bookcase between the tea room and the museum!"

"That's …" I didn't know what to say. Who doesn't love a secret passage?

"You're not the only creative person in this friendship," Adele said.

A cooling breeze lifted my hair, loose around my shoulders. The actress who'd played Cora in our trial drifted past a window, turning a wistful smile on me. The local cosplayers had done a bang-up job designing authentic-looking Victorian-western clothing. I smiled back at her and raised my glass, but she'd disappeared behind a cluster of elderly ladies.

Someone tapped my arm, and I turned.

The actress stood before me. Jolted, I blinked.

"I just wanted to tell you how much I loved playing Cora McBride," she said. "Thanks so much for arranging the trial."

"You're, uh, welcome."

She smiled and moved into the crowd.

I spun, my head whipping back and forth. The other Cora was gone. "Who …?"

"What's wrong?" Adele asked.

"Did we have two actresses playing Cora?" I asked.

"Two? Why would you have two Coras?"

"Never mind." I shook my head. There was no doubt a rational explanation.

THE END

ABOUT THE AUTHOR

Kirsten Weiss writes paranormal mysteries, blending her experiences and imagination to create a vivid world of magic and mayhem. She is also the author of the Riga Hayworth series. Follow her on her website at kirstenweiss.com.